THE VILLAGE MAID

JANE BUEHLER

Published by Emily Jane Buehler
PO Box 1285, Hillsborough, NC 27278 USA
https://janebuehler.com

Publisher's Note: This is a work of fiction. Names, characters, businesses, places, events, locales, and incidents are either the products of the author's imagination or used in a fictitious manner. Any resemblance to actual persons, living or dead, or actual events is purely coincidental.

The Village Maid (Sylvania Book 2) / Emily Jane Buehler
ISBN (print): 978-1-957350-00-4
ISBN (ebook): 978-1-957350-01-1

Library of Congress Control Number: 2021925520

Woodglen
the Grange Hall
Thorn's Print Shop
Alistair's Pub
the Park
the Wharf
the Village Square
the Boarding House
to Woods Rest and Nor Bay
Central Sylvania
Woodglen
N
W
E
S
the Forest
the Harbor
the Forest Road
the Castle
the Cliff Path
to South End and Sar Bay

Chapter 1

AVIANNA WAS NOT THE KIND of girl men courted. She never had been, and she certainly wasn't right now, trapped under a passed-out ex-soldier in the upstairs room of Woodglen's seediest pub. She shoved at Rye's hulking form, giving two big heaves before she was able to roll his sweaty body off her. He grumbled, but the whiskey in his system won, and he slumped onto the bed beside her.

"Rye?" Avianna whispered. He didn't respond, and a moment later his snores began.

What had she been thinking, tumbling Rye?

Rye wasn't husband material, that was for sure. He hadn't had a steady job since the revolution, when the king's guard had fallen apart. The new peacekeeper corps hadn't wanted him. Not that she blamed them.

As Rye snored, Avianna stared up at the cracked ceiling in the semidarkness, breathing in the stale smell of old ale. Her mind went over and over the past seven moons if she let it—if she stopped moving long enough to think. It felt like seven winters.

She'd been in this room many times in those seven moons, since the revolution had destroyed the castle court, dumping her out on the village streets. She'd missed her chance to find a wealthy husband among the courtiers, but she wasn't giving up. She'd always known her looks were her best chance to escape poverty, and she still had them—for now. If she had to tumble every man in Woodglen to find the right one, she'd do it.

Avianna had learned it was better not to stop moving long enough to think.

She sat up. Dim light seeped into the dark room from the street lamps. The shouts and laughter from the pub below came through the floorboards. She hoped they had drowned out the sounds she and Rye had been making five minutes earlier.

Again she wondered, What had she been thinking?

Ever since she'd lost her place at the castle, she'd been stumbling along, hustling to make ends meet—exactly the life she'd hoped to escape when she'd begun her deception as a courtier ten seasons ago. She hadn't had a clear goal when she went to court, other than escaping the poverty of her childhood. Maybe if she'd had a plan, she wouldn't have failed to secure a husband while she had the chance. Now here she was, just another peasant, her options for escape dwindling.

But still, she should've known better than to waste her time on Rye. She'd considered him handsome when he'd been in the king's guard. But he was mean. And he drank too much to be a decent husband, the kind who'd provide security and a comfortable home. The kind who was the opposite of what she'd grown up with—that was all she'd ever wanted.

She straightened her clothing and pushed herself off the bed. Rye hadn't waited long enough to get her dress off. Not that it would take long with these simple peasant dresses—unlike the ones with layers and hooks and ribbons they'd had in the castle.

She hadn't had much when she arrived in Woodglen, but at least she'd had her face, an unusual mix of darker skin from the north and the blue eyes of the south, and her curves. Her looks had been all she needed to move up, to win favor with the important people and get what she needed. She'd been sure she'd meet the right man, one who'd take her away to be his life mate. But she hadn't focused on finding him. She'd been having too much fun with Elspeth.

Now, Elspeth . . . Elspeth *was* the kind of girl men courted.

Avianna smiled, thinking of her friend. With those rosy cheeks and her perpetual smile, always polite, a girl from a respectable family—blah blah blah. Avianna could still hear their landlady gushing over Elspeth's virtues, praise she never had for Avianna. But Miss Flo was right, Elspeth *was* a catch, and men had courted her and proposed to her, and she'd accepted one, and he'd taken her off to his estate, and now Avianna was stuck in Woodglen with no friend to talk to, and nothing fun to do, and no coins on top of it.

Everything she'd had was gone, thanks to the sodding revolution.

She quietly crossed the room, fanning the sweat from her face. Under the thin curtain, she tugged up the window sash, and a cool night breeze stole in, smelling of autumn forest and the sea. She leaned out far enough to mute the sounds of the pub below. The street was quiet after the supper hour, with one lone horse clopping somewhere and the voices of two men drifting up as they talked at one of the tables below.

Avianna sank down onto her knees on the floorboards and rested her arms on the windowsill. The breeze touched her cheeks, and the smell of low tide overwhelmed the woodsy scent. The men drinking below were going on about crop prices and fish tallies—ugh. How had she ended up here? Elspeth was probably eating grapes from a crystal goblet, fanning herself beside a fountain at some luxurious lodge in the foothills as Drake groveled at her feet.

"Eight hours to sunrise," came a voice from below. "Better hit the hay." Mugs clanked on the table. In a few hours, those men would be raising their sails and slipping onto the ocean in the cold morning to work their nets, just as they had the previous morning, and the morning before that. The endless cycle of work to get a bite to eat . . . . There had to be something better than this.

Avianna dug her nails into the windowsill and pushed herself up. She'd been going in circles, working, sleeping, trying out a new man each chance she got. For three moons she'd thought she'd found him in Beck, one of the regulars at the pub, but Beck had ended up as big a waste of time as all the others. She needed a plan. She needed to try something different. But what?

Getting out of this room for a start. Tumbling Rye had been a mistake, and maybe the past seven moons had been as well. But it wasn't too late, not yet.

Without a glance back, Avianna let herself out the door, closing it quietly behind her. The noise of the barroom rang up through the darkened hallway. She followed it to the top of the pub's staircase and paused. She pulled out the lose pins hanging from her mussed hair and brushed back her curls, then fastened them back into place. There was no telling where her lipstick had smeared to, so she wiped her arm across her mouth, leaving a dark stain on her skin. She wiped her face with the other arm and it came away clean. She scrubbed her face over to be sure.

She descended the stair into the entryway of Alistair's Pub, and the sounds of the revelers grew louder. Through the large doorway in front of her, women and men laughed over their ales, happy in spite of their miserable lot as farmers and fish-catchers. At the far end, Beck tossed back a shot. Hopefully he wouldn't look up. She stepped for the front door.

A crash from the kitchen behind the staircase silenced the room, and all the eyes turned on Avianna. She froze. Then the door behind the stairs flew open, and a boy streaked toward her.

"Hide me, Avi!" he said, grabbing her skirts and swinging behind her.

At Alfie's appearance, the drinkers resumed, and the noise in the pub returned to its previous level.

Avianna faced the kitchen as Alfie's father puffed into the doorway, wheezing as he leaned on the doorframe. "Out of the way, Avianna," Alistair said, starting forward. He brandished a large metal stirring spoon. The boy's small fingers on her dress tightened.

"Oh, Alistair," Avianna said, softening her voice. "What's Alfie done now?" As Alistair neared, she reached out a hand to his chest and stopped him.

"Knocked over a full tray of oysters, trying to pinch one. Wouldn't even like them."

Alfie leaned around Avianna. "I heard they make you lusty."

"Just what we need around here," Alistair growled, "more lusty bastards. Get out here and take your knocks." Avianna hooked Alfie with her ankle and pushed him back behind her, as she smoothed her hand down Alistair's chest.

"It was an accident, Alistair. Let the boy go. Didn't he do errands all day?" She tilted her head and gazed up at Alistair.

His fist with the spoon lowered a bit. "Errands? Got in the way, more like it. Dug through all the jars in the pantry, teased the cat. And I caught him trying to peek up Lucinda's skirt."

"Well, he's only ten, and he misses his mother." She patted Alistair.

The spoon lowered to hang at his side. "You know, you could work here, Avianna. I know it's not the kind of work you want, but it's not bad."

"The kind of work I want?" Avianna snorted. "What I want is to be life bonded, with a house in the country and servants to do the work."

Alistair smiled. "You might meet someone if you were serving the drinks, instead of lying about upstairs."

"Lying about?" Avianna arched an eyebrow.

Alistair blushed.

"I appreciate it, Alistair, I do. I just couldn't face the crowd every night, snickering about me. At least in the laundry yard I don't have a crowd of onlookers."

"But Alfie would love to have you here. You'd be a better influence on the boy than Lucinda."

Someone else snorted. "Avi, a good influence?"

Beck stood in the doorway to the bar, gripping the doorframe above his head, his shirt sleeves taut over his bulging biceps. Those arms and his thick dark hair had once made Avianna crazy, but now she saw only the mean glint in his eye.

He shifted to face her. "Have a good time upstairs? Doesn't seem like all the tumbling's helping you find a mate."

"It can't hurt," Avianna snapped. "At least I'm meeting people." She stopped herself from saying more, knowing he was trying to bait her.

"Rye? Or did you meet someone else up there?"

Avianna turned to Beck, and Alfie crept around her side to stay away from his father. Beck stood beside Alistair's ridiculous plant—a spiky Norlian lemon tree that a merchant had given him, in spite of Sylvania's cold winters. Avianna resisted the urge to break off one of its long spikes and jab it into Beck's crotch.

"At least I meet people," she said, "instead of sitting here drunk every night."

"I assure you, I meet people," Beck said, glancing over his shoulder. A woman down the bar was watching them, and when Beck's head turned, she smirked. He turned back, eyeing Avianna up and down. "Rye didn't take very long with you, did he?"

"Now Beck—" Alistair said.

"Don't be such a hypocrite," Avianna interrupted. "Like *you* ever lasted more than a minute."

Beck's smooth smile stayed on his face, but his eye twitched and Avianna knew her barb had struck. She waited for his retort.

"At least I'm not desperate enough to tumble the likes of Rye."

Before Alistair could defend her, Avianna stepped up to Beck. "Maybe he's not the one for me. But at least I'm trying to find him. Not like you, strutting about like the prize stud as if you're too good to settle down with anyone."

"Stud?" Beck's eyebrow lifted, and an annoying smile crept across his face.

But before he could continue, a thump came from above. They all turned to look up the stairs, but no one appeared.

Then a slurred voice carried down. "Avi . . ."

Beck laughed. "Looks like Prince Charming is ready for another round."

"Shut up."

"You know what your problem is, Avi?" Beck didn't wait for a reply. "You want a husband, but you're just not the kind of girl men want for a wife."

Chapter 2

Beck's taunt hit the bullseye. Avianna didn't try to hide it. Instead she stumbled to the pub door, carrying Alfie along with her as her vision blurred. She fumbled for the latch. Alfie must have found it because the door opened and they fell out into the night. She ignored the voices behind her and fled along the cobbled street, past a handful of shops until she rounded the corner and left the pub behind.

But she couldn't rid herself of Beck's sneer. He always knew exactly how to hurt her. And the worst part was, he was right. She *wasn't* the kind of girl men wanted for a wife.

She stopped walking, wiped her eyes, and sniffed to clear her nose. The night was cool and misty, threatening an autumn rain. The light from the street lamps formed a hazy ball around each globe, with the rest of the street fuzzed into darkness.

Footsteps padded up behind her. A hand slipped into hers. "I'd bond with you, Avi," Alfie said.

Avianna squeezed his hand. "Too bad I'm not ten winters old," she replied.

"Beck's a moron. He tried to plow a field using old tin cans, all tied together on his rake."

Avianna smiled down at the boy and started walking. "He did not."

As they passed under a lamp, the light flickered on Alfie's face. "He did! Eddie saw him do it. And he was stumbling everywhere and it wasn't working but he was too stupid to stop."

As Alfie launched into the tale of what Eddie had seen, Avianna glanced along the row houses lining the narrow street. Behind her, the street sloped downhill to the wharf where the fish-catchers unloaded their stinking harvest every afternoon. She and Alfie headed uphill, but Avianna would turn before they reached the top. She seldom went that far, where the cobblestones smoothed out and the lanes widened into a square with a park at the center. Bordering one side of the square was the grange hall, where dances were held, and the cottages up there had space for a garden.

But over the rooftops, the spires of the former king's castle towered in the sky. From the top of the hill she could see them, and each time she did, her heart panged like the spires had pierced it. She'd had so much opportunity, and she'd wasted it, and now she had nothing. She should've been more like Elspeth while she'd had the chance, sitting quietly instead of always jumping in with her opinion, smiling a deferential smile instead of biting back when the courtiers made their ignorant comments. She could never seem to stop herself.

As she and Alfie neared the turn to the boarding house, she tried to focus on his story.

"Are you sure he was trying to plow with tin cans?" Avianna asked. "It sounds more like he was drunk."

"Well duh, of course he was drunk, that's why he was plowing with tin cans."

"Who was plowing with tin cans?"

Avianna looked up. They'd reached the corner, and coming from the opposite direction was a lithe man with spectacles, holding a stack of pamphlets. It was Thorn, the village printer.

"Beck," Alfie said to Thorn. "He was too stupid to bond with Avi, and he got drunk and tied a row of tin cans to his rake and tried to plow with it. Eddie saw him."

"Then it must be true," Thorn said, falling into step beside them as they turned together into the lane. "Hi, Avi."

Avianna opened her mouth to reply, but Alfie interrupted. "Do some magic, Thorn!" Avianna closed her lips and smiled.

Thorn lowered his gaze to the boy. Alfie dropped Avianna's hand.

"Want me to make Beck break out in boils?" Thorn asked.

"You can do that?" Alfie's eyes widened and his legs danced with excitement.

"No, sadly."

"Make me taller."

"I can't waste my supplies, Alfie. Fairy dust is for emergencies."

"Then do it to yourself."

Thorn stopped walking and Avianna did too, but Alfie bounced around them on his toes. Thorn bit his lip and blew upward, blowing the long dark hair off his forehead, one eyebrow dropping as if he were thinking hard. Alfie bounced harder. Then Thorn's head disappeared.

Avianna jumped back, but Alfie roared with laughter. Thorn's head reappeared, grinning.

"He did his head!" Alfie said. "Just his head, did you see? Do it again, Thorn!"

Thorn reached out and mussed Alfie's hair. "It's getting late. Shouldn't you be home?"

"My da's going to cook me."

"He's not going to cook you," Avianna said.

Alfie turned to her. "He was chasing me with the soup spoon. You saw him."

"He'll get over it. He always does. Sneak in and go to your room. And don't make any more trouble tonight."

"Why can't you come live with us, Avi?"

"I just can't." A raindrop hit Avianna's nose. "Go now, you can beat the rain."

Alfie pursed his lips together and turned to go.

"And Alfie?" Avianna reached for his shoulder. "Stop trying to peek up Lucinda's skirt. No one will court you if you behave like that."

Alfie stared at the ground, hesitating a moment. "Bye Avi. Bye Thorn." He took off back the way they'd come.

"I'm heading your way," Thorn said. "I'll walk with you?"

Avianna nodded. She studied Thorn as they resumed walking. She never would have thought she'd become friends with someone like him—certainly not when she'd first arrived from the castle, dumped on the steps of the boarding house with Elspeth and Corella and told to find work. Back then, she'd imagined herself mingling with the village's elite, still garnering the attention she'd earned at court. She wouldn't have even noticed Thorn if it hadn't been for a cat. A dog had cornered the little thing a few blocks up from the market and looked ready to kill it. Avianna couldn't stand seeing anything cornered like that, so she'd grabbed the dog's scruff and hauled it backward. Of course, the cat fled, and the dog tore loose to chase it, and they both ran right under the feet of a man holding some kind of giant wooden slab and angling to get it in the doorway of a shop.

As the man's load teetered, Avianna ran forward. She grabbed the other end of the wooden slab and helped him guide it in the door and lower it to the floor.

"The cat got away," he said, pushing up a pair of spectacles.

"What?"

That was when she saw his green eyes.

"I thought you'd want to know," he said. "The dog didn't catch her."

Avianna had nodded and bolted out the door.

Now a raindrop dripped down his spectacles. He wiped it away, and the bright green of his irises flashed in the lamplight. The fairies' green eyes still sent chills down her spine. And their skin—it was the same golden tan as most of the villagers', the ones who'd grown up near Woodglen or elsewhere in central Sylvania, but with a strange luster, something to do with their magic and their love of the moon. Everyone in the castle had said the fairies were danger-ous tricksters who lured humans into the forest to have their way with them, but since the revolution, fairies sometimes came to the village, and they never seemed particularly dangerous. Although it was unnerving how they could change their appearance or even disappear.

But Thorn was just Thorn. Avianna had grown so used to him, sometimes she honestly forgot he was a fairy. Since that first day when she'd helped him, she'd been running into him almost daily. And he was always cheery and helpful—like when she was strug-gling to bring sacks of laundry home, he'd turn up and carry half of them. Or if she was scowling at the cobblestones on a bad day, he'd still say hello when he met her on the street, and he'd ask what was wrong and listen as she ranted about Mattie's latest prank, or that she had slept through breakfast and no one had saved her any biscuits. Sometimes she'd take whatever papers he was carrying and finish his delivery to save him time. It felt nice to help, like they were becoming friends.

But more than that, he felt safe, like a castle guard who took his duties way too seriously and wouldn't try to tumble her no matter how much she flirted. There was nothing menacing about Thorn, not in the ways Avianna expected of a fairy after the stories she'd heard. He used his magic to make his head disappear, for skies' sake.

Another raindrop skidded across his spectacles.

"Why don't you just make them invisible?" she asked, nodding at his face.

"My spectacles? They'd still have raindrops on them."

Avianna could never quite grasp the intricacies of the fairies' magic. She must have looked confused because Thorn began to explain.

"They don't dematerialize when I make them invisible. They're still there, with raindrops on them. You just can't see them."

Avianna wasn't sure it made sense, so she merely shook her

head, her dark curls rustling over her shoulders. "Where are you headed?"

"The boarding house. Your landlady wanted me to bring by the new pamphlets. I only now finished them, and I thought she'd still be up." He fanned the pamphlets in his hand and showed her before tucking them away out of the rain. The top one had a drawing of a fancy hat and boots.

"It's an advertisement, then?"

"Yes." Thorn paused. "You don't read?"

"No." Only manor girls had learned to read, before the revolution. Avianna might have been a court lady, but she hadn't come from a manor. No one had known her secret, not even Elspeth.

Being at court had been her one chance to escape her past. Until the revolution destroyed it. Her fingers went to the beads at her neck.

Thorn's eyes followed them. "Those are Norlian crystal?"

Avianna nodded. "When they booted out the courtiers, they took all our things, but they let me keep these. They were the first gift I was ever given, so they've always been special to me. And now they're the only thing I have left of my old life."

"I could probably name a few other things," Thorn said, and he shot her a suggestive look.

Avianna shoved at him with her elbow, and he stumbled on the cobblestones. "Don't tease," she said. "It's been a long day."

He righted himself and caught up with her. "I could teach you to read, Avi. I've been giving lessons for the villagers' children."

"And give everyone another reason to laugh at me? No, thank you."

"You could come after, not with the children."

"I have to work. Besides, I can't learn to read."

She tensed, waiting for him to argue. But Thorn dropped it. He was like that—always offering to help, but never pushy about it. She liked that about him.

Avianna peeked sideways at him. She liked Thorn. But he

wasn't her type. If only he were a little more . . . rugged. More . . . exciting. And not poor.

And human.

It's not like she was against tumbling a fairy. But she'd gotten involved with a . . . nonhuman creature once before, and it hadn't worked out too well.

Thorn would argue he wasn't poor. The fairies didn't care much for human belongings. Most of them didn't even visit the village, where they could buy human trinkets. They lived in some sort of commune deep in the forest. But even without high-class tastes, how Thorn supported himself with the print shop was a mystery. As was how he even owned a print shop—and why. Did the fairies have some kind of plan to take over the village, and Thorn was the preliminary spy, gathering information to send home? Ha, not likely. But why live in the village? Did he just like eating fish and biscuits more than acorns, or whatever the fairies ate? How had he even learned to read, growing up in the forest?

The print shop seemed to be flourishing—Thorn's political flyers papered the walls near the docks, fodder for the conversations in the pubs—well, the nice pubs, where patrons weren't too drunk to converse. Or so she'd heard—it wasn't like she frequented those pubs often. But Avianna knew he bartered for his services half the time, to make them available to more of the villagers. And he printed the grange's flyers for free. And no matter how many flyers he actually sold, they couldn't bring in *that* many shells.

Why Thorn followed human politics, Avianna didn't know. But it was awfully easy to forget he wasn't human. At least it was when he wasn't making his head disappear for Alfie.

They neared the towering boarding house. Its front was flush with the street, with no flower beds or shrubs to settle it in place. But the stark lines of the house were broken by . . . something. Or someone. Someone lay on the road, propped against the stone foundation of the wooden house, not moving in spite of the raindrops now sprinkling down.

Avianna recognized the figure on the ground and hoped that he was passed-out drunk. He still didn't move as she and Thorn climbed the steps to the door.

Avianna reached for the latch, but the door swung open before she touched it. Mattie stepped out, blocking Avianna from entering the house. Had Mattie been watching out the window? For her? Or for Thorn? Avianna smiled smugly.

"Hi Thorn," Mattie said, running her hands down the long, dark braid that hung over her shoulder. "Did you bring us new papers?" Her voice was silky, not the harsh caw she used when she ridiculed Avianna. All the usual meanness was gone from her gaze.

Avianna rolled her eyes and crossed her arms.

"Oh, Avianna!" Mattie said, as if just noticing her. "Have you been out at the pub again? I see no one's walking you home. He must have finished with you there."

"I'm walking her—" Thorn began.

"Your boyfriend's been waiting for you." Mattie cut him off and pointed at the drunk man slumped on the ground.

"Prince Murkel is not my boyfriend," Avianna said, narrowing her eyes.

Prince Murkel. He was a man now, true, but once he'd been the leader of the merfolk. When Princess Rose and the peasants had overthrown the human king, they'd left Murkel in a dungeon cell until he dried out and lost his ability to change back into a merman. Of course, he *had* tried to drag the princess out to sea to be his love slave, so it was hard to pity him.

Mattie sniggered. "Hey Murkel!" she called. "Avianna's home!"

Avianna tried to get past Mattie, but Mattie stepped sideways to block her, keeping Avianna trapped on the stoop.

"Avianna," came a rasping voice from the body on the ground. His head tilted up, the sunken eyes opening and swerving about until they caught her. "Was waiting for you."

Heat rose up Avianna's neck. "I don't see why," she snapped. She tried again for the door, but she couldn't get in without shoving Mattie aside. She hadn't yet sunk into outright fist fighting. Mattie crossed her arms, waiting for Murkel to spew out the rest of the story.

"'Member the fun we had?"

"We did not!" Avianna said, but once Murkel started reminiscing, she could never stop him. At least it was only Thorn witnessing her humiliation this time.

Murkel propped himself up. "Back when we were royals. I should've stuck with you, Avi. You were the best one."

"See, Avi?" Mattie said. "Someone's willing to bond with you." She grinned.

Avianna's eyes welled up with tears. She could take the jeers she knew weren't true, but Mattie had hit the mark, as Beck had earlier. No one wanted a life bond with her.

Murkel rambled on. "That time in the bushes, when I made you scr—"

"So, Mattie, I have the pamphlets." Thorn stepped forward and took Mattie's arm. Her grin faltered as she glanced up at Thorn.

Such a dilemma, Avianna imagined—keep torturing Avianna, or flirt with Thorn?

Thorn smiled at Mattie, pulling her gently toward him, and his smile must have dazzled her because she disregarded Avianna.

As Thorn pulled Mattie closer to him, he opened up a space behind her.

"I *would* bond with you," Murkel said.

Avianna slipped in the door.

Chapter 3

TODAY IS GOING TO BE different, Avianna told herself. *Remember your resolve last night. You're going to find a new way to get out of this situation.*

But she kept lying on her mattress, staring sideways at the empty beds in the room and trying to find some reason to leave hers. The morning sunlight through the curtains illuminated the specks of dust on the floorboards.

Avianna had been the last to wake, as always. She shared the cheapest room at Flo's boarding house with five other women. Her bunk was the most awkward to reach, tucked into a dark corner, but it gave her some privacy. A wall had her back, if no one else did. And she could hide her things. Not that she had much to hide, other than her crystal necklace and her wages. And her identity, of course.

Besides, the other women weren't thieves. Just hateful and prone to mean pranks.

Today was a day past the new moon, Avianna remembered. Another moon's rent was due. For a brief moment, she wished she'd hunted around for Rye's purse the night before. He wouldn't even notice a few missing coins—he'd think he'd drunk them. But she hadn't yet stooped that low. Rye had to work for his living same as she did, and every coin was part of a life wasted.

With a sigh she pushed back her quilt and swung her feet to the floor. The boards were warm, the last heat of summer lingering in the thick wood. She could only imagine how cold they'd be in two moons when winter was full upon them.

At least people still needed laundry done in the winter, she thought as she pulled off her cap and nightclothes and took her clean dress off its hook. She couldn't imagine being a farmer and trying to save for three moons without an income. Of course, the farmers were used to it. They'd grown up learning how to manage a farm. They hadn't been booted out of their homes and expected to start farming without any idea how.

She hadn't learned anything growing up—except how to steal.

Avianna studied her hands as she buttoned up her dress. Once they'd been smooth and fine, but now they were chapped and rough. They caught in her hair when she pulled out the band tying it up and as she fluffed it.

Avianna headed for the door. Corella must've been the last one out of the room, because Mattie would have left the door open, hoping the noise from the house would wake Avianna. As she pressed the latch, footsteps clumped on the other side. Avianna took a deep breath and put on her most tranquil face. She opened the door.

"Good morning, Miss Flo," Avianna said before her landlady could speak. Flo's pink-stained lips opened and closed, arrested by Avianna's pleasant greeting. Not for the first time, Avianna wished she could help Flo paint her lips properly and pull her mussy tresses into a neat loop atop her head. The woman gussied herself up every morning, or tried to, even if she spent most of her time poking around the boarding house.

"You were out late," Flo said, eyes narrowed.

"Alistair needed some help with Alfie."

Flo's eyes softened immediately. "Oh, that poor child," she said. "Alistair needs to find a wife."

"Well, don't look at me," Avianna said. "The last thing I need is to live in a pub."

Flo's softness evaporated. "I'll say. What you need is to pay your rent. Last moon's *and* this moon's."

Gad. She'd forgotten she still owed last moon's. "I will, Flo. I'm ready to tackle the laundry."

"See that it doesn't win, Avianna. One more moon and you're out. I'm not a charity." Flo bustled past her into the dormitory.

That would be just what she needed—losing her home on top of everything else.

The staircase by the women's room led down to the parlor and dining room. Voices carried up, indicating the residents were still at breakfast. Avianna walked away from them and down the hall, past the open doorway to the empty men's dormitory, past the opened and closed doors of the private rooms. At the end of the hall, a creaking staircase took her down to the kitchen.

Wan fall sunlight shifted in the kitchen windows. The kitchen was blessedly empty, and the fire in the hearth added a warm cheer. The kitchen was the one place that made Avianna think she might someday enjoy her new peasant life. In the castle, meals had been served in a noisy dining hall, and she'd never even seen the kitchen.

Avianna scanned over the pots and pans. What was for breakfast—sausages, she guessed from the grease in the frying pan, and bread from the crumbs in the oven pot. No eggshells—that was disappointing. The kettle was warming on the stove. As Avianna reached for the basket of tea herbs, the kitchen door banged open. Mattie and Samantha stalked through, trailed by Corella.

"Morning, Avi," Mattie said. She eyed the basket in Avianna's hands. "Oh, we already made you tea."

Mattie lifted a cozy off Flo's teapot in the center of the table. Samantha simpered behind her. Corella watched the others with her usual blank stare.

Avianna waited for the trick. There was no way Mattie had simply made her tea to be nice. Mattie poured a cup and handed it to her.

"Thank you."

"There's a whole pot left," Mattie said. "We made a new one just for you. We thought you might need extra. You know, since you're trying so hard to find a husband."

Samantha snickered.

Avianna felt the sting, even when she'd been expecting it. She blew across the tea before taking a sip. "At least the other girls and I have a reason to drink bitter tea," she said. "There's not much chance of you getting pregnant, since you can't even get a man to kiss you." Mattie pursed her lips, but her eyes stayed hard. Avianna would have to turn the screw tighter. "Even Thorn doesn't look twice at you."

Behind Mattie, Corella winced.

"I hope you get pregnant," Mattie hissed. "I hope you end up in the gutter with Prince Murkel." She turned and stalked back to the dining room, followed by Samantha, their matching braids swinging.

Avianna glared after them as an idea formed. Today she would start to get out of here. And she'd take Mattie down while she did it.

She blew across the top of her cup again and took another sip. Every morning in the castle, they'd had honey for the bitter tea. Across the table, Corella fingered the woven napkins stacked in a basket.

"I miss being the mean girl," Avianna said.

Corella's lips twisted in a smile. Unlike Mattie and Samantha, Corella wasn't a village girl. She'd come to court from one of the northern coastal towns. She'd been at court only a moon before the villagers revolted, but she'd chosen to stay in Woodglen.

"You're still mean," Corella said.

"But I liked being the *only* mean girl."

Corella shook her head, smiling wider. "You *were* mean, weren't you? You and Elspeth always whispering and picking on the poor princess."

"Well, she got the last laugh, didn't she?"

"I don't think anyone was laughing."

"She won the handsome prince, though. She started the blasted revolution, then ran off with the fairies while the rest of us are stuck here, scrubbing endless laundry while our looks fade and we grow old, alone."

Corella dropped the napkin and lifted her chin. Her deep brown eyes bored into Avianna. "Don't you ever think of changing your life?"

"Of course I do. But how? It's impossible to save any shells. The only way out I can see is bonding with someone who already has a pile of them."

"If that's your solution, why not try meeting new men?"

"Why do you think I go to the pub every night?"

"I mean different men."

"Different how?"

Corella hesitated. "Not drunks."

"I try! There aren't any."

"There are, Avi, if you try outside the pub."

"Who has time? We have to work all day. And so do all the men, for that matter. By the time we're all done working, everyone's too tired and the pub is all there is."

"The grange dances are after work. You should come tonight. The men there might be looking for the same thing you are."

"But not with me."

Corella rolled on. "I know it's scary to try again, after what happened with Beck, but you just have to try. The men at the dances are nice."

Why'd she have to bring up Beck? Avianna had been so sure he was the one, but when she'd mentioned a life bond, he'd dropped her.

Avianna scoffed. "Nice? Boring, you mean."

"Tanner's not boring," Corella said, and her cheeks reddened.

Avianna couldn't help grinning. "From the look of you, Tanner must not be too boring in bed."

Corella held in a smile. "And, Elspeth met Drake at a dance."

"My point exactly."

"But Drake's not boring."

"Not if you like sipping citrus tea with his mother and talking about the newest imports from Esteria."

"Imports that pay for shoes and gowns."

"True."

A moment of silence passed. Avianna wondered if Corella shared her thoughts, remembering the shoes and gowns they used to wear in the castle.

"But those men aren't interested in me," Avianna said. "They're hoping for *nice* girls who smile and keep their mouths shut. Beck and Mattie are right. No one will want to court me." Especially, Avianna thought, if they knew where she'd really come from. If anyone at the castle had found out her true family history, she'd have been tossed out or worse, sent to the dungeons. She'd kept her secret for almost ten winters. She wasn't about to let it out now.

Corella sighed. "Don't listen to Mattie or even Samantha, Avi. They're just resentful. They wish they'd lived in the castle like we did."

"I don't see why. Then they'd know what they're missing."

"It bothers Mattie when the merchants treat us different and the men favor us, even though we're all supposed to be the same now."

Avianna sniffed. "It's 'cause we're new. Give it another seven moons and we'll be old news, too."

Corella shrugged. "Maybe. But I'm going to keep trying. My parents sent me to court to have a good life. I'm going to take advantage of it as long as I can."

Avianna knew she should, too. She just had to make sure no one found out the truth about her past.

After she'd had her tea and the scraps of sausage and bread, she tied up her hair, donned an apron, and followed Corella outside. Last night's rain had cleared into a cool, windy morning. The two women lugged out the wash tubs and spent an hour carrying pails of water up from the nearest village well. Corella boiled as much as would fit on the kitchen stove, while Avianna stirred the giant pot hanging over the fire pit in the yard, until they had enough hot water to start.

All through the summer, the laundry water had stayed warm all day, but now that autumn had come, it quickly grew cold. In spite of the bright fall sunshine, Avianna's hands were red and raw after a few minutes of scrubbing. Doing the laundry would be ten times worse once winter came. But maybe she would no longer be here doing it . . . .

The morning passed, and then the lunch hour, and still she and Corella worked, soaking, scrubbing, wringing, rinsing, and wringing again, then pinning the clothes and sheets up in the breezy sunshine on the lines that crisscrossed overhead. Neither of them wanted to pay the extra coin Flo charged for the midday meal. That's why they filled up on breakfast—assuming they got up on time. Corella always managed to, at least.

Now the sun headed down the sky. In spite of how briefly it had stayed warm, the laundry water had managed to steam Avianna's curls, leaving her hair frizzy in its binding. Avianna used the back of her wrist to wipe the damp strands off her forehead. Corella had pinned back her own hair tightly, protecting it under a cap to keep it tidy for the dance that night.

Corella handed her another soaking bundle. She wrung it out and began to scrub it on the ridges of the metal washboard. She was faster now than she had been seven moons ago, now that she'd had so much practice. Plus she didn't need to watch for her fingernails. Every last one was broken off.

"That's the end of it," Corella said.

"Thank the skies."

Corella began rinsing her tub, after pouring the water out into the grass. "It'll cover another two weeks' rent," Corella said.

"Lucky for you. I owe her for all last moon." When Corella

didn't reply, Avianna continued. "At this rate, neither one of us will ever afford a new dress."

Corella leaned her tub on the pole of a drying line and tugged off her damp apron. She dried her hands on her skirt and then smoothed out the fabric. The skirt was whole, but the waist and shoulders had patches. "At least we have two dresses each," Corella said. "I'd work in this one filled with holes before I'd wear my dance dress out here."

"Well let's hope you find a husband before it comes to that," Avianna said, regarding her own dress. It was the nicer of her two. Her work dress lay crumpled on the floor by her bed. She should have worn it again. Or brought it out to be laundered. Why hadn't she thought of it? She was hopeless.

The back door of the boarding house burst open, and Mattie came out, her dress starched smooth, her hair up in bows.

Avianna groaned. "I hate her stinking bows," she muttered.

Corella shot her a sympathetic look before smiling at Mattie.

Mattie perched on the stoop at the door, her feet in stockings. "You ladies look lovely," she said. "Your red faces should clear before dinner, at least. But it's too bad about your curls, Avi. They're so nice when you haven't sweated them into a frizz." Mattie reached in her pocket and came out with a golden bun. She pinched a piece off and popped it into her mouth. The yeasty bun smell wafted to Avianna's nose, mixed with the soapy smell of laundry.

"Keep scrubbing that one so we can finish out here," Corella said, nudging Avianna's elbow.

"Are you going to the dance?" Mattie asked Corella as Avianna pushed the clump of damp clothing down the washboard.

"We were just talking about it," Corella answered before Avianna could think of a provoking reply. Corella smiled encouragingly. "Right, Avi?"

Mattie's smile dimmed. "You don't usually go," she said to Avianna.

Avianna smiled.

"You probably wouldn't like it much," Mattie continued. She must really not want Avianna to go.

"Why not?"

Mattie's face hardened. "You're such a flirt. People at the dance are always polite, but you're so . . . talkative."

"I'm 'talkative'?" Anger simmered in Avianna's gut.

Mattie lifted her chin. "You always have to be the center of attention. Men don't always like that. It might work in the pub, but the dances are different."

"Maybe the dances would be more fun if more flirty, talkative girls *did* go. Fun for the men, anyway."

Mattie's lips pressed tight and she inhaled sharply. Avianna stared into her mean eyes. "You know, Mattie, I think I *will* go." She glared at Mattie. "You'll help fix my hair, won't you, Corella?"

"Of course."

Flo's voice called from inside the house. Mattie's tight lips curved into her usual mocking smile and she stood, swallowed the last bite of her bun, and licked her fingertips.

"Flo needs me for deliveries," Mattie said. "I'm so glad she has me run errands instead of helping with the laundry." She brushed imaginary crumbs from her skirt and went inside, letting the door bang shut behind her.

"I'm so glad she has me run errands," Avianna mimicked, tilting her head back and forth like a ragdoll.

Corella burst out laughing. "Ignore her. You let her get to you."

"Not today," Avianna said, and a smile broke across her face.

"What did you do?"

"I hid her shoes."

"When?"

"After I brought the water pails back inside this morning."

Corella shook her head. "She'll borrow Samantha's."

"I hid Samantha's, too."

"Where? They'll find them."

"No, they won't. And I can't tell you, or you'll be an accomplice."

Corella shook her head again as Avianna finished scrubbing and handed back the last bundle of laundry. "You don't mind rinsing this, do you? I want to go offer Flo my delivery services."

Chapter 4

MUFFINS TO THE DOCK MISTRESS, six pounds of cod. Muffins to the dock mistress, six pounds of cod." Avianna repeated Flo's errand under her breath, pulling her shawl around her shoulders with her free hand as she hurried down the shadowed lane. Flo had frowned when Avianna had asked to run the errand, and then shaken her head and refused to answer. But when half an hour had passed with no sign of Mattie's shoes, and with the dinner hour drawing ever nearer, Flo had given in.

"Don't dawdle, and don't get distracted," Flo had admonished. As if Avianna would. Someone whistled as she neared the docks, but she ignored it, clutching the coins in her pocket and the linen-wrapped muffins. She might have clutched that one muffin a little too hard, but Flo would never know. Avianna couldn't mess up this errand. If she did, Flo would never trust her again, and she'd never escape the punishing laundry duty. Besides, the pay from running this errand would remove a few days' debt.

She stepped onto the wharf. This late in the day, the fishing boats were returning to the docks. The sun had dipped almost to the rooftops, and the afternoon wind blew in from the water. The fish-catchers hoisted nets and crates out of their sloops. The fresh autumn scent of the nearby forest mixed with the salty air, striking Avianna with an exhilarating breeze that filled her with hope. Cruel Beck, drunk old Murkel, and nasty Mattie were left behind.

"Muffins to the dock mistress." Avianna spotted the dock master walking from boat to boat, tallying the catch before the fish were taken up to the market stalls. She clasped the tea towel holding the muffins to her chest and climbed carefully down the ramp, then hurried across the shifting docks toward him.

A low whistle followed her. "Hey missy, got some room in my boat!"

Without thinking, Avianna spun to face the man. "Got some room in your head is more like it," she said. The nearby fish-catchers hooted, and the one who'd called out to her grinned. Avianna turned to find the dock master watching. He was an older man in a clean shirt and polished boots that for some reason made Avianna think he might be judgmental. A heated flush crept up her neck at the realization that he'd overheard her tell off the fish-catcher.

She approached him. "I'm looking for the mistress. I have her muffins."

"She's feeling poorly today. I can take them to her." He reached for the muffins and Avianna handed them over. "I apologize for the whistles," he said. "Some of the newer lads can be disrespectful after a day out on the water. I'll have a word with him."

"I don't mind," Avianna said. "But I won't just take it."

"That's fair."

"Where do I purchase fish?"

The dock master pointed her to one side of the wharf, and she retraced her steps up from the docks. The whistler grinned again as she passed. Avianna narrowed her eyes at him, and his grin spread wider. He wasn't bad looking. If only he didn't stink like fish.

At the market stalls, villagers crowded before the tables of fish. Sellers sorted the day's catch, pulling the best ones to sell and tossing the others into bins to be salted, pickled, dried, or donated to the grange home for the residents' dinner. Avianna fingered the coins in her pocket as she elbowed her way to the front and asked which fish fillets were cod. She would show Flo and Mattie that she was capable of running errands. She would buy the best six pounds of cod Flo had ever seen.

At the front of the tables, Avianna scanned the pile of cod. This was almost like buying ribbons or sweets . . . but what did one consider in a fish? She glanced at the hands grabbing at the fish beside her. All the fillets were the same translucent white. They were all freshly caught, so that couldn't matter. The other customers were tossing back the thinner fillets. Avianna spotted a thicker one and snatched it, pushing aside the thought that she'd never had to touch anything this slimy when she lived in the castle. When she'd nabbed a few, she handed her purchase to the seller. But as soon as the seller handed her the package of fish, Avianna turned to go and found herself blocked by Rye.

"Oh, hello Avianna," he said with mock politeness, as if he hadn't known it was her.

Rye was tall and broad, and his face was always clean shaven, and plenty of girls ogled him and swooned. But Avianna knew that his anger simmered constantly. He had a mean streak, mean enough that the village guard that formed after the revolution—the peacekeepers corps, they called it—had refused to accept him. That had only made him meaner.

Now he stared down at her, standing too close as shoppers bustled around them. "Where'd you go last night?" he said. "I didn't like waking up alone."

"Then you shouldn't pass out the minute you hit the bed," Avianna said, pushing past him and escaping the crowd. He followed and gripped her arm. She dragged him along.

"I don't remember it that way," he said.

"Well you did, and I wasn't about to spend the entire night upstairs in Alistair's, waiting for you to wake up."

"Your loss."

Avianna rolled her eyes. "Sure, whatever. Will you let go of me? I'm working." She indicated the paper parcel in her hands.

But he didn't let go. He moved after her into the lane that led away from the shop-lined wharf. Now that the fish had arrived with the boats, the lane with its row houses was deserted. The daylight had dimmed as the sun sank, leaving the street in the shadows of twilight. It was an hour before the street lamps were lit. Rye jerked Avianna to face him before letting go of her arm.

"Why are you being like this?" His hard eyes glared, and he ran a hand over his stubbly hair. He still shaved his head like one of the king's soldiers.

"Like what?"

"So . . . so rude. What did I do?"

"Nothing. I'm just tired of it, Rye."

"Of what?"

"Tumbling men at Alistair's. I want something different."

"Different?"

Mattie's insults came back to her. "I'm not looking for only a tumble. I want something more."

"You mean like a life mate?" The lack of derision in Rye's voice surprised Avianna. Did he want such a thing, too?

"Y-yes. Someone to share a home with."

"And you don't think I'd do?"

She peered into his face, and he stared back with sincerity. She wanted to be nice, to not say something that would only make him angrier. But what could she say? Tell him she didn't want to partner with a drunk, like her mother had with her father? What if he quit the drinking—would that be enough to make her want him?

"It's not just about the life bond, Rye. I want someone who thinks about my needs, too."

Rye's brow scrunched in confusion. "But last night—"

Her resolve to be nice started to crack. "Last night's a perfect example. We went upstairs and you shoved your tongue into my mouth and pulled up my skirts and started thrusting away without a second thought."

"That's just how it's done."

Sadly, he was right. That *was* how it was often done. But Avianna nurtured a hope that tumbling didn't have to be that way, that it could be more.

Rye was shaking his head, and his face had started to harden into the mien he usually wore around the village. "What d'you think, I don't know how to please a woman?" His tone right now was the one she'd heard many nights in the bar, right before he pummeled someone in the face and got thrown out the door.

But Avianna's temper rose in spite of the risk. It was useless to try discussing women's needs with Rye. He was always so sure he knew best. "Well I want something else," she blurted out. "I want someone who can last long enough to give me a chance, who doesn't pass out three breaths after he finishes."

Rye's face reddened, and his eyes widened. "Don't you talk to me that way." His voice was low and menacing. Avianna stepped back, but Rye closed the distance. "Like you're some fancy lady better than the rest of us. You cleaned up nice, but I see the cracks. Your hands aren't smooth like they used to be, and your clothes are wearing out. Soon you'll be wearing out, too, and who'll want you then, Avi?"

His words hurt, but Avianna wouldn't let him see that he'd gotten to her. She glared back, until a movement behind Rye caught her gaze. Rye turned to follow where she looked. Behind Rye, leaning on the wall of a house, was Thorn. He wasn't wearing a coat, just a vest over his shirt that highlighted his thin frame. His thumbs were in his vest pockets, and he stared at her and Rye without smiling, as if he were simply bored.

"What are you looking at?" Rye snarled.

Thorn kept leaning on the wall. "I was wondering the same thing. It seems to be an ex-soldier bullying a lady half his size."

"Bullying her?" Rye scoffed. "Avianna can take care of herself. And she's no lady, not anymore."

Thorn didn't reply. He pushed his spectacles up his nose. Rye took a step toward him, away from Avianna.

"This guy's different," Rye said, taking another step toward Thorn. "This what you're looking for, Avi? He doesn't look like he could get started, much less finish."

Thorn was tall, but Rye seemed three sizes bigger. And Thorn probably couldn't knock out Alfie, much less defend himself against Rye. Avianna reached for Rye's arm and tugged him back, but he shook her off and advanced on Thorn. As Rye lifted his arms and lunged forward, Thorn ducked sideways and slipped past him. At least he was fast.

Rye turned, and Thorn stepped in front of Avianna as if he were shielding her. As if he could—but it was a sweet gesture.

Thorn backed into Avianna, and his fingers wrapped around hers. Rye jerked back. Thorn tugged Avianna's hand, wordlessly pulling her up the cobbled lane. Rye gaped back and forth.

"Blasted fairy," Rye muttered, and Avianna understood— Thorn had turned them invisible.

Relief flooded through her as they stole away from Rye, up the darkening lane. They passed one doorway, then a second and third, and Rye still stood confused in the same spot.

Something caught Avianna's foot. She lurched forward, yanking her hand from Thorn's as she grabbed to catch the package of fish. She fell hard on her knees, but the fish was spared.

Thorn reached for her, but it was too late. The moment she'd let go of Thorn's hand, his spell had broken and she'd reappeared. Apparently Thorn was too gentlemanly to abandon her, because she could see him now, even though she'd left the spell. Which meant that Rye could see him, too.

Rye barreled up the lane and into Thorn, knocking him to the ground. Avianna tried to stand, but something wrapped around her ankle. It was the thing that had tripped her. It gripped like a tentacle, growing tighter as she tried to crawl away, trying to shake it off, all the while clutching the package of fish to her chest. The tentacle held on until she kicked hard, connecting with a body. It let go.

She turned to look. Prince Murkel was slumped on the cobblestones, an empty bottle rolling beside him. His greenish merman skin had faded in the moons since he'd lost the power to change form, leaving him a sickly hue, even when he wasn't drunk.

"Avi," he slurred, his fingers again reaching for her leg.

Avianna kicked him back again.

Ten paces away, Rye's beefy hand held Thorn's head to the ground, but Thorn had twisted his legs upward and locked them around Rye's neck, apparently with some force, given Rye's bulging eyes. Rye lifted Thorn's head, but the leglock tightened and Rye gasped for breath before he could bash Thorn's head back to the stones. It was a stalemate.

Avianna stumbled to her feet, rushed forward, and shoved Rye as hard as she could. She barely moved him, but it was enough for Thorn to gain the advantage. As Thorn untwisted his legs and placed his feet on Rye's chest, Rye turned. His hand came up and closed on Avianna's necklace.

Thorn pushed his legs out, and Rye fell backward, taking a handful of beads with him. The necklace snapped.

Horror washed over Avianna as the necklace slid off her skin. She reached for it, dropping the fish, but the beads were gone, bits of crystal flying away from her, falling with a patter onto the cobblestones. They bounced and rolled into the cracks.

Her old life was gone.

She had nothing left.

And if she didn't find a way to change things soon, she would end up like the weary fish-catchers who worked every day and never got ahead. Or worse, like Murkel, lying hopeless in the gutter, getting by on whatever scraps the pitying neighbors gave him. No one was going to help her, and time was running out.

She had to change things herself. But she couldn't even manage to run one errand without screwing it up. She wasn't good enough.

The beads were scattered, barely visible in the twilight, their twinkling lights gone out. Everything in Avianna's vision began to swim. She turned and ran.

Chapter 5

AVIANNA PEERED INTO THE MURKY glass in the dim back room of the grange hall. Her locks were still frizzed, but at least the red had faded from her eyes, now that she'd finally stopped crying. Hopefully Corella would realize she wasn't coming home and would bring a comb along when she came to the dance.

Avianna's fingers groped at her neck, and she remembered that her necklace was gone. She saw the bare skin in the glass. Rye was right—her looks were fading. The work was bending her back and roughening her skin, not to mention ruining the last two dresses she owned. Her final chance had come. If she didn't find a husband, she'd spend the rest of her life doing the village's laundry and seeking pleasure from men in the pub. The work would only get harder as she aged. And when she got too old to work, what then? Alone, she'd never be able to save for her future.

Elspeth had met Drake at a grange dance. Maybe she could find someone, too.

But dancing was the last thing Avianna felt like doing. She wanted to crawl into bed and cry again, but she'd never get into the boarding house without Flo spotting her. How long could she avoid her landlady? Flo would never trust her with an errand again. How could she have failed at something so simple?

And now she owed Flo for the fish, in addition to last moon's rent. Why had she dropped it? Stupid stupid stupid. "You don't deserve to be happy," she told her reflection, and it mouthed the words back at her.

She twirled a lock of hair around her finger, willing it to form a shining curl. If this was her last chance to save herself from a life of poverty, she'd better present her best self. She needed to find a likely husband, dance his heart out, and tumble his brain into oblivion. And then get him to bond with her before he grew tired of her. She held the curl another moment for good luck. Her dress had a dark smudge across the front of the skirt where her knees had ground it into the street, but hopefully the dance hall wouldn't be too well lit. Her other dress was trapped in the boarding house, and besides, it was crumpled in a heap on the floor and probably smelled like the pub.

She released the lock of hair and it struggled to hold its curl. Her hair had about as much willpower as she did right now. Avianna sighed. Could Corella fix her? She turned away from the glass and plodded into the main hall. The dark, silent space had a peace to it, with empty chairs scattered about and a raised platform at one end. The only light came in from the street. She slumped into a chair to wait.

A few minutes later, the door creaked open and one of the grange elders entered and began lighting the lamps. More people arrived, clearing the wooden chairs to the sides of the room as they greeted each other and gossiped. No one approached her, and even when the room brightened, no one looked her way. At the far end of the hall, on the platform, the members of a string band took instruments out of cases and began to tune them.

Then the door opened again, and in came Corella and Thorn.

Corella was wearing her designated dance dress, not the faded one she'd had on earlier that day in the laundry yard. She'd obviously brushed her hair a hundred times because it shone like Esterian silk, and she'd powdered away the tiredness from her face.

Thorn had a black eye.

"Flo's having a fit," Corella said as they neared.

"I figured. That's why I didn't go home."

"She made us turnip stew for dinner and told everyone it was your fault we didn't have fish."

"At least I delivered the muffins," Avianna said. "And I had the fish, the best ones. But Rye hassled me, and then Murkel tripped me."

"Thorn told her," Corella said. "He said it wasn't your fault."

Avianna mumbled thanks in Thorn's direction, but she couldn't bring herself to look at him. His black eye was all her fault.

"I'm sorry, Avi," Thorn said. "I tried to get the fish, but Rye came at me again, and Murkel crawled over to it and by the time I was free, he was gnawing on it and I figured it was too late."

"I'm sorry about Rye," Avianna said, staring at the floor. She forced herself to look up and into his eyes. "Why did you fight Rye? He's three times your size."

Thorn shrugged and turned his head away. A few strands of his long hair slid down to cover his eyes. "I don't like bullies."

Corella touched Thorn's arm. "You must've held your own if you only got a black eye, Thorn. I think it makes you even more brave, standing up to Rye."

Thorn's face reddened, and he pushed his specs up his nose.

A niggling guilt shifted in Avianna's chest. She hadn't meant to belittle him.

"You're embarrassing him, Corella," Avianna said, pulling Corella away. "Did you bring me some powder, I hope?"

"Of course I did. I'm not a ninny. Besides, he'll need it, too."

"Me?" Thorn asked, peering up at last.

" 'Less you want to be dancing with that black eye, scaring all the girls away."

"Doesn't it make me look tough? I thought ladies liked that." He pushed his spectacles up again, over the bruise. At least those hadn't broken, although Avianna didn't see how.

Corella rolled her eyes. "Come on, both of you." She led them into the back room, taking a satchel off her shoulder.

Avianna rallied as Corella worked on her face. It was almost like having Elspeth back. And Corella didn't mention Avianna's missing necklace. Every time Avianna remembered her Norlian crystal beads lying in the cracks of the street with drunk Prince Murkel wallowing on top of them, her heart sank all over again.

Corella moved around to her back, running her fingers loosely over Avianna's hair and scrunching her curls a few times. "I wish we had time to go home and mix something for this."

"Flo wouldn't give me an extra egg for breakfast right now, much less spare one to condition my hair."

"I sneaked a little of her cooking oil," Corella said. "It was the best I could do." She got out a comb and a bottle. From the main hall, the chatter of the crowd grew, as the band practiced a tune.

"You're so lucky, with this Norlian hair and your blue eyes," Corella murmured, working her hands over Avianna's hair.

Avianna kept her mouth shut, hoping Corella wouldn't ask about her family. She had a fake history she'd used at court, but over the seasons, she'd forgotten bits, until she wasn't sure what she'd said to whom. It was better not to talk about it.

"You always were the prettiest one at court."

"Lot of good it did me," Avianna replied.

Thorn shifted on the chair across from her.

"What did you like so much about court?" he asked.

"We didn't have to do people's laundry, for one thing," Avianna said.

"What did you do?"

"Needlework. And knitting."

Corella pursed her lips. "Mostly we sat around. And walked in the gardens, and ate food prepared by other people."

"And flirted," added Avianna. Corella had missed the most obvious point of all. But Thorn barged in.

"So basically you sat around in luxury while other people supported you."

He sounded like the revolutionaries, but somehow Avianna couldn't see a way to argue with him. Now that she'd been working for seven moons, it was harder to justify the easy life she'd led before the revolution. Avianna squirmed in the chair.

"Hold still," Corella said, and she began pulling one side of Avianna's hair into a braid. Avianna stared at the wall.

"We didn't know where the riches came from," Avianna said. "And it's not like we had any choice about sitting around. That was our job. We were pretty faces to decorate the castle. We were there for the male courtiers to buy nice things for."

"Then why did you like it?"

Avianna exhaled. "Because we didn't have to worry. There was always food and something to wear and somewhere to sleep. And we knew eventually someone would bond with us, and we'd be set for life and nothing bad would happen."

"Bad things still happen even when you're bonded."

"Maybe bad things happen when you're bonded, but they don't happen every *day*. They don't even happen every *moon*."

"We're barely able to pay Flo's rent by the new moon," Corella added. She pulled a ribbon from somewhere and tied off the braid, although with Avianna's thick hair she didn't need to tie it.

"We never get ahead," Avianna added. "And now our dresses are wearing out, and winter's coming but neither of us has a coat, and there'll never be enough shells for a new anything." Corella turned Avianna's head and began braiding the other side. Now Avianna faced Thorn. "And I hate doing laundry."

Avianna knew she was scowling, but Thorn grinned back. She liked his smile. His face was usually lit up by it, not like Beck and Rye and the others who constantly scowled. Thorn's hair hung straight, the front long enough to hide those freakish fairy eyes. He was always flipping it to one side, where it caught on his spectacles and stayed back. He did it now and his grin faded to a gentle smile as he held her gaze.

"Why don't you cut it?" Avianna asked. "You'd see better."

"I'm not good with scissors. Especially not that close to my face."

"I'll do it for you sometime."

"Thank you."

"Why do you come to these dances? Don't the fairies have their own?" Rumors of the fairies' wild dances circulated throughout the village, although no one Avianna knew had ever been to one. Since the revolution, the fairies were free to come and go, but most of them still lived in the forest, not like Thorn. And the villagers were free too, but their long-standing fear of the fairies was slow to diminish. Besides, the fairy village was nearly impossible for a human to find.

"I attend those as well," Thorn said.

"Oh." Avianna hadn't realized that Thorn spent time with his own people. He always seemed to be around the village. Almost every day she ran into him.

Corella finished with the second braid. She took both and looped them high on Avianna's head, pinning them into place.

"There, now you have a crown," Corella said. Her hands turned Avianna's head back toward the glass. Avianna stared in surprise. She'd expected to see someone bedraggled, but her eyes sparkled, her skin shone, and her hair did crown her head gloriously. Corella leaned to her ear. "You look so nice when you smile, Avi. Try to smile tonight."

Thorn refused to have his blackened eye powdered, and the three of them headed back into the main hall. A crowd of villagers had gathered. The band was still practicing, but couples had already moved into places on the floor. Avianna scanned the faces. She recognized some of the men, but others were strangers. And none were men she'd ever been with.

Corella was right. This dance was filled with possibilities. Avianna smiled and felt her flirting skills come right back to her—flirting always started with a smile.

She targeted a young man in a vest who stood along one wall. The vest was plush, like it was made of some material other than the linen or leather everyone else in the hall wore. And he had some kind of chain hanging from his pocket as if he had a pocket watch. He must be well off. He didn't have Beck's enormous muscles, but he wasn't bad to look at. Could she charm him?

She'd charmed Beck, at least for a while. Beck, in his tight deer-hide trousers with his shirt hanging open—every girl in the pub had wanted him. And Avianna had bested them all. Compared to Beck? This man in the vest would be a cinch. Had he ever even tumbled a girl? No matter. Once he'd been with her, he'd be hooked.

The door opened and Mattie and Samantha paraded in. Avianna ignored them, but as soon as they'd laid aside their shawls, they came toward her. The man she'd been eyeing watched them cross the hall. Samantha peeked over at him and turned back quickly, smiling and blushing scarlet.

"Hi, Corella," Mattie said. "Hi, Thorn." Thorn's name lingered on her tongue.

Thorn gave a tight smile back and dropped his gaze. Was he shy? Or did he truly not care for Mattie's attention?

Mattie's voice sharpened. "You look lovely, Avianna."

"Thank you."

"I spent all day searching for my shoes. Samantha found them under the shed."

"It's lucky you found them in time for the dance. I'm sure you would've hated to miss it."

Mattie's eyes narrowed and air hissed out her nostrils as she snapped, "You couldn't even do an errand right. Flo is livid. She said if you didn't pay back her shells, you're out. She'll never trust you again. It serves you right." Behind Mattie, Samantha smirked.

Mattie spoke the truth, but seeing her vexed made Avianna too happy to care. She'd smooth things over with Flo somehow. She always did.

Avianna returned Samantha's smirk with a wide smile. "No doubt. But now that we're all here, let's enjoy the dance. You'll have to introduce me around." She pointed at the man in the vest. "Like that man. Who's he? He looks like a catch."

Samantha sucked in a breath, and her skin blotched over. Avianna had been right—he was Samantha's quarry. Mattie's fists clenched.

"It's Jeb Doolihan," Corella said from behind Avianna. "His family owns the horse barn. Oh!"

Avianna turned at the change in Corella's voice.

"There's Tanner," Corella said. Now Corella's face was flushed. She shot a pleading look at Avianna and dashed across the hall to the door, where another young man had entered. She wasn't a moment too soon—Tanner had turned a few heads. This dance was a regular fish market.

Avianna turned back to Mattie and Samantha. "I think I'll go introduce myself to Jeb." She stepped forward, wishing she could watch Mattie and Samantha agonize as she seduced the hapless Jeb Doolihan.

Mattie grabbed Avianna's arm. "You better be careful, Avi," she said.

Avianna snorted. "How do you mean?"

"We've been making your tea every morning," Mattie said.

"So?"

Mattie came close to Avianna's ear. "We left out the thistle and laceflower. All you drank was ginger tea."

Avianna's heart turned over. "But that won't work. The laceflower stops conception, and the thistle—"

"Exactly," Mattie said. "I guess you'd better not get too friendly with anyone tonight." Her lips curved as she stepped back. "Well, enjoy the dance." She took Samantha's arm and steered her away.

Chapter 6

Avianna's heart pounded. How long had they been sabotaging her tea? When had her last cycle been? And how many times had she tumbled in that time? She couldn't get pregnant. If she did, her life was over.

"Avi?"

Avianna turned. Thorn was still beside her.

"You look like you're about to swoon. Do you need to sit?"

Avianna stepped off the dance floor and sank into the nearest chair. Thorn sat beside her. "What did Mattie say to you?"

"They've been changing the tea—the bitter tea that stops pregnancy. They gave me the wrong kind. How could they be so mean?"

Thorn leaned in, resting his arms on his knees. "How bad is it?"

"Bad."

Thorn didn't reply, just sat quietly beside her.

"I can't support myself, much less a child."

"The father would help."

"If I knew who it was."

"And the grange hall would—"

Avi shook her head. "It's not just the coins. I don't want to raise a child, not after—" She stopped herself before she said too much. She shook her head again. "I should have been more careful. I never imagined Mattie would stoop that low."

"That is low."

Avianna sat up. Thorn was watching her. It was nice having

someone who listened. She took a deep breath and let it out. "I can't fix it now. All I can do is wait."

"And start making your own tea."

"And find a husband." She began scanning the crowd again. The musicians were still warming up, but most of the crowd had paired off and stood eagerly in the center of the hall, in a gigantic circle.

Thorn slowly shook his head, watching her.

"What?" Avianna said. "If I am pregnant, my chances will plummet. The sooner I find someone, the better. But—" Avianna stopped as horror swept through her. "Oh, Thorn!"

"What is it?" He leaned in, his face serious.

"What about tonight?" Avianna said.

"Tonight?"

"How am I supposed to meet someone if I can't . . ." She couldn't bring herself to say it to Thorn. "You know."

"No, I don't."

Avianna did a milder version of the thrusting motion people in the pub used when they joked about tumbling. She lifted her eyebrows at Thorn.

"Is that how Rye does it?" Thorn asked with a straight face, and in spite of her fear, Avianna snorted as a laugh rippled through her.

"Stop making me laugh. It's not funny."

"It's not. But I still don't understand. Are you really hoping to bed Jeb Doolihan after the dance tonight?"

"It's not like I want to tumble Jeb Doolihan. But I need him to want me."

Thorn considered her a moment. "Was this what it was like in the castle?"

Avianna stared at him.

"Getting men, I mean. Your goal was always tumbling them."

Avianna shrugged. "That was usually how it worked."

Thorn dragged his chair around until he sat facing her. "Avianna." He leaned forward, placing his elbows on his knees again. "If you want the likes of Jeb Doolihan, you have to stop thinking like you're a castle courtier. Or like you're picking up another Rye."

"What do you mean? All men want the same thing."

"I take offense."

"Well, not you. I mean all real men."

Thorn closed his eyes and shook his head. "I'm going to let that pass, because you've had a rough day. Listen. I'm not saying Jeb Doolihan doesn't want to tumble you. But you've got to make him work for it."

"How do you mean?"

"Talk to him. Flirt with him. Make him want you so he goes home thinking about you. Give him a hint of what's to come. Then he'll want to see you again, and you get another chance to get to know him and make your relationship stronger."

"But won't he give up on me?"

"Not if he really likes you. I mean, I can't say if you and Jeb Doolihan are fated to be together. But if you're not, you move on to someone else."

"Easy for you to say. You're not running out of men."

"No, I'm not. Or women. But neither are you. Have you been with anyone in this hall?"

Avianna scanned the crowd again. "No." The music had begun, and pairs of couples were circling the floor in the giant ring. "Well, maybe that fellow in the green hat. He looks kind of familiar."

"But there are a lot of new men here, right? Here to meet people and get to know each other."

"I guess. So I talk. Flirt. No sex. What about kissing?"

Thorn didn't answer. Avianna turned back to him. He swallowed. "Maybe a little."

"So I've been hurting my chances by rushing things."

"I mean, I'm no expert on the life bond, but it seems like you should get to know each other a bit and see if you like each other. Aside from tumbling."

"But in the castle, if you didn't tumble, you never got any-where."

"This isn't the castle."

"That's for sure." Avianna peered closer at Thorn. "How did I not know this? Does everyone else know this?"

Thorn sat up at last. "You were in the castle for ages. No one ever courted you properly. You'll figure it out."

"Hopefully soon. Hopefully with Jeb Doolihan."

Thorn exhaled. "Jeb Doolihan will do it right. He's the perfect gentleman. By the time you've sorted out your tea situation, he'll be begging for your hand."

"Well, I have to sleep with him before I bond with him."

"Why is that?"

"What if he's not any good?"

"Presumably, if you love him, you'll make it work," Thorn said.

"This isn't about love."

"Besides, I'm sure Jeb Doolihan will be good in bed."

"How do you know that?"

"He's Jeb Doolihan," Thorn stated, as if that were an answer.

"Stop saying his name like that."

"Like what?"

"DOO-lihan."

"That's his name. Doolihan."

"No, you're saying it funny. Like you're mocking him."

"Why would I mock Jeb DOO-lihan?" Thorn asked. "He breeds horses, for stars' sake. Could there be a more noble profes-sion?"

"You're mocking him again."

"No, I'm not."

The dancers were circling the floor in pairs, each couple's arms around each other in the "promenade" position. Jeb Doolihan and Samantha, who clung to his fingers, approached Avianna and Thorn. She glared at Avianna as they passed.

"I have another problem," Avianna said.

Thorn let out an overloud sigh. "What's that?"

"I don't know these dances."

"Didn't you dance at the castle?"

"We did, but not like this. It was all dainty, like step forward and back, and turn in a circle. This looks positively heathen by comparison."

"This?" Thorn's face cracked into a grin.

"It's that one move they do, with the spinning and the hands."

Thorn backed up his chair and stood, holding his hand out. "Come on, I'll show you."

Avianna scrutinized him as she took his hand. His grip was surprisingly strong as he pulled her up. "How do you know these dances?"

"I come here for every dance, for one thing." He took her left hand and put it on his shoulder. His body wasn't as bony as she'd expected. He kept holding her right hand. "And for another, they're all simplified versions of traditional fairy dances."

"They are?"

"Yes. Now focus. Is it okay if I put my hand on your back?"

"Why are you asking?"

"To make sure it's okay."

"Why wouldn't it be okay?"

"Never mind."

Thorn stepped toward her and his hand settled on her back, higher than she'd expected, right between her shoulder blades. For a heartbeat, she imagined that if she had wings, that's where they'd sprout from. His elbow came under hers, lifting it up. She shook her head. This close, she could smell Thorn's skin, and it didn't reek like ale or fish or any of the other things men usually smelled like. Maybe it was the smell of paper and ink from his print shop— if the shop were located in a wild forest glen filled with pungent herbs and wind-swept trees.

Thorn tilted his hand against her back and her body shifted.

"Try to pay attention to your partner's signals," he said. "Most of the folks here know what they're doing, so if you follow their lead, you'll end up in the right place." His hand shifted again, and her body followed. "Good," he said.

"Show me the spinny move."

He began walking her in a circle. "Not to be a creep, but it'll help you stay steady if you focus on my face."

The room was already starting to spin, and they weren't going half as fast as the couples on the dance floor. Avianna met Thorn's gaze, and he smiled, making it not awkward. His green eyes were growing on her. He spun faster, and the force of it pulled her outward against his hand, which pushed back and held her up. She found herself smiling. He gave a final spin, twirling her under his arm to finish it.

Avianna caught her breath as he pulled her to a stop. "It's fun."

"Yes. It *is* fun." He squeezed her hand and let go.

Avianna and Thorn both turned to the dance floor. The circle dance had been going on the whole time. It must be nearing its end. The hairs on her arm could sense Thorn beside her. Would he ask her to dance? Suddenly she dreaded the idea of being close to him for a whole dance, and how awkward it would be, especially in the middle of all these people.

She cleared her throat. "I'd better go stalk Jeb Doolihan."

Thorn glanced down at her and smiled slightly. "Good luck."

Avianna made her way around the edge of the hall. The dancers ranged from youngsters of a dozen or so winters to white-haired elders, one even dancing with a cane hanging from his arm. Older folks sat in the chairs, tapping along to the string band. She spotted Jeb and made her way nearer, swallowing the sickly feeling of nerves that filled her. For a moment, dancing with Thorn, she'd forgotten about her desperation. She needed money before Flo turned her out of the boarding house. She might be pregnant, thanks to Mattie and Samantha. She had to find a husband, and fast.

When the song finally ended, Jeb Doolihan was ten paces away.

Avianna waited while he and Samantha clapped for the band. His black hair shone in the lights, smoothed flat and glossy on his head. He actually took Samantha's hand and bent to kiss it, like a fatuous courtier would have. Avianna's chest swelled. Thorn was right. Jeb was a gentleman.

The clapping died away and everyone on the dance floor turned this way and that. Before Avianna had a chance to step forward, Jeb had turned and grasped the hand of a doe-eyed woman in a flower-print dress. Everyone suddenly had a new partner. The caller in the band gave instructions, and the couples moved to form sets of four.

As Avianna kept surveying the hall, scanning for a single man, a few people glanced her way with curious stares. She was going to be left standing alone on the sidelines.

"You've got to be fast in this crowd." A woman with streaks of gray hair stood at Avianna's elbow.

"I see that."

"Want to go fill that spot?" Across the hall stood one set of dancers with their hands raised. They needed a fourth couple.

Relief flooded Avianna. "Oh yes. Thank you."

The woman gave her a kind smile and led the way onto the floor.

"I'm new at this," Avianna said.

"You'll have it down in no time."

As they walked through the dancers, the ones who were Avianna's age turned to watch her pass. Were they intimidated by her? Curious? No one in the pub ever acted this way. Corella was still paired with Tanner. She gave Avianna a smile. Far across the room, Thorn stood with one of the youngsters on his arm.

Her partner took the lead spot, as Thorn had when he'd taught her. A band member called out the dance's steps, and the music began. Avianna was able to follow along, weaving her way in and out of the circle of eight people. It wasn't as much fun as it had been with Thorn, but the music and the movement lifted her spirits. She braced herself for the end of the dance, though, wondering whom she'd get to be her partner for the next one.

When the music ended, Avianna thanked her partner and checked the people around her. Again, couples were switching off rapidly, taking hands with new partners. Avianna's hopes sank. And then someone tapped her shoulder.

She turned to find a boy of maybe fifteen winters. He was beanpole tall and swallowed before asking, "May I have the next dance?"

"I would love that," Avianna said.

The boy took her hand and led her toward a set of dancers. "I'm Connor."

"Avianna. It's my first time here."

"I know. Thorn said so. He said you were nice"—a rush of gratitude filled Avianna—"and not to listen to the gossip." Avianna's stomach dropped.

"What gossip?"

Connor's eyes widened and his face reddened. His mouth opened but nothing came out.

"Never mind," Avianna said, squeezing his hand. "I can imagine."

After her dance with Connor, Avianna managed to find a partner for every dance. But none of them were her age. Instead, the youngsters and the old folks asked her to dance. The men her age either stared from across the room or avoided her. She fumed inside. Wretched Mattie had ruined things again—what had she told everyone that made them gawk and keep their distance?

When the band finally set down their instruments for a break, Avianna fell onto a chair along the wall. Corella dropped into the seat beside her, fanning the sweat off her brow.

"What did Mattie say?"

When Corella turned to Avianna, she grimaced. "She told everyone you have a disease."

"A disease?"

"From Prince Murkel. A merfolk sex disease that's deadly to humans."

Avianna was so angry she could barely speak. "Anything else?"

Corella stared down. "That you usually pick up men for a romp at the pubs, and that's all you're interested in—fooling around, not being serious about finding a mate. But no one there would touch you anymore, so you've come here to find men." She looked up, her face set. "It's rubbish, Avi. I told Tanner, and he said he'd defend you. People will know it's a lie."

"Thanks." Avianna leaned back and closed her eyes. Whether people believed Corella and Tanner, or Mattie's lies, everyone would notice her now. She wanted to slip out the door.

But she couldn't give up. She had to fight harder. She let out a long breath, trying to regain her composure.

She could do this. She might have been the nastiest girl in the castle, but she hadn't started that way. She'd been tricked and trod upon like everyone else, until she'd learned to fight back. The court had been a cesspit of gossip and lies. She could fight back against one little rumor. A merfolk sex disease! It was ludicrous.

But if anyone uncovered her past, she'd never lose this new reputation.

She opened her eyes. Most everyone had collapsed onto a seat or stepped outside to cool off. A few young people still moved on the floor, practicing their moves. Thorn was out there, too, dipping one of the boys. He'd removed his vest, leaving only his linen shirt under suspenders. Thorn straightened, pulling the boy up, and spoke while his hands moved about. Then he and the boy changed their stance and the boy dipped Thorn, almost dropping him. Apparently, Thorn was the village dance instructor as well as the reading teacher.

When the band members returned to the dais and picked up their instruments, Avianna and Corella stood. Thorn was coming toward them. Avianna stopped breathing. Was he going to ask her to dance? She held up her head. If Thorn asked, she'd accept. It was one dance. She could handle feeling awkward for fifteen minutes.

Thorn came to stand by them. "You were right," he said to Corella. "This black eye is a bother. Every lady I dance with wants to know how I got it. And the youngsters are even more impressed."

"What are you telling them?" Corella asked.

"Street fighting at the wharf."

Corella barked out a laugh, and Avianna couldn't suppress a smile.

"You know," Thorn continued, "at the fairy dances, the women ask the men to dance as much as the men ask the women." He raised his eyebrows at Avianna. "I'm just saying."

"Well then, Thorn," Corella said, "would you dance the next one?"

"I'd be delighted," Thorn said. They moved onto the floor together.

Avianna sagged in relief. She watched Corella take Thorn's hand as the dance floor slowly filled. Should she ask someone to dance? With Mattie's rumors circulating, the men her age were clearly avoiding her. What if she asked and they said no? But she couldn't leave this dance without meeting a single eligible bachelor. She had to try, at least.

She scanned the dance hall as people returned. Then the main door opened and Jeb Doolihan entered with a burst of cold wind.

Before she could lose her courage, Avianna walked over to him. She could do this. Flirting was the one thing she'd always been skilled at. And she'd rein herself in. She would be like Elspeth had been, smiling prettily and keeping her mouth shut.

Avianna caught Jeb's gaze as she neared. She slowed, lowering her eyes to the floor before peeking back up at him and smiling. His eyes widened, but then he gave a tentative smile back.

"You're friends with Samantha, aren't you?" she asked. "I'm Avianna Blackburn. I live with Mattie and Samantha at the boarding house."

"I heard," Jeb said. His fingers picked at a button on the front of his vest.

Avianna laughed. "Mattie played such a mean trick, telling everyone I had a merfolk disease. Can you believe it? She bested me this time, I admit."

Jeb stared like a dead fish. "But Mattie said—"

"We're always pulling pranks on each other," Avianna continued, lowering her voice as if she were confiding a secret. "I hid her shoes this morning so I could run Flo's errands instead of her. And she was livid that it took her all day to find them. Now she's gotten back at me. I'll have to think of something even better to get her with next time." She twisted her lips in a mischievous grin.

Jeb's shoulders relaxed, and his hand dropped from the button. Had he believed her? He was awfully handsome now that he wasn't staring with his mouth hanging open. He towered a head above her, his broad shoulders blocking the room.

She dropped her gaze again, willing her smile to entice him and biting her lower lip.

"I don't suppose I could have the next dance?" Jeb asked.

Avianna looked up, radiating surprise and delight. "I would love to."

Avianna took the hand Jeb offered and let him lead her out onto the floor. She tried to gently tug him to her left, where the people of their generation had gathered, but he forged ahead without noticing. He walked to a square on the right and took a place on one side. Across the formation, Thorn stood holding hands with Corella. He lifted his eyebrows at Avianna. She turned to Jeb.

"I'm Jeb DOO-lihan, by the way," Jeb said, and Avianna struggled not to glance back at Thorn.

"I know," she said suggestively.

He swallowed. "I'm surprised we've never met."

"It's my first time. At a dance, I mean." She liked how he kept staring at her. "I didn't come to the village much before the revolution. I lived in the castle."

"The castle?" Jeb's eyes lit up. "I didn't realize you'd been a courtier."

"Yes, for many seasons."

"Imagine that," Jeb said, smiling and continuing to watch her. "Your family must be well off. Why didn't you return to them after the revolution?"

Avianna struggled not to panic. Jeb would believe her story, just like everyone else had. "They lost their land. They're traveling now, hoping to find some new trading partners."

Jeb nodded. "But now, with you living here and being a friend of Samantha's, surely we'd have crossed paths."

Avianna batted her eyelashes once. "Samantha might be trying to keep you all to herself." She remembered to drop her gaze again, like a demure maiden. When she peeked up, Jeb was staring with his mouth slightly open again. His lips snapped shut and he wiped his brow.

Across the set, Thorn was swinging Corella in wild circles as her feet skipped across the floor. Thankfully, the leader called them to attention before Jeb could ask any more questions, and the dance began.

Jeb was a decent dancer. He had a firm grip and ended each move in time with the music. But he felt stiff. Dancing with him wasn't nearly as easy as it had been with Thorn or the free-wheeling youngsters. Following the caller's instructions, Avianna left Jeb to walk around the circle, and when she met Thorn halfway round, the leader called for a spin. Thorn put his arm around her as her hand came to rest on his shoulder. Through the thin shirt, his surprisingly sturdy muscles were solid and hot from dancing.

"How's it going with Jeb?" he asked, spinning her slowly enough that they could talk.

"Okay, I think," Avianna replied between catching her breath. "You were right. He's a gentleman. And he seems to like me despite . . . you know."

"Of course he does."

And then she spun away from Thorn and back around the circle to Jeb.

This time when the dance ended, Avianna thanked Jeb and headed for the back of the hall, where the grange elders had set up a table with pitchers of water and cups. Better to appear like she was taking a break than to fail to find a partner with Jeb Doolihan watching. Before she had reached the table, though, another of Thorn's young friends asked her to dance.

The remaining hours flew past. For each dance, she had a partner—still the older folks and the gawky youngsters, but each time Avianna scanned the hall, she found Jeb staring back at her. When the leader announced the final dance, Jeb made a beeline for her. Avianna almost pitied Samantha, who stood watching Jeb walk away. Throughout the final dance, Jeb held her closer than he had before.

When the dance ended, Jeb caught up Avianna's hands. "I'm thrilled you came tonight, Avianna. Did you have fun?"

"I did."

His eyes darted around and he lowered his voice. "Fancy a stroll around the park?"

Avianna almost burst into a smile but contained herself. She didn't know how they did things up here at the top of the hill, but a "stroll around the park" sounded a lot like "stepping into the alley" down by the wharf. Was Jeb trying to get her alone for a quick tumble?

She had snagged him.

But she couldn't risk it, not when she had missed who knows how many days of taking her tea. And Thorn had advised making herself hard to get. She might as well try it. Avianna batted her eyelashes a few more times and gazed downward. "I'm a bit tired from the dance. But some other time, I'd love to."

"Then permit me to call on you," Jeb said. He scanned the hall again. Who was he looking for?

"Call on me?"

"We could walk around the village, or have dinner at the inn."

Jeb wanted to spend time with her? Thorn's advice seemed to be working.

"Oh, of course! Why Jeb, that sounds delightful." Delightful? Who *was* she? Someone Jeb Doolihan courted, apparently.

Jeb beamed down at her. His teeth gleamed white. "I'm afraid it will have to be the day after tomorrow. I'm taking horses to a sale in Woods Rest tomorrow."

"That's fine, Jeb. I can wait."

Jeb's shoulders relaxed, and he dropped her hands. Some people were gathering in a circle out on the floor. Jeb took a step toward them, then stopped and stepped back to her.

"Are those your friends?" she asked.

"Yes." Without further talk, he moved toward the group. He didn't invite her along, but Avianna followed him. Some of the men eyed her askance, but hopefully Jeb would set them straight about Mattie's prank.

Jeb joined the circle, but before he could introduce her, one of the men asked, "Did you see the latest?" He pulled a pamphlet from the pocket on his vest. It looked familiar. Thorn must have printed it. Where was Thorn? She scanned past the men who surrounded her but didn't see him in the hall.

"I can't believe they're calling for that," Jeb said, shaking his head. "Haven't they given up enough? If I were a manor lord, I wouldn't stand for it."

Avianna had no idea what the men were on about—something Thorn had printed concerning the aftermath of the revolution. She considered Thorn's support of the revolutionaries and her own work experiences, and she wondered if she should disagree with Jeb, but she didn't know enough about the conversation to get involved. And besides, speaking her mind wasn't the way to win him. She had to be placid like Elspeth. Maybe she and Jeb wouldn't even disagree, once she knew more.

Thankfully no one asked her to speak. Two other women joined the circle, and both stood silently. Did they not read the papers either, or did no one in this group care for their opinion? A tinge of annoyance pricked at Avianna. These men made her think of the courtiers.

Well, in two days' time, Avianna would have an entire evening to spend with Jeb Doolihan, with no dances to take up the time, and no blathering men doing all the talking. She'd get her chance to talk with him then.

As she realized it, her heart sank. What on earth would they talk about? Jeb would think she was an imbecile.

"Of course it's an outrage." Oh, no. Mattie had inched her way into the circle, hanging on one of the men. She directed an ugly grin toward Avianna. "What do you think, Avianna?" She sneered wider, if that was possible. "About the latest flyer?"

"I haven't seen that one," Avianna said.

Mattie shook her head, no doubt preparing her next attack. Avianna didn't wait for it. "Jeb," she said, resting her hand gently on his arm. He covered it with his own. "It's been so lovely. I'll eagerly await our dinner." She squeezed his arm, batted her eyelashes twice to be safe, and smiled sweetly before turning to the door.

Chapter 7

AVIANNA COULD THINK OF ONLY one way to prepare for her date with Jeb Doolihan. It was ridiculous, but she was desperate.

The afternoon after the dance, she pushed open the door of the print shop. Stacks of printed flyers covered the counter that stretched in front of her. A child's voice spoke. "The bee makes hoe. Hoe-ney."

"Huh-ney. Very good."

Behind the counter to the left, Thorn sat at a table with two girls. He wore his suspenders, just as she'd last seen him at the dance. The small girl had a block of wood underneath her to lift her higher on her chair. Thorn glanced over at Avianna. When his gaze stopped on her, he smiled. She had forgotten about his black eye.

She quietly closed the door of the shop.

Thorn turned back to the girls. "Your turn, Cecily." The older girl began to read from a large printed sheet laid flat on the table. The children reminded Avianna that she might be pregnant, and dread swirled around her chest. She'd managed to push the possibility aside as she'd scrubbed more laundry that day.

A doorway behind the counter led to a room filled with afternoon sunlight. The light flickered with fall shadows. It fell on a large wooden contraption with a table-like surface jutting out from one side—the printing press, Avianna assumed. The table might have been the thing she'd helped Thorn carry in, the day they'd met. Shelves lined the front room, with more stacks of paper and pottery vessels and a long white feather. Avianna had seen someone write with a feather once, in the castle.

Thorn must have had a fire burning somewhere, because the shop was snug and warm. Avianna unwrapped her shawl and stretched her fingers. She'd begged Corella to let her do all the laundry that morning, since she needed the pay so badly. Besides, after seeing Corella and Tanner at the dance, it didn't seem likely Corella would be on her own much longer.

Avianna had been bent over that laundry for hours, and her fingers ached, as did her back.

She had half expected Flo would boot her from the boarding house that morning, but Alfie had stopped by, needing something or other right at the moment when Flo was rounding on Avianna. And Flo always softened around Alfie, since she was sweet on his father. Avianna had escaped to the laundry yard, where she'd been hard at work when Flo poked her head out later on.

But Avianna was on crumbling ground. Hopefully the villagers were dirtying themselves up to give her more laundry to wash, so she could pay off her debts.

At least until she could snag Jeb Doolihan.

The girls giggled. Thorn was leaning forward, pointing to something on the page. The littler girl followed his hand, but Cecily, who was maybe fourteen winters, stared at Thorn. When he noticed, she turned red as a cooked lobster and dropped her gaze.

Thorn stood, and the girls followed him out from the corner to the front of the shop. Avianna stood out of the way.

"Don't get in any more fights, Thorn," the little one said.

"Why not? Don't you think it makes me look tough?"

"It's horrible."

"I think it looks tough," Cecily said.

Thorn opened the door, and the little girl balked.

"It's crowded, Thorn. Will you walk us home?"

"I can't, I have to help this customer. But Cecily isn't scared, right?"

Cecily couldn't hide the strain from her face. Torn, Avianna imagined, between being brave in Thorn's eyes, and getting Thorn to walk her home.

But before Cecily answered, the other girl said, "Cecily's scared too, ever since the drunk man grabbed her ankle."

Avianna had a good guess who that was.

"What did you do?" Thorn asked Cecily.

"I kicked him."

"Good. You can take care of yourself and your sister. But why don't I get a cat to walk you home?"

A cat?

The little girl waved her fists, delight washing over her face. Cecily was less joyous, but when Thorn stepped out the door, she watched the street along with her sister. Avianna peeked out after them. A moment later, a giant brown tabby cat appeared on the rooftop and leapt down to the stones. It sidled up to them and rubbed itself on Thorn's trousers.

Thorn picked up the cat and handed it to Cecily. She stumbled under its weight but held on.

"Girls," Thorn said, "this is Finnegan. He'd be happy to escort you home. Should anyone bother you, his claws will protect you." The little girl reached up to scratch Finnegan's rump, and he began to purr.

"Thanks, Thorn," Cecily said, snuggling into Finnegan's fur. Apparently the cat would do as well as Thorn for a companion. The girls set off along the lane, Cecily staggering a bit and her sister trying to pet the cat. Ten steps on, Cecily dropped Finnegan, who landed on his feet, paused to lick a paw, and set off, followed by the girls.

Thorn watched them go. Then he turned to Avianna.

"Thanks for waiting."

"A cat?"

"Have you ever fought one?"

"No."

"Besides, nothing should bother them. I don't think Prince Murkel could harm anyone anymore."

Thorn came inside and closed the door behind himself. Suddenly it was quiet in the shop. Now she could hear that a fire crackled in the hearth over by the table where the girls had been reading. Thorn leaned back on the closed door and waited with his thumbs hooked in his suspenders.

"I guess you're wondering why I'm here," Avianna said.

"Are you ready to tell me, or would you like some tea first?"

"Tea?"

"Normal tea. Hibiscus. Although I assume you had the right tea this morning."

Her heart tightened again at the reminder. She nodded.

Thorn pushed himself up and headed behind the counter. "Come on in."

The fire flickered in the small fireplace. Thorn lifted a kettle from the hearth, jostled it around while listening to the water slosh, and hung it over the fire. As he prepared two cups of tea, Avianna slid into a chair at the table and studied the printed sheet the girls had been reading from. The page had flowers twined along the edges, one with a bee hovering over it. Her finger traced the letters beside it. Were those the letters for "bee"? Or "honey"?

"Are you here to learn to read?" Thorn asked gently. He watched her from beside the hearth.

"Did you make this? It's beautiful."

"I did. That one's for the flowery types. I've got others, with swords and ships and things. I think it helps if the children like the pictures."

"Would I be flowers or swords?"

Thorn smiled. "You'd need a custom-made poster."

Avianna stared at her lap. "Well you better get to work because that's why I'm here."

His smile widened. "Okay. Stay right here."

"Where would I go?" Avianna said, but he was walking away into the back room. A moment later he returned with a card.

"This is what we start with. I started printing them when I realized most of the human children couldn't read." He placed it on the table before her.

The card had giant letters on it, filling the entire space.

"Me and the children. Wonderful."

"Not just you, Avianna. Lots of people. The dock master was learning just last spring. The revolution gave people hope for something better."

"Did you print a flyer about the revolution, or the government?"

"That's where most of my business comes from, unfortunately. There's not a lot of pay in flowers. Why?"

"They had it at the dance. The men were talking about it. What did it say?"

"Which one? There's a new one every week."

"How do you write that many?"

"I don't write them. Not most of them. I'm the printer, Avi. Other people bring me the words and order a hundred copies or whatever, and I create the pamphlet and print them. I only write my own when there's, um, a gap in the knowledge."

Avianna tilted her head and waited.

"So," Thorn continued, "say someone, say a horse-breeding someone"—Avianna bit back a retort—"thinks his horses should be able to graze in the park, basically getting a free dinner and pooping everywhere that the children play, and nibbling on the flowers and biting the apples off the trees, just so he can make an extra coin by not buying them food. And he asks me to print a flyer espousing the virtues of the park being a common area that all can share, but leaving out the poop and flowers and apples. I might print a flyer with poop on it so that the villagers get the whole story."

"Do you sell them?"

"I generally give my own away."

"That's noble of you."

"Not really. I just want a park with apples and flowers and no horse droppings."

"So you don't know what Jeb and the others were discussing at the dance."

"I can guess," Thorn said. The kettle was steaming. He turned to pour the water and brought two cups to the table, sitting beside Avianna. "The Council thinks the lords should give up their manor houses."

"But they already have to pay the servants, and the tenant farmers were all given the land they farm."

"True. But the Council found Lord Amberfeld stockpiling munitions and feared he might be planning to cause trouble. They had reports of him recruiting fighters in the nearby village, promising future favors in exchange for loyalty. He could have gained enough followers to threaten the villagers and scare them into supporting him. And besides, do you think those lords do a bit of work? They still run their households like they're in power."

"I just feel bad for them, having their lives swept away."

"That's why the Council proposed a compromise."

"A compromise?"

"Jeb's flyer didn't mention that."

"But yours did."

"Yes. The lords can stay in their homes if their older children volunteer in their local village, helping the poor. They'd stay in the local grange home and work and learn what life is like away from a manor."

"And the lords won't do it?"

"Some of them are still refusing. I think they'll come around. I mean, they can no longer ship their children off to court when they reach fifteen seasons and become sullen brats."

"That makes me feel sorry for the villagers."

"There is that. How old were you when you came to court?"

The question caught Avianna by surprise. Talking with Thorn was so easy that she was tempted to blurt out the truth. She regrouped and recited her well-rehearsed story. "I was fourteen when Father died, and Mother's new husband wanted to sail for Esteria to pursue a trading opportunity. So I talked her into sending me to court. Of course, we both expected I'd be life bonded as soon as I reached a suitable age."

"What happened?"

Avianna slipped back into honesty. "It was so fun, I didn't want to leave. I got caught up in it, I guess. I knew I had to find a life mate, to secure a future, but it was such a vague idea, always in the back of my head. Each man I met, I'd think, This one? But he never seemed like the right man.

"And I'd never been good at anything, Thorn. And there I was, and all I had to do was lie with a man and he'd give me things, and seat me beside him in the hall, and it felt amazing. Like I had value for the first time.

"And then the king wanted to sell off the princess, and all these foreign princes started visiting to see her. I was sure I could land with one of them. But they lied, one after another. Prince Murkel lied worst of all, the monster."

"Literally."

"I waited too long. Who ever imagined the people would take over the castle and carry off the king and leave the rest of us as laundry maids?"

"You know there are other professions."

"None I could do. I have no skills."

"Well let's change that." He pushed the card in front of her. "Starting with the alphabet."

Avianna covered her face with her hands. "This is so embarrassing. I don't even know the letters. I'll never be able to, Thorn."

"Just try, that's all. I have a present for you, if you'll give it a try."

"What kind of present?"

"A sparkly one."

"Can I have it now?"

"No. Now focus." Thorn leaned over the card beside her. He began pronouncing the names of each letter, having Avianna repeat each after him. Avianna could feel his warmth off her shoulder. Other than dancing, she'd never been this close to a man who wasn't about to plunge himself inside her. It gave her a chance to appreciate him, somehow. Thorn might be scrawny, and he probably couldn't build a house or stockpile the larder with smoked venison, but he sure did smell nice.

"*T* as in Treasure," Thorn said.

"What?"

"The letter *T*," he repeated. "You drifted off."

"*T* as in Treasure."

"You know what else begins with *T*?"

Avianna rolled her eyes. "What?"

"Thorn."

"Shouldn't it be Torn then?"

"You'll have to keep coming to reading lessons to find out why it's not. Now stop daydreaming about your beau and focus."

They went through the list a few times. The sun slid lower outside the window. The thick stone walls of the shop muffled the sounds of the village, and in the stillness, Avianna realized a clock had been ticking loudly the whole time. Trust Thorn to have a human clock. Some fairy.

"That's good, Avi," Thorn said as she finished reading the alphabet by herself. "What do you think about writing?"

"Writing?"

"You could learn to keep the books for one of the shops, or help Alistair keep track of his inventory."

"Alistair? Have you ever seen Alistair keep track of anything?"

"But he might want to start. With the children, I stick with reading for a bit, but writing would be a useful skill for you to have."

"Would I get to use the feather?"

Thorn smiled. "Not this time." From the shelf he retrieved a small board and a white rock. He used the rock to draw an *A* on the board in white lines. Then he handed the board to Avianna. "You try."

"I can't," Avianna said. "I'll mess it up."

"No, look, it erases." He smudged his hand across the board and the *A* disappeared. He handed the rock to Avianna. It was softer than most rocks and flaked onto her fingers.

The door opened behind Avianna, but she focused on the letter she was forming—*A* as in Avianna. She made one slope up, then the other down, then carefully crossed the space between them.

"Look, Thorn, I did it."

Thorn was staring past her, his lips parted and dismay on his face.

"Oh, what a perfect *A*!"

No. Not Mattie. Not here. Why did she always turn up with her nastiness to ruin things? In an instant, the thrilling feeling of reading the alphabet and forming her first letter turned into a feeling of plummeting off a cliff. Avianna's eyes threatened tears.

She wanted to be mean, to throw back a spiteful comment in Mattie's face, but her meanness abandoned her. All she could do was stare at the *A*, noticing how lopsided it was, the lines wobbly.

"Mattie, did you need something?" Thorn asked, rising and walking to the counter.

"No. I was passing by and I saw you two in here. And I thought you must have something new to read, to be poring over it so intently. But writing lessons! That's very exciting." She said it so smugly that Avianna knew Mattie was laughing at her.

But Thorn didn't seem to realize it. "It is. Avianna's doing well."

Avianna kept her back to them and wiped her eyes on her sleeve, hoping they couldn't see her do it.

Behind her, Mattie continued, "Maybe she can impress Jeb on their date tomorrow. Write 'I love you' in the sand with a stick."

An awkward silence followed. Avianna composed her face before looking up. Thorn was shuffling a stack of papers on the counter. Mattie stood opposite with her lips pursed like mating slugs.

"I'm sure Jeb and I will have better things to talk about than my reading and writing lessons," Avianna said, lifting her chin.

"Especially because he'll assume you can read," Mattie replied. "You being a *manor* girl."

"Mattie, lay off," Thorn said. His body was stiff, and he kept stacking and restacking the papers.

At the rebuke, Mattie's face blanched.

"No, she's right," Avianna said. "I should have learned, and I missed my chance. I'm glad you're giving me a chance now, Thorn."

Something softened in Thorn's stance. He rested the papers on the counter, placing a rock as a weight on top of them. Mattie's eyes darted once from Thorn to Avianna and back. Then she zeroed in on Avianna.

"Flo said you had one chance left before you were booted out," Mattie said. "You might want to get home soon and pack your things."

"I have one chance left."

"Not for long."

Panic rose up in Avianna's chest and she stood. "What did you do?"

"I didn't do anything. But it appears *you* invited old Murkel to our room and left him there when you finished with him. You must've needed a tumble after all that laundry you did. I found him in your bed shortly after you left."

"You found Prince Murkel *in my bed*?"

"Or maybe I let him in the house, and told him you'd do it with him when you came home, if he just waited. And then I pretended that I'd found him . . . ."

"You set me up? How could you?"

"Didn't you set me up when you stole my shoes?"

"I cost you one errand—it's not like I got you kicked out onto the street."

Mattie shrugged. "With your new reading skills, I'm sure you'll find an admirable position soon. Everyone needs someone to write an *A* for them. Maybe, by next spring, you'll have the whole alphabet down. Besides, I didn't get you kicked out. I screamed, of course. Imagine stumbling upon that in your room. Unfortunately Flo was out, but I passed her coming up the hill from the market. She'll be home in minutes."

Avianna flew around the counter and out the door. If she ran, she might overtake Flo. Although how she'd get Murkel out of the house, she had no idea.

Her feet pounded on the hard road, jarring her bones. She barely noticed the sunset painting the sky or the leaves skittering across the cobblestones. By the time she reached the main road, her lungs threatened to burst. She slowed a bit as she turned down the hill, scanning for Flo, then remembered she had nowhere to go if she lost her lodging and spurred herself to keep running. The villagers watched her pass, questioning expressions on their faces.

By the turn to the boarding house, she could barely breathe. She halted, leaning over and wheezing. People milled in the street between her and home, blocking her view. Was Flo already back? Was it too late?

"Avi!" Alfie darted up and hung on her elbow. "What's going on?"

Alfie! The boy ran faster than anyone.

"Alfie," Avianna panted, doubled over. "I need your help. Stop Flo. Don't let her go home. Lead her away." She jutted her chin in the direction of the boarding house.

Alfie's face hardened as his lips pressed tight. He spun away and burst off down the lane toward the boarding house. After a few more deep inhales, Avianna jogged after him, her heart pounding and her breathing jagged.

Seven buildings away. Six. Five. There was the boarding house towering over the end of the street in the twilight. And there in front of it was Flo, struggling to hang on to her packages as Alfie tugged at her arm.

Avianna composed herself and assumed a stately walk as she neared the house. She glanced over as she passed Alfie and Flo, but Flo was too distracted to notice her. Alfie was carrying on about something at the docks that Flo had to come see. Avianna breezed past them and into the house.

Corella, Samantha, and the other girls clustered in the parlor.

"I didn't do it," Avianna said at once. "Mattie set me up."

"Oh come off it, Avianna," Samantha replied. "I can't believe you did it with that creep in our room."

Avianna glared at the others. "You don't all think I did this, do you?"

"You disappeared a few hours ago."

"I was with Thorn! Ask him."

Finally Corella stepped forward. "We all know Mattie's out to get Avianna. Let's just figure out how to get rid of him before Flo gets back."

"I'm not going near him," said Samantha. "You'd better open all the windows once he's gone." She picked up her sewing and turned away, and the other girls joined her, all except Corella. She wasn't smiling, but at least she stayed by Avianna.

"Fine." Avianna turned to Corella. "You'll help me, won't you?" Corella nodded quietly, slowly, as if she had to force her chin to move up and down.

Avianna headed for the front staircase with Corella reluctantly following.

Murkel's snores reverberated in the upstairs hallway. Mattie must have left the girls' door open, probably to hasten Flo discovering Murkel in the house. The room was dark in the twilight, but the hump of a body sprawled on Avianna's bed, his boots still on. Revolting. She'd thought she was done with the laundry for a few days, but now she'd have to wash her own bedsheets. She forced herself to approach.

Avianna hesitated a moment, peering down at Murkel. Was this what would happen to her if she lost her bed at the boarding house—would she end up toothless and dirty with snarled hair and grimy fingernails? What if she had a baby to feed on top of it?

She shook Murkel's shoulder until he sputtered awake in a cloud of whiskey breath.

"Avi," he said. "I'm ready for you. She said you'd be home if I waited. Who's your friend? She looks nice."

"Prince Murkel. We have to go."

"Go where?"

"The landlady's coming. We need to leave."

"But what about our tryst?"

"Skies help me," Avianna muttered. She put on her charming face and leaned close to Murkel's ear. "I got us a room at Alistair's Pub," she said breathily. "I don't want my roommates to hear me moaning in delight."

Murkel reached for her, struggling to sit up. Avianna tugged him off the bed, keeping her face averted as well as she could as she lifted him up from under his shoulder.

"Get the other side," she said to Corella. "Please."

"You owe me for this."

With Corella's help, Avianna hefted Murkel out of the room. Voices carried up from the parlor—the girls, fussing and talking, and then a boy's voice. "I really think you should come see the mermaid they found at the docks!" It was Alfie.

"Down the back stairs, quick," Avianna said. Murkel stumbled along between them. They turned sideways to fit him into the staircase. At least down was the direction he tended to go, as they thumped from step to step. If only they could drop him.

In the dark kitchen, they tugged him out the door. Behind the house, the washbasins stood where she'd left them to drip that afternoon. Clean laundry hung on a series of lines, flapping in the breeze. Once they'd moved behind a few rows of sheets, Avianna calmed. They helped Murkel out the back gate into the alley and took him out to the street.

"Here's a nice doorway for you to sit in," Avianna said, lowering him to the ground.

"What about Alistair's?"

"We're not going to Alistair's," Avianna said. "I'm sorry. Mattie lied to you. I'm not going to tumble you."

Murkel's lopsided smile fell. Even through his drunken haze, disappointment dulled his eyes. "Not even a quick one?"

"No. Stop asking."

She took Corella's hand and started back toward the boarding house, pulling her friend along.

"That was close," Corella said. She brushed herself off where Murkel had leaned against her.

"Stinking Mattie. She barged in to the print shop to torment me. Even Thorn told her to lay off."

"Yes, about that—what's up between you and Thorn?"

"Me and Thorn?" Avianna asked. Corella lifted her eyebrows suggestively. "Oh, nothing like that. The truth is . . . I needed to learn to read. For my date tomorrow. Thorn had offered to teach me."

"You needed to learn to read before tomorrow?" Corella squinted and shook her head, confused.

"Not only reading. After the dance, Jeb and his friends were talking about politics and trade and all that, and I had no idea about any of it. And tomorrow, we won't have dances to take up the time. I'll have to talk to him. Thorn always knows so much, and he's so kind about helping me. I just don't want Jeb to think I'm ignorant."

"Avi, plenty of people can't read. The kingdom wasn't exactly known for serving the people, much less women. And once the whole court thing started, some parents didn't bother to teach girls."

"Really? I thought it was just me."

"But don't change the subject. Thorn likes you."

Avianna shook her head as she ducked around the sheets. "Thorn likes everyone."

"He fought Rye for you."

"He would have done it for anyone. He hates bullies, remember?"

Now Corella shook her head. They stopped outside the back door. "I don't know, Avi. He's always glancing at you and watching out for you—"

"But why would Thorn like me? I'm the mean girl, remember? And he's not shallow enough to like a girl for how she looks."

"Maybe he sees past all that. You're not mean on the inside."

"I'm not?"

Corella shrugged.

"Why didn't he ask me to dance, then?" Avianna said. "Instead of sending all his young friends to do it?"

"Maybe he would have asked you if you'd acted interested. Thorn's not pushy, Avi. If he thinks you're not interested, he won't ask because he's respecting you not wanting to dance with him."

Avianna didn't reply. She'd have to think about that.

Corella turned and pulled open the door. From the front of the house, the commotion they'd heard earlier continued.

"I told Alfie to distract Flo," Avianna said. "He seems to be doing a remarkable job. We'd better go stop him."

They headed through the dark dining room into the front hall. As Avianna came into the parlor, the crowd parted. A couple stood in the center of the room. They wore disheveled hats and coats, as if they'd arrived from a long trip. A small suitcase stood by their feet.

"There's my girl," the woman said, turning toward Avianna. It was Avianna's mother.

Chapter 8

HOW HAD HER PARENTS FOUND her? And after almost ten winters—Avianna had never expected to see them again.

Her mother was smiling at her, a bright and strange smile. She had never smiled like that when Avianna was a girl. The other boarders stepped aside, clearing a wider path between her and her parents, but Avianna made no move toward them. The traveling case by her mother's feet was unscuffed, as if it were new—so were her mother's shoes. Had she stolen them? Her mother looked different, beyond the smile. She should have been bent over and decaying with age, but instead she was upright, and . . . and *lively*. Behind her mother's shoulder, her father peeked out, also smiling. He'd lost more teeth in the ten seasons since she'd left them, but his face was somewhat shaven and he appeared sober.

What was going on?

"Ma," Avianna said slowly, nodding once. "Da."

"We're sorry to arrive unexpected, Avi," her mother said. "Only we didn't know how to reach you with a message."

"How did you find me?"

"We asked around."

The room had gone silent. Everyone was watching her. She needed to say something, but what? Avianna tried to piece together all the lies she'd told about her past, or even just the lies she'd told to the people in the boarding house the last few moons, but her thoughts felt like they were stuck in mud. Her mother had remarried, she'd said. That was good, since it was obvious from her looks that one of her biological parents must be from the north, and her mother and stepfather were both southern. But then what?

Corella stepped forward. "How long have you been back in Sylvania?" she said, turning her pleasant smile on Avianna's parents.

Avianna's mother broke her gaze from Avianna to turn to Corella, and her father cocked his head, squinting.

Heat flushed up Avianna's face as she remembered. She'd told everyone at the boarding house that her parents had lost their property in the revolution—that they'd sailed back to Esteria to find a new trading opportunity, so that she'd had no home to return to. That was why she'd stayed in Woodglen, she had said, instead of leaving like many of the other courtiers.

Only she'd made it all up.

And now they were here, and they'd been chatting up a storm with her housemates before she'd walked in. What had they been saying?

Her parents had always put on airs. They had always pretended they had more than they did. Maybe they hadn't revealed the truth—that they were paupers. And they always had been. Certainly her mother wouldn't have told anyone the truth about Avianna's birth.

Corella's innocent question hung in the air.

"Just a little while," Avianna's mother said slowly, turning back to Avianna.

Avianna blushed harder, avoiding her mother's gaze.

Flo licked her lips, opening her mouth to speak. Beside her, Samantha slouched with her eyes narrowed. Thank the skies Mattie wasn't home yet.

Her parents couldn't stay here. Flo didn't have an extra room, for starters. But Avianna couldn't have her parents talking with this many people or her secrets were bound to come out. Maybe she wouldn't get locked in a dungeon for lying, but everyone would know that she'd invented her whole past—that she never should have been allowed at court, that she was a fraud. She'd be ridiculed. Jeb Doolihan would never consider bonding with her, if the entire village was laughing at her. And as soon as Mattie returned, she'd be prying at Avianna's parents for details, for anything she could use against Avianna. Her parents might put on airs, but they weren't exactly clever. Mattie would manipulate them into spilling her story in no time. And once Mattie knew the truth, she was sure to spin it into some worse lie about Avianna, worse than a merfolk sex disease.

Avianna had to get her parents out of the boarding house now, before Mattie saw them and learned the truth about her background. And they definitely couldn't be hanging around when Jeb came to pick her up tomorrow. She couldn't let them spoil her date.

She stepped forward before Flo could speak.

"I'm in such shock," she said. "I never expected to see you." She rested her hand on her mother's arm, and her mother's eyes misted over. What in the skies? Her mother never cried.

Avianna tapped the suitcase with her foot. "You must be tired from the journey. How far did you come?"

"All the way from South End," her father said. "You'll never guess, Avi, how we ended up—"

She and her mother interrupted him at once. Avianna let her mother finish.

"We'll tell her later, John."

"Let's get you somewhere to sleep," Avianna added.

Both Flo and her father opened their mouths, but Avianna continued.

"Flo's rooms are all full, and Alistair's is cheaper."

Flo's lips flattened in a frown. "You can't put your parents at Alistair's Pub, Avi. Those rooms are cramped, and the pub is noisy. And who knows when Alistair last cleaned anything."

Avianna faced Flo. "The room at the end of the hall is roomy enough."

"You should know," Samantha muttered, shifting to slouch on her other foot.

"And they'll like the atmosphere, Flo. Your house is more, um, temperate. Besides, I already owe you rent."

"We can pay," her father said.

How often had she heard that before?

But Flo backed down, although the frown stayed on her face.

"I'll get you settled at Alistair's," Avianna said, "and then we can catch up, how's that? And we'll come back here to meet everyone properly after you've had a rest."

She almost had them moving, and Mattie hadn't returned. What was keeping Mattie, anyway? She was probably still batting her eyelashes at Thorn over in the print shop. Irritation stirred in Avianna's chest at the picture of the two of them, but she ignored it.

Avianna scanned the room. Alfie slumped in a chair in the corner, staring morosely at the crowd.

"Come on, Alfie," she said. "Grab that bag for my ma, would you?" Alfie pushed himself up from the chair with a sigh and came over. Avianna tugged her mother out of the circle of boarders. Her father tipped his hat to Flo, beaming at the silent crowd as he bumbled after them. The other boarders were sure to gossip as soon as Avianna was gone, but she couldn't help that.

Her father chuckled as he came out the door. The sun was down now. A crescent moon hung low in the western sky, and the first stars were out. The breeze off the ocean carried the salty smell through the street.

"So many friends, Avi," her father said, coming up on her left. Ahead of them, Alfie stumbled along with the suitcase. "I can get that case," her father added.

"I got it," Alfie yelled over his shoulder without stopping.

"We're sorry for just turning up—" her mother began again.

"It's fine, Ma. I'm glad to see you, and you look well. Both of you."

"We are, Avi. We'll tell you all about it when we're settled."

As they turned into the main road, the wind off the ocean caught them. Avianna shivered, and her mother's arm came around her.

"Don't you have a shawl?"

"I left it somewhere," Avianna said, remembering that it was in Thorn's shop. She again pictured Thorn in there with Mattie. Ugh, she thought, stop thinking about it. Think about the cool evening breeze. Soon she'd need a real coat—another expense. The ones from the castle had all been furs and deemed too costly to let the demoted courtiers keep, and no one had considered replacements in the springtime when the weather had been warm.

Her mother was saying something about shells—enough shells to buy her a new shawl. That would be the day. At least she'd gotten them out of the boarding house before they'd said anything damaging or before Mattie came home. Seriously, what was Mattie doing all this time?

Avianna followed Alfie through the streets, barely listening to her mother's chatter. She still couldn't believe they had found her. Why? Why now? Right when she was about to turn her life around. She could feel herself slipping, wanting to whine at her mother like she had as a youngster—each time they had had some new scheme she was forced to participate in. She inhaled deeply and let it out. She was responsible for herself now, and she wasn't going to let her parents mess up her plans.

At the bottom of the hill, they turned toward Alistair's. Lights shone out the windows, and people moved inside, their muted laughter filtering out into the street.

Her parents talked on about their newest escapade and all the riches it had brought them. As she pulled open the door, the buzz of the pub's crowd spilled out, along with the smell of ale. Avianna cut off her mother as Alfie plopped their suitcase down in the entryway.

"Alfie, will you ask your da to find a room for them upstairs?"

"Da's sick with a fever. He's been passed out in bed all day."

Avianna sighed. "Well, you find them an empty room then, and I'll sort it out with your father later." Alfie began up the stairs, hefting the suitcase after him.

She turned to her parents. "I suppose you want a drink after you get settled?" Another debt she would owe Alistair.

But her mother shook her head. "Your father gave up drinking."

Avianna stared in shock.

"But . . ."

Her father winked, grinning.

"Just wait," her mother said. "We have so much to tell you. And we want to hear all about you. But we've been on the road all day. We had a bite of dinner when we arrived. I think we might need to turn in and wait to talk tomorrow. Goodnight, Avi." And with that, her mother took her father's arm and headed up the stairs. Avianna stared after them as they disappeared into the hallway.

She stared another minute after they had vanished, again wondering over their sudden appearance. Her parents! She'd never thought to see them again. And now they were here for some unknown reason. And they'd ask all about her. She smoothed her hands down the front of her dress. What would she tell them? That she had no money or prospects? That she worked as a laundry maid? That she might be pregnant? They'd probably imagined her running away to marry a rich man and already bragged about it to everyone in South End. They'd be so disappointed.

Not that their opinion mattered.

She glanced over the chattering crowd in the pub room. The usual suspects, including Beck at the far end with a new woman, but no Alistair behind the bar, and Lucinda wasn't in sight. Was anyone working at all? Avianna stepped into the kitchen.

Lucinda was making a potpie at the table, with her hands covered in flour and dough. Her hair sagged out of its usual bun, messy even for Lucinda, and her apron was twisted sideways. Bits of dough and clouds of flour were scattered across the kitchen floor.

A shout came from the front room, and Lucinda started, her eyes desperate. "Oh, Avi, thank the skies!" she said. "I can't take another minute. Bunch of drunk louts. And one of them wants dinner."

"Are you alone?"

"Alistair caught a fever and I couldn't get anyone else to help. I've been here by myself since we opened. You have to help me."

A crash sounded in the bar room.

"I can't work the bar," Avianna said. "Let me finish the pie. I don't know what I'm doing out there."

Lucinda's face fell. "Oh, please Avi. You can handle them. I'm that tired. You pour their drinks and take their coins—that's all it is, really."

"But—"

"You keep the tips. They tip better when they're soused. And Alistair will pay you on top of it."

Avianna hesitated only a moment. It didn't matter if she felt ashamed to be out there. She needed the money, especially with her parents now here. Maybe Alistair would trade her for their room.

"Okay," she said. She took a deep breath and regarded the door. Beck was out there. Maybe Beck and Rye. But she could handle a few drunk men. She needed to do this to keep her parents here, to keep them out of trouble. The last thing she needed was for them to draw attention to themselves and spill the details of her past, ruining any chance of a decent future.

She pushed the door open and headed into the pub.

It really wasn't that much of a crowd, given the noise they were making. She scanned the familiar faces as she slid behind the bar, all the men and women laughing and shouting to be heard. Sure enough, Rye's hulking form brooded in a corner. He had his back to her and she guessed he was nursing an ale. Near the door was someone she didn't know, a broad-shouldered man with tattoos on his muscular arms and a sailor's cap pulled low on his head. He didn't have a drink. At least he wasn't unruly. With those arms, he could cause some damage if he tried.

A man called her over and ordered an ale. As she brought it, a harsh laugh drew her attention. She knew that laugh. She steeled herself and glanced down at the end of the bar. Beck sat with his bulging forearms on the bar top, and next to him, perched on a stool, was Mattie.

Avianna almost tripped at the sight of Mattie. What was she doing here? She never drank ale or hung out down by the docks. Beck would chew her up and spit her out. Avianna delivered the drink and returned to the center of the space. Mattie's eyes were red-rimmed, and she had an empty mug in front of her. Avianna's first instinct was to rescue her.

Avianna swallowed and picked up a rag to wipe a spill of beer on the bar.

"What're you doing back there?" Beck called. He couldn't not sneer, apparently. "Shouldn't you be upstairs testing out someone new?"

Mattie cracked a smile. But she didn't join in Beck's ribbing. She sat stiffly on her bar stool.

Avianna took calming breaths as she made her way toward them. "Lucinda asked me to help. Now can I get you anything?"

"No, you don't have anything I want." Beck turned to Mattie.

"I'll have another ale," Mattie said. Her voice was quiet, but when Avianna met her gaze, she exhaled and her eyes narrowed.

What was up with her?

Avianna took Mattie's mug and poured the ale. She'd seen Alistair do it a thousand times. But she had no idea how much a mug cost—it wasn't like she paid for her own drinks.

"Please leave the coins on the bar," she said, sliding the mug to Mattie. Then she took a tray and walked away.

She stepped out from the bar and circled the room. A few people flagged her over for refills or pressed coins into her hand before heaving themselves up and staggering out the door. She approached the stranger with the tattoos. He did have a mug of ale after all, and when she asked if he needed anything, he only shook his head. She didn't bother with Rye. Chances were, he had enough alcohol in him already.

She took the used mugs back to the kitchen. Lucinda's potpie sat steaming on the stovetop. Lucinda had disappeared. Avianna found a mitt and carried the pie out to the front, where a couple waved her over.

The minutes ticked past, and Avianna began to relax. Tending the bar wasn't hard at all. How much would Alistair give her—enough to cover the room for her parents? Maybe there'd be extra to go toward her debts with Flo. And the tips were all hers. She straightened the mugs on a shelf behind the bar. Maybe she should walk around again and sell a few more drinks before everyone went home, to make Alistair more grateful for her help.

Beck was whispering in Mattie's ear, and his hand rested on her knee. So that's where that was headed, then. How had Mattie ended up in Alistair's Pub? It wasn't exactly her kind of place. Avianna watched from behind them as they slid off their seats and left. She let out a long whistle. Good riddance.

As midnight neared, only two customers remained. Rye slumped onto his arms in the corner, and the man with the tattoos still sat by the door, sipping the same ale he'd had since she'd arrived. Avianna cleared tables and carried the remains of the potpie back to the kitchen. Her stomach rumbled as the scent of the gravy wafted up to her nose. She'd completely forgotten to eat supper, between getting Murkel out of her bed and her parents' surprise arrival.

Avianna returned to the front, wishing both men would leave. Rye looked like he might be asleep, and the stranger . . . he stared into his mug like he planned to sit there all night.

Of course, if the stranger left, she'd be alone with Rye.

A ripple of nervousness shot through her. The last time Rye had seen her, he'd gotten angry. He'd given Thorn a black eye.

Calm down, she told herself. He was probably so drunk he couldn't even stand.

And it wasn't like she'd never dealt with an angry man before. No one ever liked being dropped, or worse, left for another man, and she'd left plenty of men in her days at the castle. She'd had to navigate some messy situations and to soothe hurt prides, if not broken hearts.

And she and Rye had tumbled a total of once. It wasn't like they'd even been a thing. Besides, he'd probably forgotten all about their fight in the street.

A shout sounded outside, and both Rye and the stranger lifted their heads.

Rye pushed himself to his feet. He pushed back the chair without stumbling. A few glasses littered his table, but Avianna hadn't brought him a single drink in the past few hours. Maybe he wasn't as drunk as she'd hoped.

He turned to her.

His face twitched, and he exhaled like a bull about to charge.

"Rye," Avianna said, keeping her voice calm. "Ready to call it a night?" She smiled gently.

He exhaled again and shook his head. "Why are you here?"

"I'm helping Alistair," she said. "Do you have a coat?"

Another shout sounded, this one louder. Then the door opened and two men fell in, one grabbing the other to stop himself from toppling over. These two were clearly drunk. They had cropped hair like Rye's and arms as big as his.

"Rye!" one of them slurred, as they stumbled into the pub. "Knew you'd be here."

Rye kept his eyes on Avianna, and the other men glanced over at her.

"Whoa, Rye, what's up?" one of the men asked, tugging on his arm.

Rye jutted out his chin at her.

"What, the bar wench?"

"She's the bitch that screwed me over."

"I never—" Avianna said in a flash of anger. But the men weren't listening. They were staring at her.

Avianna moved toward the end of the bar, and the closest man moved to block her escape. She backed up, trapped as he came around the corner. Rye leaned forward, a gleam in his watery eyes.

"Now what're you going to do, eh, Avi?" Rye said, leering across the bar.

Chapter 9

THE MAN TRAPPING AVIANNA BEHIND the bar moved closer. She reached for a bottle of whiskey—aged Esterian whiskey, curse it all. She'd owe Alistair three moons' rent if she broke it over the man's head. He snickered at the bottle in her hands and took another step toward her.

Avianna stared down the man stalking her, her fist tightening on the neck of the bottle.

And then the stranger with the tattoos stood up. In two strides, he crossed the room and shoved Rye into his friend. They pitched to the floor in a heap.

The stalker trapping her in looked drunkenly at his friends. Avianna leaned away from him, lifted her leg, and kicked him in the stomach, pushing with all her might. He toppled backward and fell.

The stranger vaulted onto the bar and crouched down. He held out his arms. Sandy strands of hair poked out from beneath his cap, partially obscuring his eyes, and his lips were set in a tight line.

Rye was sitting up. The other men were moving. They'd be up again in moments.

Avianna put down the whiskey and held her arms out to the stranger.

He gripped her waist and stood, lifting her out of the trap. She wobbled, struggling to balance her feet on the bar, and clung to him. He locked an arm around her waist and jumped down to the floor, carrying her with him. In two heartbeats, he had her out the door.

The men inside Alistair's shouted. Avianna barely had time to breathe in the night air before the stranger tilted her back, swept her legs up in his other arm, and ran up the dark street.

What was he going to do with her?

It couldn't be worse than whatever Rye's friends would've done. She slid her arms around his neck and held on.

He carried her out toward the wharf. They turned the corner and headed up the main hill into the village before he slowed. The street was deserted and silent. His chest panted against her body. His hands felt sturdy beneath her, and his arms solid. He lowered her feet to the ground, holding her up as she found her footing.

"Thank you," Avianna said, staring up at him. The moon was down and the street dark. The man's face was still shadowed by his hat, but he broke into an unexpected grin.

"Anytime," he said.

She recognized the voice. No, it couldn't be.

His face wavered, and she blinked and Thorn was standing before her, the sailor's cap gone from his head.

"Thorn!"

"You just keep getting into trouble."

"That was you? The whole time?"

He nodded.

She reached for his arm. The tattoos were gone. "How did you do that? I thought you could turn invisible."

"I can use illusions, too," Thorn said. "I'm not very good at them, but I can use them a little. Here, I'll show you." He held out his hand, and in the dim lamplight, a curling tattoo flickered once and appeared on his hand, and then faded out of view.

"That's amazing. I never would have guessed it was you. But what were you doing in Alistair's?"

"I saw you heading in and I knew Rye was in there, so I followed you. In case he caused trouble. Not that you can't take care of yourself, I just . . . I didn't want you to get hurt."

"But how did you do that—with your muscles?"

"What?"

"I thought fairy illusions couldn't change what's really there."

"They can't."

"Then how did you give yourself such strong arms?"

Thorn shook his head. "You are too much." Shouts sounded around the corner. "Let's get out of here." He took her hand and pulled her up the hill and away from the pub. When she followed along, he dropped her hand. For some reason, she wished he hadn't.

"What were *you* doing in Alistair's?" he asked. "You're not really working there, are you? Rye's in there just about every night."

"Oh, Thorn, it's terrible," Avianna said. "My *parents* showed up at the boarding house."

"Your parents? How is that terrible?"

"You don't understand."

"Wait, was this before or after you got Prince Murkel out of your bed? Assuming you managed that."

"I did, thank the skies. I crossed paths with Alfie, and he distracted Flo long enough that Corella and I dragged Murkel out the back stairs and dumped him by the alley."

"Poor Murkel."

"He's revolting! He actually thought I would come home and tumble him. I think he wanted Corella to join us. And he wouldn't leave. I had to tell him I had a room for us, just to get him moving. And we practically had to carry him. Poor Corella was traumatized. And I don't think any amount of washing will make my bed sheets feel clean again."

"That *is* revolting."

"But Flo didn't catch me."

"And your parents came."

"I can't believe they found me. I had to get them out of Flo's before they talked, so I took them to Alistair's. And he'd offered me work once, and Lucinda was all alone and asked for help. I'm so behind on my rent, and the coins for the fish, and now a room for my parents. So I got behind the bar."

"What's so bad about your parents? Other than costing you shells."

Avianna blew out her breath. There was no way to explain her reaction without telling the truth. What would Thorn say? She couldn't see him throwing her over as a friend just because of her past. Maybe it would help to share her secret with someone.

"You can't tell anyone."

"Never."

"My parents are paupers."

"So is half the village, Avi."

"No, I mean, they've always been. I told everyone they lost their property in the revolution, but it's not true. They never had any. I didn't grow up in a manor with servants and ball gowns. I grew up on the streets, stealing my dinner."

"I don't think anyone—"

"It's worse."

"Go on," Thorn said.

"My da . . . he's not my real father. My mother tumbled lots of people, back before she met him. That's how she got by, always finding someone to buy her a meal. She even took straight money for it sometimes. I don't know who my father was. And with Mattie telling everyone I'm diseased? If they found out about my past, they'd believe whatever horrible new rumors Mattie would spread about me. And I've lied to so many people. The whole village would laugh at me if the truth came out. No one would want me." She paused. In the silence she studied Thorn.

He watched her in return, as he always did. "I didn't know my father either."

"You didn't?"

He shook his head.

"But weren't all the fairies trapped in the caverns? How could he have gotten away?"

"He didn't leave," Thorn replied. "It's just that my ma tumbled so many men, she had no idea which one was the father."

Avianna stared. Thorn showed no embarrassment as he ambled along beside her. As if the fairies hadn't treated him any differently because of his parentage.

"How did you end up at court?" he asked.

Avianna paused before answering. "I just decided to go." She took a moment to collect herself. She'd never told anyone the real story.

"I spent my whole childhood watching my parents hustle. We never knew where our next meal was coming from, stealing it half the time. Then men started looking my way, and I knew I was in for it. They'd always smiled at me, and I knew how to talk to them, how to make them laugh. I knew I was pretty. But this was different, it sent chills down my back. I knew enough to know what they were after. And I didn't want it, not with them. I'd end up stuck in some horrid situation and poor for the rest of my life, just like my parents. I was desperate to get out, but I had no options.

"And then one day, it was spring and the roads were muddy, and I'd left town on an errand, and I came upon a carriage stuck with its wheel in the mud. The driver was trying to figure how to lift it out. He tipped his hat at me, and I offered to help. And next thing I knew, he was helping a young woman out of the carriage door, and he sat us on the bank and told us to visit while he fixed the carriage. She was older than me, a lord's daughter from near Sar Bay. She'd been at court for many seasons, and she'd become engaged and was traveling back to her parents to plan for the ceremony. I wanted to hear all about court and about her beau—I was fourteen. I think she liked how I admired her.

"That's when it came to me. I had to go to court. It sounded wonderful, the gardens and dancing, and all you had to do was knit and stay pretty and flirt with men, and eventually one would court you and bond with you. No more hustling for food or moving from one shambles to another. I knew I could succeed there, if only I could get in. And once I fell in love and bonded with someone, we'd have a home—a place I could stay and never have to worry.

"I started asking how it worked, and who else was there, and from where. She mentioned one girl who'd been there, the farthest one from way up north, the daughter of the Scroddington de Pleuves from Nor Bay, on the sea that faces Norland. But that girl had met someone and left the court, she said, and then *she'd* been the one farthest from home. So I remembered that name. And I admired her dress and told her how poor we were, and she made the driver get out her chests so she could give me some of her old dresses. For being nice and keeping her company, she said. She'd be getting new ones before her ceremony, anyway. She even gave me a pair of shoes."

"So you just walked into the castle and told them you were . . . ?"

"I used my real name. But I said we were cousins of the Scroddington de Pleuves, and my father had died and my mother needed to travel with her new husband, so they sent me to court with a merchant friend. Really I'd stolen the coins for the coach ride, and after we reached Woodglen, I scrubbed myself clean in a farmyard after dark, and put on a decent dress and did up my hair. I was young, so I could pass as a manor girl without having jewelry."

"Avianna Blackburn, that is an amazing story."

"That was my one chance to make a new life for myself. And I blew it."

Thorn sighed, sounding exasperated. "We've been over this. You have not blown it. There's plenty you can do."

"But now my parents are here. People will see it immediately, that we're not from a noble family. I'm a fraud."

"And you think that matters?"

"Of course it does."

"No, it really doesn't. That's the beauty of the revolution. All those old ideas about status and value, they were tossed off the cliff. You had nothing and you made something of yourself. You have more value than Lord Skiddle-de-Puff's sodding heirs."

They had stopped walking. Avianna had been so focused on recalling her history that she hadn't realized where they were. They stood at the door of the print shop. They'd passed right by the turn to the boarding house.

"I thought you might want dinner," Thorn said, gazing down.

For a brief moment, Avianna had that feeling she got sometimes—the feeling that hinted to her that a man was interested. Like a scent on the air that she sensed in her skin. Thorn was inviting her to dinner—what did it mean?

But as fast as she felt it, it was gone. She must have imagined it. This was Thorn, after all—there was no way he was putting the moves on her, no matter what nonsense Corella made up about his feelings. He was the least presumptuous person she'd ever met.

And besides, she and Thorn had nothing in common. He probably liked sensible girls who'd grown up in the village, like Mattie, not women who'd been ruined by a life of luxury in the castle. He'd nearly said as much at the dance, when he went off talking about the unfortunate people who'd had to wait on the king and the courtiers.

Avianna fought off the nerves that pricked up at the idea of Thorn courting her. He was merely being friendly and offering her dinner. And he had just helped her escape a situation that could have ended dreadfully. She couldn't bring herself to turn him down, even if it gave him the wrong idea—which it wouldn't.

"I did miss dinner," she replied. Thorn clicked open the lock and showed her in.

As he followed her inside, he closed the door behind them. She stood still until he led her through the darkness into the back room. The press was in the shadows, but enough light came in the windows to show the way. On one side, a lopsided staircase climbed up. Thorn stopped at the hearth, back-to-back with the hearth in the front room where he had boiled water for their tea that afternoon. He lit a candle from the embers.

He held out his hand, and she slipped her fingers into his. They were rough, from handling papers and inks and whatever else he did, she imagined. But they were warm and held hers tightly. He ascended the narrow stairs, leading her up after him. The candle illuminated their steps, casting tall shadows on the close walls as they neared the top.

Upstairs was a neat room under the sloping roof of the building. Dormer windows on either side overlooked the street and the back alley. Thorn placed the candle at the center of a plain wooden table. Behind it was a makeshift kitchen, with a hearth above the one downstairs, and a wash basin with cups and plates stacked clean beside it. A bed with a worn-out quilt stood in one shadowy corner. The room smelled nice—like the ink and paper smells of the shop, but with fried onion and candle smoke blended in.

"Do you live up here?" Avianna asked. Somehow she had never considered where he slept, or where he went when he wasn't running into her on the street.

"Sometimes." Thorn was rummaging through some sacks and jars in the candlelight. "How about a stuffed potato?"

"A potato? For dinner?"

"I have some cheese, and some broccoli I could add, and of course potatoes."

"Oh right, fairy food," Avianna said. Thorn blushed, and immediately she wished she could take back her words. It wasn't sausages, but it was free dinner, and no one else had thought to give her any.

"I'm sorry Thorn, I would love a potato. I forgot is all." She felt so bad at her inconsiderate words that she stepped forward, slipping her hand into his again and squeezing.

Thorn squeezed back without turning to her. He pushed his spectacles up his nose. "Let me get a fire started."

Avianna pulled out a chair, picked up a folded piece of fabric that hung over the back, and sat. She was expecting a kitchen towel or napkins, but realized the fabric was the shawl she'd left in the shop when she'd fled that afternoon. Thorn must have planned to return it to her. He was fiddling with kindling at the hearth. He tipped the candle into the small pieces of wood, setting them ablaze, and as the light flared up, it shone on his spectacles and the curve of his lips. And suddenly he wasn't just gangly Thorn the printer, but an exciting mysterious stranger who'd lifted her in his arms only twenty minutes ago. And they were alone. In what appeared to be his bedroom, of all places.

What would it be like to pull him down on that rather small bed in the corner and have her way with him?

The bed was probably cold, the upstairs room not having had a fire all day. And she probably had loads more experience than Thorn did. Avianna was used to men who took charge—who tossed her onto the bed and immediately began unbuckling their belts and didn't much wait for anything. Thorn might be awkward and hesitant. She'd probably have to undo his trousers for him— she couldn't imagine him being forward enough to do it himself. But maybe . . .

Maybe she'd like it. What would it be like to be with someone like Thorn—quiet and polite, and always thinking about her? Someone who wanted to hear her ideas, and seemed to like her no matter what? What would it be like to kiss, or to fool around with, or to have sex with someone like that? She imagined there might be more kissing and tumbling about before they reached the actual moment of intercourse.

"Avi?"

Her head jerked up, tearing her eyes away from the scratch on the table she'd been running her fingertip over. Skies, the fire was hot. It wasn't even that big yet, and Avianna was completely flushed.

"Where'd you go off to?" Thorn asked. Now the firelight was

dancing on his skin. He'd put out the candle. She could barely make out the darkish ring of his fading black eye.

Where *had* she gone off to? "Nowhere. Just thinking."

"About your date?"

"No. Yes. I hope I don't make a fool of myself."

"You won't. You'll enchant him."

Avianna didn't know what to say to that.

"Speaking of dates," she said, "Mattie was at Alistair's before you got there. She was sitting with Beck. I . . . I felt sort of worried for her."

"I saw. I *was* there, remember?"

"Oh, right."

"Why were you worried?"

"I don't know. He's not as bad as Rye. But he's still a mean sort. I don't trust him to be kind to anyone."

"Mattie's pretty mean herself. Maybe they'll hit it off," Thorn said.

"Maybe you're right. Thank you for telling her to lay off me today. Coming from you, I'm sure it smarted."

"Coming from me?"

"She's sweet on you, Thorn. She's always trying to get your attention."

Thorn sighed. "After you left this afternoon, she . . . let's just say it was embarrassing. I had to tell her I wasn't interested."

Why did Thorn's words make Avianna so happy?

Thorn was her friend, that was all—she wouldn't want a friend dating someone mean like Mattie. And his words explained why Mattie had ventured into Alistair's Pub looking all mopey eyed. Being rejected by Thorn after all her weeks of fawning over him must have stung.

Thorn poked around in the fire. He'd placed two potatoes on the hearth. He inched them closer to the heat, staring at the flames.

Clearly he wasn't going to expound on rejecting Mattie. What could Avianna ask him about? How to talk to cats? Everything coming into her head to say was completely silly.

"How long have you worn spectacles?"

"Since the revolution. The fairies don't make them, so I didn't get them until we were free to come to the village."

"I'd forgotten it was a revolution for the fairies, too."

"Yes."

"Before that you couldn't see?"

"I couldn't see far from me. But I could read," Thorn said.

"Ah."

Thorn left the hearth and fell into the seat across from her. "Most fairies have perfect eyesight. Something went wrong with mine, though. I was the only child who couldn't see well enough to play. I could never keep up with the other children or catch a ball. No one ever wanted me on their team. I ended up staying home mostly, and playing by myself. So one day, one of the elders asked my ma to send me over. I thought she'd want help fixing something, but she shut her door and latched it and pulled out a book.

"She said I couldn't tell, because most human things were forbidden in the fairy realm, back then I mean, and especially books about happy fairies living free in the forest. But she suspected I'd like reading and writing and drawing, too, since I could see close up. Drawing was allowed, as long as it was flowers and things. And of course, you had to make the queen beautiful if you were drawing her."

"But she *was* beautiful, right?" Avianna asked.

Thorn snorted. "If by beautiful you mean cruel and selfish."

"But she had long flowing tresses, and wore a crown of emeralds as bright as her eyes, and her gown—"

Thorn's laughter cut Avianna off. "Where did you hear this crap?" he asked.

"As a matter of fact, it was in a *book*." That sobered him up. "When I first arrived at court, there were still books in the castle library. Some of the ladies would read them aloud, especially the romantic ones. And when I was lonely, I'd sneak in there and find the ones with pictures. And there was one with fairies, and it showed the queen walking through the forest. It was my favorite picture."

"That must have been some long-ago queen, Avi, because the last queen never would've walked in the forest. She'd have made servants carry her. She wasn't a normal fairy at all. She kidnapped human children and used them as servants, for skies' sake, even though living underground made them ill."

"I'd forgotten that bit." Avianna frowned, trying to remember the rumors that had circulated after the revolution. "The ones who were underground too long never made it out, did they?" she said quietly.

Thorn shifted in his seat. He had a strange expression on his face. He shook his head once to move the hair off his face, and the look disappeared. "What happened to the books?"

"Of course you care about the books."

"Books are hard to come by. I'm planning to make some, as soon as I have the time and the shells saved. Being able to read, and to read a book, will make such a difference to the children here. It made such a difference to me."

"And you think reading will benefit me?"

He shrugged, looking down. "It couldn't hurt anything." Then he looked up at her from under his long hair and he grinned. "And it gives me an excuse to see you."

Avianna flushed first hot and then cold at that. She wasn't used to Thorn flirting. Or at least, she wasn't used to noticing it when he did. He was still staring at her, grinning.

"I don't know what happened to the books," she said. "And you're one to talk about normal fairies—leaving the forest to live in the village, wearing spectacles and printing flyers about human politics, and teaching all the children to read. You're not much of a fairy at all. You have a clock in the print shop, for skies' sake."

"What's wrong with my clock?"

"Fairies are supposed to live by the moon and the sun and all that, not care what human hour of the day it is."

"The clock helps, living in the village. I need to know when to open the shop, and when to go to the dance, and when it's the hour when I'm most likely to see you walking past and can go outside and pretend to run into you." He grinned again, and now she wasn't sure if he was flirting or being his goofy self. But her heart gave a weird little squirm at his words.

"You do not."

He only smiled in reply.

"Besides," Avianna continued, "fairies name their children after the trees and flowers. Whoever named you got it wrong. You might as well be Stem or Petal."

Thorn burst out laughing. "Avi, you ninny, Thorn is short for Hawthorn."

Hawthorn. His real name was Hawthorn.

The silence that followed his laugh unnerved her. "So you love the humans," she said, to break it, "and you want to make books for us all."

He grew serious. "I know my dream is odd, but I don't care. I'm going to pursue it anyway. And you can never have enough to read, whether it's books or pamphlets. Reading's how you visit places you can't get to in this world."

"What was your favorite place then?" Avianna asked.

"I always wanted to be on a pirate ship."

"Me too!"

"Only you probably wanted to bed the pirates, right?"

She wanted to be offended, but he'd guessed right.

He continued, "I wanted to climb the rigging and spot new islands and go exploring with a Sarlian gull on my shoulder. Which was ironic since I couldn't see ten feet in front of me."

"I wanted to wear all the jewels they'd stolen," Avianna said. "After the pirate captain fell in love with me, of course. When I was young, in South End, I would imagine they robbed the nearest manor, and I'd come up with all these ways that I ended up on their ship so I could meet the captain. And when I lived at the castle, I imagined they came to rob the king and the captain saw me and fell in love and took me, too."

Thorn smiled. "That reminds me, you left the shop before I could give you your present." He reached back onto the counter and brought a bundled kerchief to the table. He opened it to reveal a pile of crystal beads.

"My necklace!"

Avianna stared in shock, and then seeing it truly was her beads, became dizzy with joy. She'd believed her necklace was gone forever. He placed the beads in her hand, like a bundle of hope. Maybe her life was not at a dead end.

Thorn must've used a fairy finding spell to gather up the crystal beads after she'd run off, and after Rye had left. Something strung them together, but Avianna couldn't see what—the chain was missing. She held them up, turning them over and trying to figure it out.

"It's fairy thread," Thorn said.

"I can't see it."

"You have to hold it to the light just right."

"What's it made of?"

"You'll turn up your nose if I tell you."

"No I won't."

"Spider webs."

Avianna held her face steady to avoid turning up her nose. "But it's strong. How do you manage that?"

"Magic."

"Right. Help me put it on?"

He stood, came around the table, and took the necklace from her. She pulled her mass of curls away from her neck and waited. Thorn stood behind her, and for a moment she imagined he might bend down and kiss the back of her neck, and at the thought, little jolts of heat shot through her. But instead he looped the necklace around her neck and began fastening it. When his knuckles brushed against her skin, she started.

He finished and lightly rested his hands on her shoulders. She let go her hair. If she turned her head up and twisted around to him, would he bend down and kiss her? Did she want him to?

Just look up, she told herself. But she only fingered her necklace and stared at the table. Thorn squeezed her shoulders and went to the fire.

He pulled out the potatoes and cut them open on two plates. He began adding the toppings as steam curled up from inside them. She couldn't stop watching him—the muscle twitching in his forearm where he'd pushed his sleeve up, or the place where his shirt tucked neatly into his trousers.

"So you need more income." His words broke her trance.

"Yes."

"Are you going back to Alistair's? For work, I mean."

"I don't want to, not if it means fending off Rye again. But I don't have many options. There's only so much laundry available. Corella's been letting me do most of it as it is."

"I have a job idea."

"For me?"

Thorn nodded. "I help sometimes at the grange home."

"The grange? Like, where the old people live?"

"Someday you'll be old, Avi."

She shut her mouth. Thorn was trying to help her, and all she could do was say rude things. "What do you do there?" she asked.

"I fix things sometimes, but mostly I visit with the residents. Most of them don't have any family, obviously, since they live in the grange. I think they like to see a young person."

"They pay you to visit?"

"There's pay for it in the grange's budget."

"But I can't take your job."

"I don't need it. I'd rather have the time in my shop, actually, but I hated to leave if they didn't have another person. Another qualified person."

"And you think I'm qualified? They'd be horrified by me. I'm the girl that grandmothers point at as a warning to their offspring, saying they should never behave like me."

Thorn paused, holding a knife over a potato, and turned to her. "You might be surprised. Old people can be a rowdy bunch. Besides, these are the 'grandmothers' without offspring, remember? Maybe they were like you when they were young."

"Wonderful, you think I'll end up alone in the grange home."

"You know I didn't mean that." He turned back to the potatoes.

Avi didn't see a bunch of sweet old ladies wanting to visit with her, but she needed to pay her debts. If Thorn believed she could do it, she would give it a try.

"So I would go there . . . ?"

"Tomorrow. I go midmorning, so they're up and they've had breakfast. Let yourself in the main door and head into the parlor, and someone will probably be there. That's where they sit most of the day if it's too cold to go to the park. I stay through lunch and then it's nap time. For them, I mean. Well, sometimes for me, too."

A picture appeared in Avianna's mind of Thorn asleep in the bed in the corner, with dusty sunlight streaming in through the thick glass panes, as the villagers went about their lives on the street outside. She imagined it would be warm to curl up beside him, lazing about in the middle of the workday. Brushing his long hair out of his face. Waking him, and his eyes would open already fixed on her, always waiting on her. And she'd reach for him—

"So you'll do it?"

Avianna jerked back to the present. And suddenly the truth dawned on her, the horrible truth. She didn't want to believe it. But it was the only explanation for all the strange feelings she'd had this evening.

Thorn had put her under a love spell.

Chapter 10

A FAIRY LOVE SPELL, AVIANNA THOUGHT in shock. Like the spell the fairy prince had used to lure in Princess Rose last spring. Thorn must have put her under one. How else could she explain all the new feelings she'd been having—the way her thoughts kept turning to Thorn, and the way she kept imagining what it would be like to touch him?

She'd never had any interest in bookish types, or in fairies, and then she'd started running into Thorn on the street—he'd *tried* to run into her, he'd said as much! And at some point, he'd done his magic, and she'd started thinking about him, liking the touch of his hand, and wondering about kissing him. He'd used a fairy love spell on her, and now she was as good as his, doomed to have feelings for him no matter where she turned. No wonder he kept popping into her head, and one glimpse of his sad little bed gave her visions of pulling him down onto it and wrapping herself around him.

He was watching her. He'd asked about the grange job. She had to reply. "Y-y-yes, I'll go tomorrow."

He turned back to their supper. "Do you want me to meet you there?"

"No! No. You get to work in your shop. I'll be fine."

Avianna studied his back in the firelight, the edge where his shoulder blade curved under his shirt, pinned down by his suspenders, and predictably, her blood raced. She wanted to go stand behind him and hug her arms around him.

Innocent Thorn the human-loving fairy. Hah! Devious Hawthorn was more like it. Who was he? Was he the quiet being she knew, but more lovelorn than she'd realized, enough that he'd use a spell to gain companionship? Or was he something else entirely, capable of who knows what? She couldn't let him know she was onto him.

But he'd rescued her from Rye and his thugs, Avianna's mind argued. Twice! He'd gotten a black eye for her. He'd given back her Norlian crystals—she reached for them, and thankfulness filled her. He'd told Mattie to lay off, and now he'd found a new job for her. As much as she hated the idea of someone using a spell on her, she couldn't bring herself to think badly of Thorn. Maybe he was terribly lonely. What if he was desperate enough to use a spell to end his loneliness?

Thorn turned and placed two plates on the table. Each had a potato, cut down the middle and mashed flat, glistening with butter and piled with roasted bits of broccoli and melted cheese, and drizzled with some kind of white sauce. He slid one plate toward her, and the smell wafted up on the steam coming off the potato. Avianna's mouth watered. Maybe the love spell made her enchanted by anything he did, even a meal he'd prepared. He handed her a fork.

She took the fork without touching his fingers and swallowed hard. "That smells amazing. I hadn't expected something so . . . fancy."

"Did you think I'd feed you a plain old potato?" He smiled at her as he retrieved two cups of water and sat by his own plate.

Avianna blew to cool it, then forced herself to take a bite. Gingerly, she put it into her mouth. The sauce was delicious and not like anything she normally ate at the boarding house. It wasn't even like anything that she could remember having at the castle.

"The sauce is scrumptious," she said, taking another forkful. "What's in it?"

"Secret fairy ingredients."

Avianna choked.

"I'm kidding," Thorn said, cutting into his own potato. "It's acidified cream. Humans make it with milk and buttermilk, but we didn't have a lot of cows growing up, so when we had any milk, we used a different recipe, with over-fermented wine. It gives it kind of a zing."

Avianna hoped that "a zing" was all the sauce was giving and kept eating.

"So you left your parents at Alistair's?" Thorn asked.

"It'll be cheaper than having them stay at the boarding house. Plus I didn't think Flo would give me any more credit."

"What will they do tomorrow?"

"Oh." Avianna lowered her fork. "I hadn't considered that yet."

"You don't have to go to the grange—"

"No, I want to. I'll think of something to occupy them while I work." She'd just as soon put off talking to them. Who knew what scam they were planning now? She didn't want any part of it, not when she was trying so hard to turn things around.

"And while you go on your date," Thorn added.

She'd forgotten that. Of course, the spell was probably making her forget.

Was Thorn bitter about her date with Jeb Doolihan? He took another bite as if nothing were the matter. His behavior didn't make sense. He'd helped her meet Jeb at the dance, but why would he do that? Maybe his spell followed some complicated logic that involved foisting her off on dolts like Jeb Doolihan, to make himself appear better by comparison. That would be just like Thorn to create some elaborate spell. He'd probably learned how in one of the fairy books. She wished she could go on a date with him instead. It would be a lot more fun.

No. What was she thinking? Jeb wasn't a dolt, he was a successful merchant with fine clothing who was interested in her. Their date would be fun.

She had to get out of Thorn's apartment before his spell consumed her.

She focused on eating her dinner, and Thorn didn't break the silence. When she licked her fork clean, Thorn was sitting, his plate empty, staring into the fire. She clinked her fork onto the table and he looked up.

"After two Rye attacks in two days, you must be exhausted," he said.

"Me? You're the one doing most of the fighting."

"Give me a moment and I'll walk you home."

Avianna could see it now—if Thorn walked her home, there'd come that moment when they parted, and what if he tried to kiss her? She wasn't sure she could resist, not the way she twisted inside every time she watched him. She had to get herself together. She couldn't kiss Thorn, not with her date tomorrow. If she gave in to these feelings for Thorn, her date with Jeb would be a disaster.

"I'll be fine," she said. "You must be tired, too. But thank you for making me dinner."

Thorn considered her a moment. "At least let me get Finnegan. In case Rye is lurking out there."

Avianna smiled. "Okay, Finnegan it is."

She stood and wrapped her shawl around her shoulders. Thorn headed down the narrow stair ahead of her. She'd expected him to take her hand to lead her down the staircase, or help wrap the shawl around her, instead of walking off without her. No doubt his behavior was all part of his plan. Her fingers went to her beads as she headed down after him.

It was cooler in the shop without the cozy fire. The dormitory back at the boarding house would be cold as well. Avianna wished she could stay in the snug attic at the print shop, with no laundry to do and no date with Jeb Doolihan.

She was nervous, she told herself. The date would be fine. Once she was out of the shop, her head would clear.

Thorn opened the door to the street and waited, and a moment later, a long "Merrrowww" drifted in the doorway. Finnegan walked into sight from an alley. He sauntered over and wound himself around Thorn's ankles.

"He doesn't mind?" Avianna asked.

"He says he hopes you meet Rye on the way home, so he can disfigure him."

"Skies, Finnegan, I hope I never get on your bad side."

Finnegan peered up at her. "Merrrowww," he said again.

Thorn reached out a hand, and Avianna swallowed as she took it. But he only squeezed hers.

"You'll do fine tomorrow," he said. "At the grange, and on your date." He let go of her hand. Avianna made herself follow Finnegan out the door.

Chapter 11

THE NEXT MORNING, AVIANNA STOOD at the front door of the grange home, collecting herself before she entered. Thanks to Thorn, she had another chance to make some coins today. Perhaps she could even land steady work with the residents here. Work like that would help with her bills, and it wouldn't involve being in a pub with Rye or scraping her fingers to the bone over laundry. She couldn't screw this job up like she had Flo's errands.

She'd managed only a few hours of sleep the night before. After Finnegan had left her at the boarding house, she'd lain awake in bed, trying not to think of Thorn. Then she'd been up early to see to her parents. Alistair was still in bed, so she'd raided his pantry to make breakfast for her parents and Alfie. She'd also cleaned up the mess Rye and his buddies had left in the bar room, before Alistair ever saw it. Thankfully they hadn't stolen the Esterian whiskey or broken the furniture.

She'd talked Alfie into showing her parents the castle gardens while she worked. Other than that, she'd avoided standing still long enough to give her parents a chance to speak. She didn't want to hear whatever racket they had cooked up this time. And she hadn't told them about her date. She'd apologized and said she'd have more time to see them the next day. Her da had seemed awfully happy about how much work she had, at least.

So, she told herself now, facing the door to the grange. She'd succeeded at tending bar, more or less, in spite of how the night had ended. She could succeed today, too, although visiting the residents of the grange home was about as different a job from last night's as she could get.

The grange home sat on the edge of the town square, facing the park that filled the center. The square was in the nice part of town, at the top of the hill and close to the castle road. Adjacent to this building was the grange hall where she'd gone for the dance. Thorn had been so at home at the dance, walking among the crowd and talking to everyone. Did he come up to this part of the village often? What was he doing this morning—working on stitching together a book, now that he had more time in his shop?

Gad! She'd been determined not to think about Thorn, and here he was, popping into her thoughts. At least visiting with the old people would distract her. If she wasn't thinking, she couldn't be thinking about Thorn.

Avianna depressed the latch and the door swung open. Inside, a hallway led into the building and a room opened off to the left— the parlor. She stepped in and found a circle of white-haired ladies with wrinkled skin, all sitting with a patchwork quilt laid out in the center. Some of the faces she recognized from the dance—they'd been Thorn's dance partners.

Don't think about Thorn.

The ladies were greeting her all at once.

Avianna smiled. "Thorn asked me to come," she said, wincing at his name. "He needed to work at his shop."

"Well come in, dear," one of the women said. "You can help us with the quilt."

Avianna sat in the chair they indicated as they told her their names, all five women. She repeated each name, but within a few breaths she had forgotten. They showed her the pattern outlined on the fabric where she was to stitch. Did they have Thorn help with quilting when he visited them? He probably knew how to sew, industrious as he was. He'd need his sewing skills for his new book enterprise.

Don't think about Thorn.

"You're a friend of Thorn's?" one of the women said, smiling. Margaret was her name. Or Martha?

Avianna scowled at the quilt, trying not to think of Thorn. Her needle popped up in the wrong location, her stitch gone crooked. She pressed her lips tight and smiled. "Yes, we know each other from around the village."

"He's such a dear."

"And so handsome."

Avianna rolled her eyes. This was impossible! How was she supposed to not think about Thorn, sitting in a circle of admirers all waxing on about him?

"What a catch he'll be for some lucky girl."

He'd put the ladies up to it—that had to be it. He'd sent Avianna here to sit with these seemingly oblivious elders on the pretext of helping her find work, knowing they'd sing his praises and nudge her toward giving in to his charms. Or the spell's charms, rather. He must have spells on all of them, because the ladies talked as if they genuinely liked him.

And she was stuck here for hours.

She should sabotage Thorn. Tell all the ladies some made-up stories about him to ruin his apparently spotless reputation. How he'd pickpocketed a merchant one time and claimed it wasn't stealing if the person had more shells than you. Or how she had seen him drunk on the wharf, catcalling the women fish-catchers. Or how she'd walked into the print shop and found him sprawled naked on the printing press with one of the wharf girls atop him.

But she couldn't bring herself to do it, not to these nice ladies. And now she was thinking about Thorn lying naked on the printing press. She focused on her stitching.

"You were at the dance, weren't you?" Margaret said.

"Yes. It was my first time."

"You must've been popular. You have such a pretty face."

"I used to have curls like that," another one said.

"I was asked to dance almost every dance," Avianna said. "My feet were all but worn out by the end."

"Did you find any nice young men?"

Avianna felt herself blushing. "Actually, I have a date tonight."

A chorus of ohhs and sighs rose up. "What's his name?"

"Jeb. Jeb Doolihan."

"Jeb is Reginald Doolihan's son. He *is* handsome. You must be excited to spend time with him."

"A little. I hope we have enough to talk about."

"If talking doesn't work out, there's always kissing."

The ladies cackled as Avianna's cheeks flushed even hotter. Now more than ever she hoped that she could think of enough to say to Jeb. And that Jeb wouldn't try to get her alone in the park again, or pull any other stunts.

Why did the idea of kissing Jeb get under her skin? Kissing had never been a big deal to her, but suddenly it put her off. And Jeb might try to kiss her—it was likely, in fact, and she wasn't sure what she'd do.

Then she remembered Thorn's spell. That explained things—the spell must ruin all your feelings for anyone else. Of course she'd kiss Jeb Doolihan back.

"Now you've embarrassed her, Margery," one of the ladies said. It was Margery then, not Margaret.

Margery patted Avianna's hand. "You'll be fine."

Beside her hand, a row of crooked stitches zigzagged across the quilt. Margery's eyes moved toward them and she tilted her head.

Avianna stared at her lap. "I'm not sure I'm the best person to help with your quilt."

"Not much of a seamstress?"

Across the quilt, another woman spoke. "Don't worry, dear. We never let Hilda help with the quilts. She can't sew two stitches straight." Next to the speaker, a woman looked up from a pamphlet she was reading and rolled her eyes.

No one seemed disappointed in Avianna as she handed the needle back to Margery. They just kept on with their own work.

"My parents weren't terribly, um, meticulous about teaching me things like sewing," Avianna said. "And I went to live in the castle when I was still young, and we mostly did needlework or knitted. The maids did the sewing." Not that she'd spent much time at needlework, either. Hopefully they wouldn't ask what she *was* skilled at.

But at the mention of the castle, several heads had turned. They began to pepper her with questions. The ladies wanted to hear all about life in the castle and particularly what Princess Rose was like. Rose had practically been a captive, kept by her father in the tower until she escaped with the fairy prince. Some of them remembered Rose's mother, who'd apparently been a shining example of virtue, bringing medicine and food to the sick and poor before she died.

"And she always brought Rose with her when she visited the village," Margery said. "She was such a sweet child."

Avianna couldn't bring herself to make a snide reply about the princess, not to all these besotted women. "She stayed sweet," she said instead. "She was meek—I never would've imagined she had it in her, sneaking out her tower window in the middle of the night to go in the forest with the prince."

"But she was under his fairy spell—it could've changed her."

Avianna hadn't considered that, despite her own enchantment. She didn't feel any different than she had two moons ago. Had the princess changed when the prince cast his spell on her? She hadn't behaved differently during the daylight hours, although it certainly had been a shock to learn she'd climbed out the window of the tallest tower in the castle.

But the rumors indicated the princess had had no idea she was under a spell, whereas Avianna could feel Thorn's spell at work, time and again. Then again, the princess had been so naïve, she probably wouldn't have noticed ten fairy spells. Avianna already had a lot more experience.

"Well," Avianna said, anticipating the ladies' delight, "being seduced by Prince Dustan would've changed anyone."

"Did you get to see him?"

"What was he like?"

"I saw him once after the revolution," Margery chimed in. "His face would charm a dragon."

"They were all dashing," Avianna said, "all the princes who came to court the princess."

"Even Prince Murkel?" Hilda asked.

Usually Avianna avoided talking about Murkel, but in the circle of eager women, she couldn't resist. "Especially Prince Murkel," she said, and they leaned closer as she lowered her voice. "If it hadn't been for the fairy love spell, I'm sure Rose would've wanted him. He was a foot taller than he is now, at least, and his hair was dark and shiny, and, well, the rest of him was just as fine. Trust me."

Hilda wagged a finger. "You're the one he dallied with," she said. "I've heard about you."

Avianna tensed.

But Hilda grinned. "In the king's own castle, right under his nose. I'd never have dared."

"Where did you grow up, Avianna?" Margery asked. "You've got northern looks, with those curls! But your blue eyes are southern."

Avianna imagined telling these women about her childhood, and that her mother had tumbled men for a living. She'd told Thorn and he hadn't recoiled in disgust. She shouldn't tell them, of course. There was no telling who else they gossiped with.

"I'm from South End," she said. "My mother's people are from the south. I'm . . . I'm not sure who my real father was, but I guess the dark skin and curly hair must be from him."

"Your mother never told you?"

"I'm not sure she knew."

Across the quilt, Hilda smirked. "I remember those days. I used to have three beaus at once, all crying at my window like tomcats."

"Used to?" Margery said, and everyone laughed as Hilda flattened her fingers to her chest and closed her eyes, smiling.

Avianna helped make sandwiches for lunch, and since the day was sunny, after eating they walked out into the village park. Directly across from the grange home, an area of the park had been planted with vibrant flowers. As Avianna paced up and down the garden walkways with the women, she had to admit—since the king had been deposed and the villagers relieved of his taxes, the garden was a whole lot nicer. Late summer flowers still bloomed in the beds, with brightly painted benches along the paths.

The sun seemed warmer up here, and the breeze slighter than down by the docks where she and Thorn lived. After fifteen minutes basking in the sun and breeze, Avianna could see how a nap would soon be in order.

Back inside, everyone settled into their chairs in the parlor. Maybe they were excited to have Avianna there and willing to forego their naps. Hilda took another pamphlet off the shelf. Were the pamphlets Thorn's? Probably, given how much the ladies loved him.

"Perhaps you'd read to us?" she said to Avianna. "My eyes have tired, and I'm sure your voice would be nicer than mine."

Avianna stared at her lap again. After telling them all about life in the castle—a life of luxury where she hadn't had to worry about a thing—how could she admit she hadn't bothered to learn to read? They'd be tired of uncovering things she couldn't do.

But it was the truth. Even if she felt ashamed, she couldn't deny it.

"I'd like to," she said, scanning the faces around her. "I'm only now learning to read, though. Thorn's helping me. He taught me the letters."

She waited to see if Hilda would throw down the flyer and ask what she could do.

But instead, Hilda folded it into her lap. "That's wonderful that you're learning to read," she said. "You're such a determined young lady."

"And lucky you, with Thorn as a teacher," Margery said. And they set off sighing over Thorn again.

Avianna warmed at the mention of him, and her fingers went to the necklace at her throat. She tried to remind herself of the spell, but the longer she was away from him, the harder it grew to believe it was real. It was as if she was meant to daydream of Thorn. His name was like a fly in the room, continually buzzing into her thoughts. Thorn. Thorn. Thorn. And she couldn't feel angry with him, not after all the times he'd helped her and stood up for her when no one else did. Thorn simply wasn't her enemy.

The ladies started in on Jeb—they remembered him as a youth delivering produce to the village for the farmers, always keen to make some coins. His horse-breeding business was new, apparently, an opportunity he'd taken advantage of after the revolution.

The more they talked about Jeb, the more nervous Avianna became. What if he asked if she'd read the latest news? Or if he asked about her childhood? The truth was, she wasn't looking forward to the date at all.

Now if the date had been with Thorn . . . how nice that would be. Thorn was always easy to talk to. She wouldn't feel nervous at all, if it were him picking her up tonight and taking her to dinner. She wished it were Thorn—but then she remembered his spell. Maybe a date with Jeb was exactly what she needed to break Thorn's hold on her.

At least she had one comfort. In a few hours, the whole thing would be over.

Chapter 12

AVIANNA SAT UP STRAIGHT, STARING out the front window of the dining room at the Boar's Head Inn. All those times she had rolled past in the carriage on her way back to the castle . . . she had never imagined that one day, she'd be sitting inside with a villager, watching the people walk by on the tree-lined street from the other side. And these days, when she scuffled past in her worn-out shoes, it was just as hard to imagine sitting here.

Yet here she was.

She peeked at Jeb. He was peering out the window, too, and hadn't started talking since they'd arrived. Should she say something? Instead, she kept reminiscing.

She'd been in most of the shops around the village square. She'd always liked visiting the shops, back when she had coins to spend. The castle steward used to send her with coins and a list. Then she'd talk down the shopkeepers into giving her a deal and pocket the change, or use it to buy a sweet or a trinket or sometimes a gift for Elspeth. In fact, she'd been licking the sticky sugar of a bonbon off her fingers the first time she'd met Prince Murkel.

That day, she'd walked to the village. Murkel's carriage had overtaken her on the way home. Mattie and the others might tease her about tumbling Murkel, but they didn't know how fine he'd been back then, with his broad build and shining curls, just as she'd told the ladies at the grange home. Of course, he'd been a sea monster in disguise, but how could she have known? He'd been a handsome one.

No carriages rolled past the Boar's Head now, since most villagers couldn't afford a work horse, much less a horse to pull a carriage. But one carriage sat ostentatiously out front in the misty twilight—Jeb Doolihan's.

Avianna still couldn't believe he'd come to pick her up at Flo's boarding house in a carriage. She couldn't even see how the contraption had fit through the narrow streets at the bottom of the hill. With Flo waving and Samantha glaring, she'd let Jeb help her up the step and into the plush interior. Jeb had on a new vest, a different color but the same furry material as the one he'd worn at the dance—velvet, Corella had called it, a new fabric from Esteria. Avianna, on the other hand, wore the exact same dress. Maybe Jeb would think she'd worn her Norlian crystal beads just for him.

Corella had done something extra fancy with Avianna's hair, involving multiple braids and ribbons and loose tendrils hanging down to frame her face. Then, as Avianna had watched out the dormitory window, a fog had rolled in off the bay, shrouding the bottom of the village in white mist. The damp air might have done in her perfect curls, if she'd had to walk to the inn.

Regardless, it was a bit ridiculous to take a carriage to travel ten blocks. Avianna had been glad she could sit back and avoid anyone seeing her inside, especially when Jeb's driver almost ran down Alfie and Jeb yelled out the window at the poor boy and shook his fist. Within the hour it was likely everyone would know she had a date with Jeb, though, and that she'd ridden through the wharf district in a carriage, mowing down the peasants. Oh well. It wouldn't be the worst gossip that had gone around about her.

Jeb said something about wine, and Avianna turned to him. He sat across the table like a peacock with his tail spread, looking ridiculous and hoping to lure her in. His vest had a useless silken kerchief poking out of one pocket. It reminded Avianna of life in the castle court all over again, but now it rankled in Avianna's mind. Who had shells to waste on decorative kerchiefs?

She was thinking like Thorn. She had to focus on her date. Jeb was a first-rate catch and she had a chance to nab him, right now.

"That would be lovely," she said, wondering what she'd agreed to. Hopefully nothing too difficult, since it was only about wine.

Jeb snapped his fingers, frowning toward the kitchen door. The inn's waitstaff hurried over, and Jeb demanded two glasses of wine. His face wasn't so handsome when he was giving orders.

Jeb turned back to her and his expression softened with its usual charm. He reached across the table and took her hand, pulling it over to his side. "I've been thinking of you all day."

"How was your trip to Woods Rest?"

"Excellent. The buyer there wanted all the horses I'd brought, so I made a pretty sum." He turned over her hand, wiping his thumb down her palm. Her stomach turned. If she'd expected an evening with Jeb to be the antidote to Thorn's love spell, she'd been sorely wrong. Being with Jeb made her desperate to be anywhere else.

He kept talking about horses and rubbing her hand until she thought she'd go mad. Blast politeness. When he paused to sip his wine, she took the opportunity to interrupt him.

"I had an adventure last night."

Jeb's eyebrows went up, signaling alarm more than interest.

Avianna started to speak and remembered how many pitfalls her story had. Working in a pub by the wharf. Being ridiculed by her ex-lover. Being attacked by her other ex-lover. Being rescued by her future—

She stopped herself. Being rescued by her friend Thorn. And going back to his room for supper, where she'd contemplated kissing him.

Why hadn't she told Jeb about her visit at the grange home? That seemed more his style.

He was waiting.

"Do you know Alistair's Pub?"

Jeb shook his head.

"Alistair's wife died last spring, and he was desperate for some help last night, so I pitched in."

"In a pub?" Jeb squinted like he couldn't comprehend it.

"I know! I never would have thought I could do it. But I managed to run things all night." Until she'd been attacked, anyway.

"What were you doing in a pub by the docks in the first place?" So Jeb *did* know Alistair's Pub.

"Oh, I wasn't there to start with. I was at the boarding house. But Alistair's little boy came by." After she asked him to, to help her sneak Prince Murkel out of her bed.

Jeb shook his head and grimaced. "That's not always a savory crowd, down there."

"Where do you like to go out, then? Other than the dances?"

She'd meant it as an innocent question, but Jeb hesitated to answer. Maybe he *wasn't* the gentleman she'd imagined. "I, uh, always enjoy dinner here," he said.

An awkward moment passed.

"Um, I spent today at the grange home," she offered.

"With the old people?"

"You'll be old someday, Jeb."

"But I won't be living at the grange. I'll be able to take care of myself."

He was insufferable! Avianna gave up trying to converse. "What are your plans, now that you've sold all those horses?" she asked.

As she'd expected, Jeb launched into another round of animated blathering about his business and his properties. She tried to respond with pleasantries at the right moments while only half listening. What was she doing here? She'd been excited to have Jeb interested in her, but could she really handle a lifetime of this verbal drudgery, merely to gain financial security? She'd been trying so hard to be proper in Jeb's eyes, and the moment she acted like herself, he grew uncomfortable. Did she want that?

She knew she shouldn't give in, but she wanted to daydream about Thorn more than anything. As Jeb clutched her hand and started in on a description of all the ways he planned to multiply his wealth before old age arrived, Avianna let herself dream.

What if she gave in to Thorn's spell and let herself be seduced? Would the spell last? What if she could be happy for the rest of her life simply by giving in to the longings that kept tugging at her?

But what did Thorn want? Did he want a partner for life or only someone for a tumble? She couldn't see him pursuing a mere fling. That wasn't who he was. And she'd assumed he wanted a pretty girl and that he couldn't get one on his own and had resorted to using a spell. But he'd rejected Mattie, and she was pretty enough. Did he truly want *her*, Avianna?

That wasn't the question. The question was, after this interminable date ended, would she walk over to Thorn's shop and slip inside and lock the door behind her and draw the curtains closed and—

A body slammed against the window. Jeb leapt from his seat, almost yanking Avianna across the table until she snatched back her hand. A face mushed against the glass, its thick lips spread open to show rotting teeth.

Avianna sighed. "It's only Prince Murkel," she said. "He's probably drunk." She was glad to have her hand back from Jeb at last. She wiped the clamminess that remained onto her skirt and folded her hands in her lap.

Jeb edged back into his seat, appearing hesitant to be too close to Murkel even with the glass between them. Behind Murkel, the mist swirled around the village square in the glowing light of the lampposts. Murkel's tongue slid between his teeth. Avianna sipped her wine. Some sort of commotion occurred among the waitstaff, and the owner of the Boar's Head appeared beside Murkel, pulling him away from the window.

A moment later, their food arrived.

Jeb turned from peering into the mist to regard the massive hunk of meat on his plate. He lifted his fork and knife and began sawing into it. Avianna hadn't been able to stomach the idea of eating an animal—no doubt another result of the blasted fairy love spell—so she'd gotten fish, which had still appealed to her. The baked fish lay on a bed of roasted, steamed grains with delicate greens surrounding it and a sauce drizzled across the top. It smelled delicious. If she got nothing else out of this date, she'd at least get the best meal she'd had since the revolution. She lifted a bite on her fork.

Someone else banged into the window. "Not again," Jeb muttered, buttering his roll.

Avianna lowered her fork and peered out into the almost-darkness. Figures raced through the town garden, the mist swirling around them. The distant sound of a pistol crack made the window glass shiver.

"Jeb, something's happening."

Sniffing, Jeb turned his head slightly to glance out. He forked a chunk of beef into his mouth.

More people were in the square now, all hurrying about. It was the supper hour. They should be home with their families. What was going on?

The door slammed open and the inn's owner staggered in. "Pirates," he gasped. "The village is under attack."

Chapter 13

JEB'S CARRIAGE CAREENED OUT OF the village square and disappeared into the fog. The moment the innkeeper had said "pirates," Jeb had been up and out the door. He hadn't even offered to take Avianna.

Avianna stood in the doorway of the inn as the last of the twilight faded in the square. Villagers scurried past in the mist, some carrying bundles of belongings and others running empty-handed. Fear laced the air, but for some reason, Avianna felt only excited.

Pirates! Her childhood fantasy had been living on a pirate ship with a dashing captain who looted castles along the coastline to bring her jewels and made love to her all night. Of course, most pirates weren't actually like that. And there was no telling if this pirate captain was handsome, or searching for someone to share his adventures and his bed.

Well, handsome pirate captain or not, she needed to find her parents and make sure they'd secured themselves inside. Hopefully they were at Alistair's, but if not, she might find them at the boarding house. She'd have to head down toward the wharf, and if she happened to see the pirates rowing in from their ship in the bay, so much the better. Besides, so many villagers were running about, no pirate would pick her as a target. She didn't have a coin for them to steal.

Avianna set off toward the wharf in the coming darkness, breathing in the cool, damp air. As she left the square behind, clusters of villagers streamed past in the opposite direction. One even called out to her, something about the castle. All the king's treasure was still locked in the castle, waiting for the Council of Villages to decide what to do with it. That must be what the villager had been shouting about. The villagers would want to protect the treasure.

As Avianna started down the hill, the swirling mist condensed into the thick fog that had rolled in earlier. By the time she reached the turn for the boarding house, she could barely see twenty paces. Ahead, the near edge of the wharf disappeared into dim grayness. She couldn't even see the lights that lined the docks. How did anyone even know there were pirates? Had they come ashore already? She'd hoped she'd get to inspect them as they rowed in from their ship, but what if she ran right into them?

She stopped. Around her, the village had quieted. The lanes had certainly emptied fast. She could hear only an occasional shout from up the hill. A chill went up Avianna's spine.

She peeked around the corner toward the boarding house. The lane was deserted, at least as far as she could see in the dark haze that hung over the street, pierced at long intervals by the street lamps' light. Suddenly she wished to be in the boarding house, locked in with the others. But were they even there? It was completely quiet. What if she braved the fog to go down the road to the boarding house, and no one was inside? What if they'd taken shelter elsewhere, and Flo had locked the door to stop the pirates from pilfering?

Something flashed overhead, and Avianna leapt back, but it was only the tail of a cat disappearing over a rooftop.

Avianna contemplated the street leading to the wharf. Alistair's was another block down the hill, out of sight around a corner. Were her parents even there? Was anyone? She quivered with nerves when she peered into the darkness.

She couldn't do it. She couldn't walk into that deserted fog to go to Alistair's to search for her parents. Her parents were resourceful. They would have to secure themselves.

She stepped into the nearest doorway, glad to have the walls hiding her from the street. Stay calm, she told herself. It wouldn't do to panic. She had to brave the fog and walk the one short block to the boarding house. And if Flo and the others had left, she'd make a new plan.

But instead of moving, Avianna flattened herself into the doorway. She was frozen, scared to leave her shelter. The only sound was a drip on the cobblestones and the distant washing of the ocean waves against the docks. The abandoned lanes made prickles creep up her skin, and her heart thumped extra hard in her skull. Where had everyone gone?

The castle, that man had said. Everyone had been heading up the hill, and crossing the square . . . . The villagers had all gone to the castle.

Avianna groaned. Of course. No one could breach the castle walls. The villagers had headed to the castle because they'd be sure to be safe there. No doubt Flo and the others were already there—meaning she was all alone in the village. All alone with the—

Voices sounded from the bottom of the hill.

They were men's voices, coming from the wharf. They sounded odd. The men spoke with an unfamiliar accent. It had to be the pirates. Now that she could hear them, she no longer wanted to see them at all. But the voices were growing louder, ringing out through the fog. She had to get to the castle before the villagers locked up the gates.

If she ran up the lane, the pirates might round the corner and see her, unless she got far enough to disappear in the mist. But if she stayed huddled in the doorway, they might pass right by. If that happened, they would see her for sure.

The thought of being out in the lane was terrifying, but the thought of being found huddling in fear in a doorway was worse.

Avianna stopped thinking. She darted out from the doorway and ran up the hill. This time there was no Alfie to save her—she had to keep running. The windows and doorways flew by, her feet pounding on the cobblestones. She pushed herself up the incline, even as her calves burned and her lungs gasped. She didn't dare check back to see if the fog hid the end of the lane. The voices grew clear all at once as the pirates rounded the corner down below. And someone grabbed her.

She squirmed and kicked but an arm held her fast and a hand clamped over her mouth. A voice whispered insistently in her ear. "Avi, shh, it's me." Avianna went limp with relief. Thorn dragged her into a doorway.

She'd never been so glad to see anyone in her life. His hands loosened their grip, and she turned and threw her arms around him.

"Shh, come on now," he said in a low voice, rubbing her back. The voices were coming up the lane. "Avi, take my hand and stay quiet."

She froze, hanging on to Thorn's hand and struggling not to pant or hiccup as the voices came closer and closer. Then the pirates passed by. They wore fur-trimmed coats and odd metal helmets, and pistols hung from their belts. The closest of them glared right at the spot where she and Thorn stood, but she couldn't make out his face in the darkness, just his bright white hair. The pirates must be Sarlian. He stared right through her, thanks to Thorn's invisibility.

The captain might be the tall one, walking in the middle and talking—saying something about how they'd have to start rooting out the peasants if they didn't find someone soon. She didn't get a clear view of him. The pirates moved away up the hill.

"We have to get to the castle," Thorn said quietly, and he peeked out from the doorway. The voices were fading. "Come on." He kept ahold of her hand as he stepped into the dark lane. Avianna knew it was for safety, in case they needed to disappear, but she couldn't stop thinking that they were holding hands like lovers.

As they headed up the hill, Finnegan dropped out of the mist from a rooftop to join them. Avianna let Thorn lead her up the street, with Finnegan trotting before them.

"Is everyone in the castle? My parents—"

"Alistair has them."

"But how did everyone think to go there?" she asked.

Thorn's brow scrunched as he squinted at her. "It's the plan. For situations just like this."

"The plan?"

"The local Council members came up with it. The emergency plan."

How had she not known? People must have talked about it after the revolution, but she'd been focused on Beck and on how much she hated her life, and she'd never learned about this plan. What else had she missed?

"Why are you still in the village?" Avianna asked.

"I was searching for you. I helped the grange ladies to safety, and Flo arrived with the girls but hadn't seen you, and there was no sign of Jeb Doolihan."

"You came back for me?"

"Of course I did. I'm not going to leave you to a bunch of pirates. Much as you'd probably like it."

Avianna's face heated. Thorn could read her thoughts. And he'd come back for her. She wasn't sure which was making her blush.

"You really think they're that bad?" she asked, hoping he wouldn't notice her embarrassment.

"Who?"

"The pirates."

"They're *pirates*, Avi. They're not like in the stories. They don't sing and dance jigs while hoisting the sails and take captives they fall in love with. They kill people. And worse."

"How do you know?"

"I don't. But do you want to risk it?"

She didn't have an answer.

They came out from the cover of the buildings into the square and paused. When she'd left it, the square had had people rushing through, but now it was silent. The lamp light diffused in the damp air. Thorn started toward the park in the center. His face was drawn.

"Is it safe?" Avianna asked, glancing about as they left the shelter of the buildings.

"Finnegan's team hasn't spotted anyone in this part of the village."

"Finnegan has a team?"

"You didn't hear that from me."

"That's how you found me, then."

"Yes."

Finnegan sat when he reached the grass in the park. He began cleaning his paw as they walked past him. Thorn headed down the road to the castle—the same road Jeb's carriage had raced away on only an hour earlier. Jeb had fled without her. But Thorn had come back for her.

Where the row of shops ended, the cottages began. Soon they reached the end of the dark and empty homes and came to the last stretch of the road. Ahead, far down at the end of the road, the forest was on the right. To the left, the darkness and fog hid the castle towers.

Thorn hesitated. "Finnegan won't leave the village," he said. "I don't know what's ahead. And this area is exposed. But I want to get us into the castle where it's safe."

"They'll have closed the gates by now anyway," Avianna said. "How about the beach gate? We could shout through that."

"That's what I was thinking."

They turned away from the road and crept along the back sides of the cottages, staying in the shadows until they came to the trail that led out along the oceanside cliff. At the far end, the trail reached the castle gardens. When Avianna had lived in the castle, a massive stone wall had barred any of the villagers from entering the gardens, and on the inside, thick hedges had ringed the perimeter. But once the villagers had taken over the castle, they'd broken down a section of the wall and cut a path through the hedges so that anyone could visit the gardens easily from the village.

They'd also installed a tall iron gate that usually stood open. Avianna hoped they hadn't remembered to close it yet, although truthfully, that seemed unlikely. But the other gates were solid and thick and sure to be shut tight. At least at the garden entrance, anyone inside would be able to see that they were friends and let them in.

"I'm glad it's dark," Thorn said. "This next stretch is open."

"Could you hide us with your magic again?"

"I could, but if we met someone on the path, we'd have to scramble up the hillside to get out of the way. They'd hear us. I think it's better if we just go quickly."

"I thought fairy illusions felt real—that the person seeing them felt whatever he believed to be true. Wouldn't they pass through us, if they didn't think we were there?"

"Illusions work different from invisibility."

"At least we can see that no one is waiting to ambush us."

"True. Come on." He darted out and jogged along the path. Avianna kept up behind him. For once she was glad of the sensible shoes the villagers wore. She never could have moved this fast in palace slippers.

For the first minute, the land rose up around them, hiding them but also trapping them on the narrow trail. Then the bushes shrank back and the trail headed out onto the open cliff, and the wind howled off the ocean. Avianna was too nervous to be cold. Another minute and the massive wall came into view, along with the gate. It was closed.

They ran up to the gate. Thorn rattled it and tried the latch, but the bolt was tight in the lock. Avianna peered through, but nothing moved in the gardens. Thorn dug around in his pocket. He came out with a metal tool.

"That's not a key," Avianna said.

"No, it's a printer's stick. But I might be able to force the lock."

He knelt down and peered closely at the lock.

A shout sounded behind them, causing Avianna to turn. A torch blazed in the darkness, rounding the bend on the village path and moving their way.

Thorn cursed. "Quick," he said. "Let's hide and see if they go away."

Thorn and Avianna scrambled over the rocks beside the gate. Now she was even more grateful for her shoes. Palace slippers would have slipped off and fallen into the crevices. Thorn gave her a hand down to a ledge. Below, the jagged rocks turned into a smooth cliff face, dropping away to the ocean.

The torch was almost upon then. She and Thorn crouched down on the ledge, pressing themselves close to the rock. The darkness at least would help them. And then Thorn took her hand, and Avianna remembered that he could make them disappear, although she wasn't sure how long he could keep it up.

"I told you I saw a gate, Captain," came a rough voice.

"Unfortunately it appears locked." The captain's voice was smoother and menacing.

"Nothing we can't file through." The familiar rattle of the gate sounded.

"And did you bring a file?"

"Uh, no Captain."

An exaggerated sigh sounded. "Let's get on with it." Footsteps moved away down the path. Avianna lifted her head. The torch bobbed away with the men.

"How long do you think we have?" Avianna stood and straightened her skirt.

"I've no idea. But . . ."

"What?"

Thorn sighed, leaning his head back on the rocks. "I dropped the printer's stick."

"You what?"

"I dropped it when we were hurrying to hide. It's fallen in the cracks somewhere."

"So use a finding spell," Avianna said.

He cocked his head at her. "A what?"

"A fairy finding spell. Like you used to find my beads."

Now that her eyes had adjusted to the darkness, she could make out the bewilderment on Thorn's face.

"Avi, there's no such thing. Where did you hear that?"

"I figured you must have used one to find my crystal beads. They were all over the street. How did you get them then?"

Thorn shook his head as he stood. "I crawled around on the cobblestones and picked them up with my fingers, while Prince Murkel threw fish bones at me."

"You did that for me?"

He shifted and faced away. "Of course. We'd better get out of here before the pirates return."

Avianna climbed back up the rocks with Thorn beside her. She pictured the street where he'd gotten a black eye defending her and how her beads had been lying in all the cracks. Thorn had gone back, after Rye left, and crawled around on his hands and knees picking up the beads from her necklace so he could fix it for her. No one had ever done anything that nice for her.

Thorn gave her a hand off the rocks. "We'd better not take the cliff path. They'll be returning that way with their file."

Avianna and Thorn headed onto the grass and walked along the castle wall. The next gate was all the way at the main part of the castle, where the road came in from the village. The stone wall—three times Thorn's height—continued on, unbroken. It had been polished smooth so there was no chance of scaling it.

Thorn let out a deep breath. His head bent forward. His pace had slackened as if he'd been walking for miles. Avianna wished he would smile at her.

"It's so dark in the fog," she said to break the silence.

"I'm glad the moon is hidden. Otherwise it would be shining down on us right now."

"How do you know?"

"It's waxing. It's always up after sunset when it's approaching the full moon."

"But how do you *know* it's approaching full?"

"Don't you ever notice the moon?" Thorn finally regarded her.

"I notice the new moon. Flo always points it out because the rent is due."

He pushed his spectacles up his nose and studied her. "Maybe it's a fairy thing. There's a dance in the forest on the night the full moon rises. I usually go home for them."

"Home?"

"Well, home is in the village now. But where I grew up, that's still home in a way, even if it was crummy sometimes. Don't you feel anything for South End?"

A sound behind them caught their attention. The torch light bobbed along the cliff path again. They hastened their steps, but they were far enough away not to be seen in the darkness.

Avianna tried to remember anything nice about South End and the seasons she'd spent there. All that came to her was feeling hungry. And feeling ashamed when her parents stole or cheated someone in the market and she stood by, knowing it was wrong but wanting to eat.

"I wish I had a nice memory of it, but I don't."

"I'm sorry."

After another minute, they reached the castle—Avianna sensed the towers rising overhead, even if she couldn't see them. They ducked into a copse of trees. It was even darker inside the branches.

"This is the base of Princess Rose's tower," Avianna said.

Thorn turned to her. "Really?"

"Too bad Prince Dustan's ladder is gone or we could climb in." Avianna fingered the beads at her neck, now held together with fairy thread since Thorn had restrung them for her. It was the same material the prince's ladder had been made of. Prince Dustan had hung it in the tower so he could sneak in to seduce the princess. But later, it had enabled Rose and the villagers to breach the castle and capture the king. She could blame the ladder for her current poverty, but her bitterness about the revolution seemed to have faded.

More shouting sounded nearby. Avianna and Thorn peered out from the trees. The torchlight at the cliff's edge had moved out of sight. But now, more torches headed their way along the road from the village—a lot of torches.

Thorn ran both hands through his hair, pulling it off his face into his fists. "We need to get out of here."

Chapter 14

THORN PACED UNDER THE TREES, his head down and his fingers massaging his forehead. "I don't think there's any way we can get into the castle, not with the pirates swarming all over."

"Where can we go?"

"I have an idea. We just have to get past them without being seen."

"Can you keep me invisible long enough?"

"I think so, if I focus."

"And if nothing trips me and breaks the spell."

"I know," Thorn said. "We'll be more careful."

"I don't suppose there's a cat nearby who'd come attack them for you, just in case?"

Thorn bit his lower lip and closed his eyes. "Actually . . ."

"Are you serious?"

"Wait." He held up his hand, and she realized he was listening. Then he began to smile. "There's a horse nearby."

"A horse? Honestly?"

"The pirates took her from the village and are using her to carry wood to light a bonfire out in the fields beside the castle. She doesn't much care for them. They keep smacking her."

"Can she get to us?"

"They have her tethered. No wait. Someone's only holding her reins. She's—um, get ready."

"Ready for what?"

Thorn took Avianna's hand and pulled her out of the trees as shouts and curses rose up. A short way off, the faint flicker of a small fire shone through the fog. Hoofbeats thundered toward them and the horse appeared from the darkness, reins flying. The horse nearly bowled them over but pulled up short. Thorn dropped Avianna's hand and vaulted himself onto the horse's bare back in one strong motion. He bent down for Avianna and lifted her clear off the ground, drawing her on behind him. She got her leg over the horse's back just as Thorn turned away.

"Hang on," he said, gathering the reins. Avianna slipped her arms around him. The horse shot away from the castle.

They galloped out across the field, giving a wide berth to the growing bonfire. Avianna clung to Thorn. She'd been on horseback plenty of times but never like this. A village work horse probably wasn't used to carrying people, and the mare's stride was jarring. The shouts of the pirates running after them grew quieter as the mare left them behind, carrying Thorn and Avianna away with her.

The faint shouts were eventually drowned out under the hoofbeats of the horse. They galloped past the turn to the village and for another half-league down the road before Thorn leaned forward and patted the horse, and she slowed. She cantered a ways and dropped into a walk.

"You okay back there?" Thorn asked over his shoulder.

Avianna was wrapped around Thorn. She let go of him and sat upright.

"I think so."

The horse walked along the forest road, snorting in the cool night air. This far from the village, the road narrowed and the trees encroached closer on the left, with faint tendrils of mist curling at the branches. To their right, the fields disappeared in utter darkness. Now that they weren't escaping the pirates, the night chill seeped through Avianna's dress. The motion of the horse nudged her body up against Thorn's back. He was warm, and she wanted to wrap her arms around him again. She edged herself away from his body.

"Where are we going?"

"Into the forest."

Fear swirled within Avianna's breast and she started to protest, but then she remembered who she was with. The fairies lived in the forest all the time. They knew how to be safe there. Surely Thorn wouldn't let anything happen to her. If there even was any danger. She'd been told that the forest was filled with wild creatures, but since the revolution, many people had said that the dangers had all been invented to keep the people under the king's control—to stop them from abandoning the village or hunting game for food.

A few minutes later, the horse stopped.

"Are you controlling her with your mind?" Avianna asked.

Thorn laughed. "You're so ridiculous. I don't control anyone with my mind. I asked her for help. She was glad to have a run."

So he didn't control anyone with his mind, eh? Avianna considered having it out with him about his spell. After all, he was basically controlling her mind with it.

He wouldn't hurt her, she didn't think, if she confronted him about the spell. He'd probably be embarrassed. But a tiny bit of her wondered if there was more to Thorn than she knew—such as, if his alter ego, Hawthorn, would be unhappy that she'd discovered his plan to seduce her. What if he tried something else, like tampering with her memory or strengthening the love spell? A thrill went through her, and she couldn't tell if she was scared or excited by the prospect of meeting Hawthorn.

"And just now I told her we've arrived," Thorn continued.

"Arrived where?" As far as Avianna could tell, they were on the road alongside the forest at a spot no different from any other. On their left, the trees extended endlessly. If they kept going, the road would eventually be surrounded on both sides by trees and lead them through the forest to Woods Rest. And on their right, the cultivated fields spread all the way from the forest to the cliff over the ocean.

Thorn didn't reply. Instead he twisted around and placed his hands on her sides to lift her and lower her down off the horse. He slipped off beside her and looped the horse's reins together and tied them so they didn't drag on the ground. Then he patted the horse and she trotted away.

"Where's she headed?" Avianna asked.

Thorn inhaled deeply and let it out slowly. "Back to her barn. I don't think the pirates would check there twice." He turned to Avianna beside the dark forest. "Are you up for a little walk?"

"I guess. Where are we going?"

"It's a surprise," he said and let out another deep breath, stretching his neck one way and the other, his hand rubbing the back of it. He wasn't smiling. He rubbed his eyes beneath his spectacles.

"Okay, let's see here," he said. He walked to the trees and stopped, peering up and placing his hand on one thick trunk. A moment later, a light began to glow up in the branches. It grew brighter, until it resolved into a lamp shining among the leaves. Another glow started farther in among the trees, and another. As the lamps lit, one after another, they formed a path into the forest. The lamps brightened until they shone softly on the forest floor.

Avianna stared in wonder. "How did you do that?"

"The fairies hung these lamps to show the way from the village. In case anyone needs to travel the path by night."

"Wait—are we going to the fairies?"

Thorn nodded.

Anticipation washed over Avianna. Since the revolution, a few people had visited the fairies' village in the forest. Stories circulated about the system of caves the fairies had built as a home and the vast gardens they tended and how they climbed the trees so easily—but no one who went to the fairy village ever seemed to tell about their visit in detail. And Avianna had never had someone offer to take her.

Thorn headed into the trees and she hurried after him. He checked back once as if to make sure Avianna was following. As they walked, more lights came on ahead, so that they could always see the next steps to take. The fog didn't creep past the first few rows of trees. But when Avianna turned back, the lamps they'd passed had gone out, leaving the path in darkness, as if the lamps knew they'd gone by.

"They're not flame, the lamps. How do they work?"

"They trap sunlight and store it. And the trees are the switch to turn them on. You just have to send thoughts to the trees, asking them to light the lamps. Once the first one goes, the others follow. They send the message on themselves."

"The trees are a team."

"Something like that."

Bushes hung over the trail with brambles that caught at Avianna's dress and hair. Only hours ago had she left the boarding house on her date with Jeb. By the time she eventually made it home from the date, if she ever did, her nice dress would be ruined. From hiding to the horse ride and brambles, her hair had been pulled out in wisps around her head.

As they went deeper into the forest, they had to climb over downed tree limbs and push branches to the side. It wasn't much of a path, but Avianna supposed it would stop tourists from getting in. You had to want to go all the way.

"How was your date?" Thorn asked.

Avianna rolled her eyes. "Terrible. We have nothing in common. I probably should have just tumbled him."

Thorn kept walking ahead of her. Avianna continued, "Anyway, the chef sent out my meal and it looked divine, almost like the food at the castle. So I was able to inhale the aroma of probably the best meal I'll never have again before the pirates ruined it." Her stomach rumbled as she remembered the dinner placed before her on the table right before the alarm had sounded. "I should have taken the plate when I left."

"What did Jeb think of the pirates?"

Avianna huffed. "His carriage was flying away from the inn before I even got to the door."

"He left you there?"

"Yes."

"I'm sorry, Avi."

"That's okay. I'm over it."

They walked a little way in silence, and the night sounds of the forest became clear—an owl hooting and rustlings in the dry autumn leaves. She'd forgotten to be scared, with Thorn leading her, but now the stories she'd heard in the castle came back to her. Corella assured her they weren't true. Corella said that Tanner went in the forest all the time and had never encountered anything more menacing than a spooked deer that ran into him as it tried to escape.

Still, away from the fairy lamps, it was pitch dark. Avianna could easily imagine the eyes of wild animals on her and evil spirits lurking behind the tree trunks, waiting to pounce . . . . She hurried to stay close behind Thorn.

She watched him as he picked out the trail and his arm lifted a blackberry bush clear of her head. Shouldn't she be feeling attracted to him? She searched her heart, looking for the feelings, but couldn't detect any. She kept waiting for his spell to kick in, but nothing happened. Where had it gone? Why wasn't she thinking of kissing him or of how she'd have her way with him once they got to the fairies' village?

"So," she said to avoid the silence, "what was crummy about growing up with the fairies?"

Even from behind she could tell he pushed the spectacles up his nose before replying.

"Fairy children play all the time. I guess it's the same with human children, unless they're made to work. Mother'd never worried about her men not sticking around because she figured if she had a kid, it would take care of itself, like most kids.

"But I couldn't see well enough to play with the others, so I had to stay home with my mother. The fairies are communal and all, but they also have tasks to do. Sometimes the elders would watch me, but other times she was stuck with me. She wanted to drink and dance but she always had to drag me around. It wasn't a lot of fun is all."

"But then you learned to read."

"I was still lonely, but it made it better."

"And your friend who taught you, she had books even though they were forbidden?"

"Not all of them were forbidden. The first book I read on my own was a fairy soup cookbook."

Avianna almost burst out laughing. "Fairies eat soup?"

"Of course. Who doesn't eat soup?"

"And they have cookbooks?"

"We don't make books the way humans do. They're scrolls of parchment that you unroll to read."

"Who was the fairy who taught you?"

"Her name's Larkspur."

"She's still alive?"

"Yes. I don't think she'll ever die. She had old histories of the fairies and books about living above ground—on subjects like building design and gardening. And she had a human book about art and it talked about printmaking, the process used to make human books. And it caught my attention because hawthorn bark was used in one of the recipes to make ink. As my name plant, it might help me as a printmaker. Sometimes we can do special things with the plant we're named for."

"Can you?"

Thorn glanced back at her, finally breaking into a slow, mischievous smile. Avianna tripped and caught herself.

He kept walking.

"So how did you get the shop?" Avianna said to his back.

"When we finally escaped Oleander—the queen—I knew I wanted to print things. Larkspur helped me. She had human coins from before Oleander's time. They had no value in the caverns, but she let people pay her with them for all those winters and she'd saved a bundle. She gave them to me and I rented the building the shop is in. Things were run down in the village last spring, with everyone just starting to think about life without the monarch. It was dirt cheap. And I bought what I needed to build my press."

"No one printed pamphlets when the king was in power?"

"Not if they wanted to live."

"But they did after?"

"Not at first. It was such a novel idea." Thorn looked down, and Avianna glimpsed that smile again. "I had to get it started."

"How'd you manage that?"

"I printed flyers to stir things up. Like I did one about how a king should be put back into power because of all the benefits the previous king had offered the people."

"You didn't Thorn! That's utter rubbish."

"I know. But it was so obviously rubbish, I didn't think it could hurt. And I used hawthorn ink." He chewed his lip. "Somehow, it makes the words I print 'pop,' like they leap off the page and get into people's minds."

"You do control their minds!"

He laughed. "No, Avi. It's not like that. I can't change anyone's mind. But I can get them to notice, and then it's up to them."

Avianna shook her head. "I don't know."

"Anyway, it worked. The dock master showed up wanting to know who had printed it. I told him I had to protect the privacy of my clients but that I'd be happy to print an opposing viewpoint for him. He got uncomfortable and I thought I'd failed. That was when I realized half the village couldn't write or even read. I quickly offered to write it down if he would dictate. And he was so proud of it, he went around the village passing them out and telling everyone about my shop. I never lacked work again."

"I'm glad."

"Me too."

They walked on for a moment. "I went to the grange," Avianna said at last.

"I heard. They wouldn't stop going on about you, all the time I was trying to get them to safety. What did you think?"

"They were lovely. That Margery—she's crazy about you."

Avianna could hear the smile in Thorn's voice. "She's a doll. I told one of the grange elders that you'd likely be taking the post if you liked it okay."

"Thank you, Thorn. It means a lot that you're watching out for me."

He only nodded.

After that, they walked in silence for a long way. She would never be able to find her way back on her own, even in the daylight, not without the lamps as a guide. The trees enclosed them, and all was darkness and quiet rustling, until she thought she heard voices. Then she was certain that voices were speaking, but she didn't see anyone around them.

"Do you want to see the village?" Thorn asked, his voice dull.

"Of course. Don't you want to go?"

"It's been a long day."

"I'll say. Are you tired?"

"A bit."

"We could save it for another time," Avianna said.

Thorn looked back and smiled. "I can show you quickly. It's not much of a village by human standards. Besides, there might be some food left."

"Are we near?"

"Yes."

More lamps appeared and spread over a wider area overhead, and now as they walked, the lamps didn't go dark after they had passed by. The way had become an actual path with the grass and leaves beaten down into hard-packed dirt, and it widened enough that she could walk by Thorn's side.

"Why do I keep hearing voices?" Avianna asked finally.

Thorn laughed. He surveyed the forest, and then he stopped walking and stepped close to Avianna. He pointed up.

At first all she saw were branches. But then she made out a platform of some sort, with a roof on top.

"The village is in the trees?" Avianna had known fairies could climb trees, but she hadn't realized they built in them. Why had no one ever mentioned this?

"Not all of it. Just the new homes—well, the summer homes. Once the cold comes, only a few fairies will stick it out. Most everyone will go back underground. This up here is all new, since we've been allowed to come above ground again."

"What will you do this winter?" The thought of Thorn returning to the fairy caverns for the entire season distressed her.

Thorn continued walking. "I think I'll stay in Woodglen. If I have to return here this winter, I'd bring a lot of blankets and sleep outside. I don't like it underground. I spent the first twenty winters of my life trapped down there."

"Would I be able to go there? I thought humans couldn't see the way in."

"That's how it used to be when it was guarded. But the illusions are gone now. You just have to know where the entrance is."

More voices echoed through the trees now, and ahead, a light shone. Two figures appeared on the path, talking close in a way that suggested gossip. Avianna had assumed the fairies were above all that, but these two made her think of Mattie and Samantha, or of herself and Elspeth, if she were honest. They were slim and feminine with long dark hair, and as they passed beneath a lamp, the same luster shone on their skin that she sometimes noticed on Thorn. Their clothes were loose and shapeless on their willowy forms. Thorn greeted them and moved to one side. They passed without a second glance, only hushing until they had gone by.

Thorn and Avianna came into a clearing surrounded by lamps—enough lamps that the space was as bright as Alistair's Pub in the evening. It was deserted but clearly had been occupied recently. Sections of a tree trunk stood as seats around a smoldering fire pit, and a long board set up on supports served as a table along one side. The remains of a large meal were scattered across the top. A knitted scarf lay draped across a tree branch, just as a lost scarf would be in the village.

Thorn made a beeline for the food table and began poking around. "The nice thing about being last is you can take as much as you want," he said, reaching for a loaf of bread half-wrapped in a linen towel. "It would be easier to eat here, but I'm getting a bit cold since I ran out of the shop without a coat. Are you warm enough?"

No wind blew in the clearing, but the chill autumn air sank down from the trees and rose up from the forest floor, penetrating her shoes. "Now that you mention it, no."

"I can build a fire once we get home. Here."

He handed Avianna a covered pottery bowl.

"It's nice and warm."

"It'll warm your fingers until we get home. Keep it upright. It's our supper."

Thorn continued hunting until he had two apples and a wedge of cheese in his hands, along with the bread.

"Where is everyone?" Avianna said, scanning the edges of the clearing.

"It's late. We were walking for some time."

"It didn't seem long."

"No, it didn't."

She turned to him. Thorn was watching her. Something shivered inside her.

The spell. Maybe it had waited until he had her in the fairy village—alone with him, in the middle of the forest, and heading for some kind of treehouse where she was apparently going to spend the night with him.

What was she doing here?

When she met his gaze, the shivers moved through her. Avianna's lips parted, but she couldn't think what to say. She stared

helplessly at Thorn. In the forest, his moss-green eyes were no longer strange but bewitching.

He broke his gaze and set off across the clearing. Avianna
gulped and followed.

Chapter 15

THORN WON'T HURT ME, AVIANNA told herself as she followed him across the clearing. She was sure of that.

But what was going to happen between them? If she stayed here in the forest with him, she was sure they would end up doing something more than talking. But would spending the night with Thorn because of a fairy love spell be any worse than what she'd been doing with Rye or the others at Alistair's Pub? It's not like she'd loved them. Beck maybe, but he hadn't loved her back—he'd put a spell on her as much as Thorn ever had, treating her like his one and only when he had no intention of making a life bond.

At least Thorn was kind to her, and if his spell made her attracted to him, why fight it? She could have fun with him while it lasted. She hated the idea of ruining their easy friendship, which often happened once you tumbled someone. But Thorn had started this, and she didn't see a way to go back. She could play his game, and if things got complicated, she'd extract herself and move on. It was possible to escape a fairy love spell—it must be, because the princess had done it. Of course, she'd ended up bonded with the fairy prince in the end, even without his spell on her.

Thorn reached the far side of the clearing and pointed into the dark trees.

"The orchard's through there," he said. He began explaining the fairies' system of gardening. As he talked, the feeling that had overcome Avianna moments earlier when he'd looked at her faded.

He certainly wasn't rushing to take advantage of her. Could his spell be wearing off?

Still, she couldn't relax, not like she usually could around Thorn. No matter how nonchalant he seemed now, it was different knowing he wanted her. Although, he still hadn't made any moves. What was he waiting for?

Thorn explained that down in the caverns, the fairies had something like a village center, although smaller than the human village. But now that so many were living in the forest, they'd built some huts near the clearing to store things they might need. He led her past the structures. She peeked through one doorway. All sorts of strange things were neatly arranged on shelves—a roll of shimmering twine that she guessed to be a long, long length of fairy thread, bottles of liquid that sparkled even in the subdued lighting, and folded lengths of fabric.

"This one is all the human-made things," Thorn said, moving to the next hut. He walked in and Avianna followed him, gazing around at the shelves holding tools and supplies. Thorn gathered his food in one arm and reached for a piece of flint and a steel band from small piles of each. "I haven't been home in a while," he said, "and I don't remember the state of my woodstove."

"Is there only one of most things?" Avianna asked, trying to ignore her nerves. A single lantern sat on a shelf by a wood saw and a hammer.

"Mostly. Humans like to have their own of everything, from what I've seen. Here you borrow what you need and put it back when you're done."

"It makes sense."

"So that's the village."

"That's it?" she asked.

"Pretty much. Fairies don't have all the cluttery things humans have. They mostly just . . . gather. Hang out. Eat."

"Dance."

"Dance."

Avianna almost blurted out "Tumble" but stopped herself. That was the last thing she needed to put into Thorn's head. If it wasn't there already.

He reached out to the shelf again and picked up a tool, and a blade flashed.

As the blade glinted in the lamplight, Avianna's heart thumped and she almost dropped the warm bowl she carried.

Thorn was holding scissors.

"I thought maybe we could have that haircut," he said. He slipped the scissors, blades down, into a loop on the side of his trousers as he exited the hut.

"So," he said, leading her off along another path, "my place is a short way past this." A few moments later, he stopped at the base of a tree. Overhead, all was dark. He deposited the apples on a wide rock at the base.

"Give me a moment," he said. "I'll get the ladder." And with that, he reached his free arm up into the branches and pulled himself up. Avianna's lips parted in awe as he scaled the tree one-handed, still holding the bread and cheese, moving higher and higher until the branches and darkness obscured her view.

A soft noise thumped overhead, and a rope ladder came tumbling down the trunk toward her. Thorn's shoes appeared, climbing down, as a few lamps began to glow among the leaves. He stepped off by her side.

"Have you ever climbed a ladder?"

"No."

"It's got fairy thread woven into the rope, the same thread I strung your beads on."

"That's not altogether reassuring," Avianna said, "but if the princess could do it, so can I."

Thorn gave a tired smile. "I'll come right behind you, just in case. Here—" He took the covered bowl from her hands.

"One foot after another, right?" She gripped the sides of the ladder and started to climb.

In the low light, she could barely see the ground moving away from her feet. The feeling of hanging in space, the nothing of it, made her insides twist. She ascended into the branches. After about a hundred steps, she reached an opening in a platform and climbed through. The ladder was fastened high enough that she was able to climb all the way up. She stepped onto the platform.

In front of her was a small open doorway into what looked like a cottage in the village, but smaller and attached to the tree's trunk. She turned slowly in a circle as Thorn slipped through the opening, balancing the covered bowl and the apples. A railing lined the edge of the platform, and opposite the cottage sat chairs under an awning—not the usual straight-backed chairs that the village chair-maker made but odd, sloping chairs with miniature tables attached to their sides. More of the solar lamps hung all around the space, glowing softly. It was like nothing she'd ever seen—certainly not like the extravagance of the castle that she often daydreamed about. But it felt like a home, like a place she could be happy. Which was unnerving.

"Come on inside," Thorn said, and he entered the cottage.

Avianna stepped gingerly over the threshold. The lights inside were cozy in spite of the chill air. Thorn placed the food down on the table in the center and moved to a small woodstove, holding the flint and steel. He picked up a small box and pried up the lid.

"Perfect," Thorn said, looking into the box. He hooked the steel back onto the loop on his trousers and placed the flint on the table. "Guess I didn't need these. Normally I wouldn't waste fairy dust, but it makes a different fire. It'll warm up the place quicker."

He knelt down at the stove and opened the door to peer in, then took a single piece of split wood from a bin next to the stove and placed it inside. From the box, he took a pinch of something. He dropped it on the wood and pulled his hand back as a fire sprang into being. He closed the stove door partway and regarded Avianna where she hovered inside the doorway.

The chill from outside seeped in around her, but Avianna didn't step farther inside. She couldn't move. Thorn was still Thorn, but she couldn't stop seeing him in a new way. He seemed bigger somehow, broader. Had he always appeared this way, or was it another illusion?

Behind him, a doorway led into a dark back room. That would be his bedroom. She swallowed.

Thorn stood and smiled at Avianna. "What did you think of your first glimpse of the fairy forest?" he said. He moved toward her, and her heart jolted, but he only reached for the door. She stepped out of the way, linking her hands together. He pulled the door shut.

Avianna stared at Thorn and her lips parted but she couldn't speak.

He tilted his head. "Are you nervous?" he asked, his voice concerned.

She wrung her fingers together and at last words came. "I don't know. I'm just disoriented. So much keeps happening. How are you so unconcerned?"

He leaned back against the door, hooking his thumbs in his vest pockets. "I'm concerned. But the villagers made it into the castle so they're safe enough. They have all the king's firepower in there, and a lot of them were soldiers or are peacekeepers. And it's only one ship of pirates—once the people organize, they'll take care of it. And I don't think the printing press is going to be a target." He smiled. "That's the bright side of being poor. You don't have much pirates would want."

Avianna's hand went to her beads.

"Here," Thorn said, pushing himself up and moving to pull a chair—a normal chair—out from the table. "Have some supper. You'll feel better." He moved to a side cupboard and took out some plates and bowls and a small knife. He sat in the other chair.

Avianna slid into the seat, watching as Thorn lifted the lid off the bowl. Steam wafted out. Inside was soup—the fairies really did make soup.

"It won't enchant me, will it?" Avianna asked, only halfway kidding.

Thorn leaned forward and sniffed the soup. "No, not this one," he said. She couldn't tell if he was kidding at all.

He ladled some soup into a bowl, passed it to her, spread out the linen with the bread, and broke off a piece, before cutting a few slices off the wedge of cheese. Avianna took a spoonful of soup. It was savory, with a nutty, meaty flavor unfamiliar to her, but it probably didn't have any meat in it, given the fairies' connection with animals. Thorn got up to tend the fire, and then he sat on the woven rug on the floor, staring at the flames through the open stove door and picking pieces off his hunk of bread.

It was like she was on a second date that evening. A date that was the exact opposite of the first one, with Jeb. Her time with Jeb seemed like it had happened a week ago.

Now that she was sitting and eating, she calmed down. This was how she liked feeling around Thorn, like she could be herself and he liked her anyway. And Thorn stayed silent, so unlike Jeb Doolihan prattling away during her first date.

Avianna ate the soup. Spoonful after spoonful. It tasted so wonderful, and the room was so peaceful. And then she blinked as she scraped the bottom of her bowl. She'd been focused on eating, and she'd eaten the last spoonful without even realizing it. She looked up. Thorn lay stretched out on his stomach on the woven rug with his eyes closed.

Maybe he had lied to her about the soup being enchanted. She certainly felt odd, like she had floated off into a different world while she was eating. The fire crackled, the flames high even without additional fuel, and the faint creaking of branches came from outside. The cottage had become downright toasty. She slipped off her shawl and reached for the bread and cheese. Thorn didn't move. He might have been asleep.

Now Avianna took the time to scan the cottage interior. There wasn't much in it—no trinkets like at the boarding house and only the simply made table and chairs and cupboard for furniture. Wooden beams ran overhead, and the walls were some kind of cobb material. A few prints were tacked on the wall—Avianna recognized the reading chart with flowers from Cecily's reading lesson. There were some printed flyers—maybe the ones Thorn was proud of—and some sketches of landscapes and one of a woman's face—a woman with hair as curly as Avianna's, but smiling with light in her eyes. Who was she? Avianna tried to quell the jealous feeling that rose up inside.

Thorn's cheek rested on his arms, crossed in front of him. His vest lay crumpled beside him on the floor, and his suspenders were off his shoulders and hanging down the sides of his hips. His back rose and fell under his plain white shirt as he breathed. The shirt was halfway untucked from his trousers. Avianna wished he were snoring or drooling or anything to make him appear less perfect, lying asleep with the firelight flickering on his skin.

She watched him lying there as she reached to unpin her hair where Corella had fastened it to her head for her date. Two messy braids tumbled down. She pulled the ribbons off the ends and worked her fingers through the braids, unwinding the strands until her hair came free.

Chapter 16

AVIANNA STOOD CAREFULLY, NOT MAKING a sound in the quiet room. Out of curiosity, she crept to the dark doorway and peeked in. The back room was barely large enough for the mattress that filled it, held up from the floor on a wooden frame. Windows overlooked the lamplit forest, and as she stood in the doorway, tiny lights began to twinkle at the ceiling. She glanced back at Thorn but he still slept.

Did the lights know she was there? She wasn't sure if she should be captivated or alarmed. Avianna backed out of the room and they faded out.

She returned to the table and took the scissors and sat on the floor beside Thorn. The fire was delightful with the flames dancing about in the stove. Thorn stirred and opened an eye.

"Time for your haircut," Avianna said. She reached out to touch his shoulder. "Sit up."

His eye closed and he rolled onto his back. He reached his arms over his head, and the stretch lengthened through his whole body, pulling his shirt the rest of the way out of his trousers before he relaxed. He rocked forward and pulled himself up to sitting, and the thought that he must have strong stomach muscles to sit up that easily popped unbidden into Avianna's mind. He rubbed his sleepy eyes and turned to face her, crossing his legs so that his knees almost touched hers.

"I'm not being much of a host," he said.

"I can hardly complain, since you were up late last night saving me from a gang of thugs. Not to mention tonight's rescue."

"You would have kicked your way out of the pub."

"I'm glad I didn't have to."

Avianna reached forward with her left hand, sliding two fingers around the long hair that fell in front of Thorn's eyes, gently pulling it straight. It was satiny like the fancy yarn the courtiers had had at the castle, wool blended with soft fur. It stretched down to his nose.

"Do you have a particular style in mind?" she asked.

"Don't make me look ridiculous," he said. "And don't cut it short like Rye's."

"I would never do that." She ran her fingers through his hair again, pressing the back of her hand against his spectacles to protect his eyes. Her knees bumped into his, but she focused on the scissors. She moved them carefully into place and sheared away some hair.

She positioned the scissors at an angle to leave one side of the hair in front long. He'd be able to see better, but it would still be long enough to flip out of his face in that endearing way of his. She trimmed away the last bits. He watched her face, but his gaze wasn't demanding or off-putting or creepy. If he'd looked away, she'd have felt disappointed.

She placed a knuckle to his chin and turned his head to one side. Then she scooted closer, her knees shifting to fit with his so she could reach his hair. She started at the top of his head, finding where each lock fell before deciding where to trim, moving in rows down from the top. The cut hair sifted down to her lap.

"We forgot to use a shawl to catch the clippings," she said. "I'm making a mess."

"I'll sweep them later."

She kept cutting and shifting her seat until she made it to the back of his head. She cut the shaggy fringe that hung over the back of his neck, and brushed away the clippings. Then she pushed herself up onto her knees to reach the top of his head, and her body wobbled against his, and she put her free hand onto his shoulder to steady herself. His body was warm from the fire, and she noticed the bare skin at the back of his neck and wondered how warm his skin would be there. She stared at his neck, her heart pumping with sudden desire, her chest heaving in and out with breath.

The love spell was back in full force. She'd believed it was fading, but here it was and she was powerless. She wanted to kiss him, and if she did, she'd be a goner for sure.

But what was her alternative? Wouldn't she be a little bit disappointed if she walked out of the woods without having kissed him?

Avianna hung on to Thorn's shoulder as her knees slid back out, lowering herself down until she sat on her feet. She silently placed the scissors on the floor under the nearest chair. Then she leaned forward, steadying herself against him, and pressed her lips to Thorn's neck.

He sucked in a breath. After her kiss, she waited for him to turn, to take charge, but he was still as a stone. Was he really going to keep playing his game?

"Did you like that?" she whispered, and he nodded. Now he seemed to be holding his breath. Her lips curved in a smile.

She dropped another kiss on his neck, slightly on the side and a little higher up. And another with a little more force, sucking until she heard him gasp. She put her other hand on his other shoulder and pressed against his back.

She couldn't reach any farther to kiss him so she slowly pulled herself up, kissing his jawline as she went. Her loose tresses tumbled over his shoulder. She began to throb down between her legs and wanted to rub herself against him, her knees spread wide, but she could only get so close. Instead, she leaned forward and found his lips.

Her arms slid around his neck as she kissed him, and he returned her kiss, but carefully. His reticence pushed her to give him more, opening her lips to stroke his. She abandoned his lips to plant kisses across his face, on the bridge of his nose and his cheeks. He leaned back, giving her better access. His eyes were closed, his arms braced against the floor.

She paused to slide off his spectacles, placing them on a chair, and returned to his mouth, cradling his face in her hands.

When her knees began to give out, she pulled him down to the rug, away from the fire that had grown too hot. She twisted him around to face her, lying side by side.

As Avianna gazed into Thorn's eyes, something inside her wrung tight like the last piece of laundry. His eyes were wide, almost lost.

"Are you okay?" she whispered, reaching up to stroke his face.

He swallowed. "Yes."

"I don't know if I believe you." She leaned up to kiss his lips once, watching him with her hand on his chest.

His hand settled on her waist. He whispered into her lips, "Can I touch you?"

"You're already touching me."

"But here," he said, and he touched her bare leg where her dress had ridden up her thigh. A thrill shot up her, echoed in her center.

"You're already touching me there, too." She leaned in again to kiss him. "Don't stop."

She kept kissing him as his hand ran over her thigh, until the feel of his hand exploring her skin became too distracting. She nuzzled against his neck, breathing in that scent of wild forest and wind as his fingers traced slowly up her leg, pausing only to squeeze, and taking her skirt up with them.

When he reached her undergarments, he paused. She waited for his hand to lift off her. Now was when he would pull back and open the front of his trousers and—

His fingers caressed her hip once more. They didn't leave, but trailed along the line of her underpants to her front. They slid under the top hem, nudging her clothing down until his knuckles stroked her curls and brushed against her in the place between her legs where she'd been dying to be touched.

She forgot all about holding him as feelings shot through her. He brushed her again, then once again harder, until his fingers settled against her, rubbing in a slow rhythm.

What was he doing? Why hadn't he gotten his own clothing off? Did she care? His touch felt so wonderful, it overcame the thoughts scrambling about in her head. He knew exactly when to press harder, when to move faster. His free arm slipped under her head, cradling her as his fingers massaged her. Clinging to his shirt, her mind went blank as he brought her higher and higher.

"Thorn," she whimpered.

He turned his fingers, sliding them back to where she was wet for him, rubbing her in front with his thumb as his fingers delved inside her. Her body shuddered, spasms racking through her as she dug her nails into his shoulders and held on. He didn't stop. He kept swirling inside her, and the spasms kept coming, one after another as cries escaped her parted lips. She tried to twist away but he held her fast, working her body until finally the shaking slowed. He stayed inside her until every last spasm had been released.

Avianna wilted into the rug, avoiding looking at him. She reached down and pulled his hand from her, hanging on to it. Then she didn't move, except for her chest panting. Tears stung her eyes, and she felt embarrassed and strange and overcome by what had happened. She gave Thorn back his hand and pushed him away, and he rolled back on the rug beside her, moving his arm from under her head.

With all the men she'd tumbled, no one had ever touched her like that—like it was all about her. It had always been up to her to satisfy herself, while her partner thrust about inside her and finished when he was done. She bit back a sob, knowing Thorn would be distressed if he saw her crying. She took a deep, careful breath and wiped the corners of her eyes.

Beside her, Thorn stared at the ceiling. She reached for his hand across the floor.

"All right?" she whispered.

"Did that really just happen?" he whispered back.

"I think so."

"You're okay?" he said.

"Of course I'm okay," Avianna said. "I'm more worried about you."

"Me?" Thorn's head tilted slightly toward her.

"Being that you've never touched a woman before."

Thorn moaned as he found her gaze. "Was it that obvious?"

She rolled toward him and wrapped her arms around his head, pulling him sideways under her chin. "No, Thorn, you were wonderful. I only meant you never court anyone. And you don't seem like the type to fool around otherwise. In fact"—she paused to plant a kiss on the top of his head—"it strikes me as odd that you *were* that good. You knew exactly what to do."

He rolled to face her and his lips pressed against the base of her throat. "The fairies have a book."

"A book?"

"A scroll. *The Art of Love*. Written by Queen Delphinium over 700 winters ago. I read it."

Of course he had. A book on having sex, written by a woman. And he had read it. He was too much.

"What else was in it?" she asked.

"Lots of pictures." His smile curved against her neck. "I actually found it when I was a boy, hidden in the fairy caverns. It was a treasure."

"I can imagine. Tell me how you found it."

"I'd read everything the library had. Most of it was boring. Everything had been censored, so there were no books about history or life in the woods or anywhere else. But I liked it in there better than anywhere so I'd go every day. No one was ever there, except this mouse who lived there. I'd bring her bits of food. And one day,

I must've conveyed boredom, and she questioned it, and I sent her a picture of the books, that they were all old and I'd read them so many times."

"You sent her a picture?"

"We don't really talk with the animals. It's like we send them thoughts and emotions, and theirs come to us. And the mouse, she sent me this image of a space filled with books, ten times what the library had. I knew the books had to be in there somewhere because she must have seen them. It took me only a day to find them. There was a door hidden in the wall that led to another room, where the queen had piled them."

"The queen?"

"Queen Oleander. The one who kept us locked up underground until Princess Rose set us all free."

Avianna snorted.

Thorn tilted his chin up to her. "What?"

"It's just hard to imagine Rose saving anyone."

"I always forget that you knew her," he said.

"She was so docile, always doing what she was told. Now she's a hero."

"People change. Maybe she was different inside and she finally let it out."

"Or maybe the fairy love spell changed her and gave her courage," Avianna said lightly, hoping Thorn couldn't sense the way that speaking those words and hinting about his own spell made her pulse begin to race.

But Thorn only shook his head slightly, as if her words had no special meaning to him. "Fairy spells can't truly change you," he said, "not if you don't have it inside you to begin with. Princess Rose was trapped for a long time in the castle, but she still had the will to be free."

"But what about her love of the prince? She didn't even know him before he cast his love spell."

Thorn bit his lip and squinted, thinking. "I'm no expert, but

I think the spell would have only gotten her attention. He'd still have to win her heart."

So he was no expert? What an actor her Hawthorn was! Avianna let it go and relaxed with him in her arms, stroking the still-long side of his hair as he rested against her.

What did Avianna have inside her? She recalled her life in the castle. She'd slept with all those courtiers, and the princes, and finally Prince Murkel, and none of them had offered her the stable life she wanted. And after the revolution, she'd thought she'd found something different in Beck. Three moons they'd courted, tumbling every night, until she asked about committing to each other and building a life together. He'd simply stopped coming around. She'd found him in the pub and demanded an answer, and he'd humiliated her by ending things in front of everyone.

Now she was tumbling around on the floor of a treehouse with a fairy who'd reeled her in with a magic spell, to keep her for how long, the skies only knew. People might change, but not Avianna. She'd always be the girl no one wanted as a wife.

Sadness crept over her, and she pushed it away. "So you found the sex book?"

"Love book. *The Art of Love.* But yeah, it was a sex book."

She nudged him with a knee. "And?"

"And what?"

"What else was in it?" She leaned back so she could see Thorn's face and lifted her eyebrows.

He blushed. "I don't know, all kinds of stuff. It's embarrassing."

"Why?"

"I don't know how to talk about it."

"I'm not asking you to *talk* about it."

Thorn blushed harder, and hid his face against her skin, but now he was smiling. She ran her fingers through his hair, first the side she'd cut and then the side that was still long, coaxing him to relax. Down where his body met her thigh, he grew hard against her.

"Well, there was this," he said.

Avianna rolled to her back and started to slide under him, but he stopped her.

"Stay still," he whispered. "Let me do it this time."

She lay her head back on the floor and loosened her arms as Thorn pulled away from her. Towering over her, kneeling between her legs, he seemed more impressive than she would've expected.

He grinned at her before lifting the hem of his shirt and pulling it off in one smooth motion. Avianna had to stop herself from gasping. In the firelight, the muscles of his lean, hard torso stood out, neat rows leading down to his trousers, where his erection strained against the buttons. Something about the suspenders hanging by his hips made him even sexier. His muscles weren't huge and bulging like Rye's, but they were nothing to scoff at.

Then she remembered.

"Stop with the illusions, Thorn. Let me see the real you."

His grin faded. "What are you talking about?"

"You've made your body look like a Sarlian warlord's, for skies' sake."

His lips quirked but he held back his smile. "Maybe I do look like a Sarlian warlord."

"You work in a print shop! All you do is read."

"I climb trees."

"Not every day."

He leaned forward, planting a hand on either side of her body. "Touch them."

"What?"

"Touch these fake illusion muscles I've supposedly created to impress you."

Suddenly, Avianna wasn't so sure of herself. She reached out, hesitating a finger's width away from his skin. When her eyes darted to his face, he was focusing on her, his usual quiet confidence restored. She swallowed and contemplated her finger. This wasn't real, she told herself. His smooth, muscular torso was not real, and she would feel what was actually there.

She moved her finger forward and touched his skin.

She let out the breath she hadn't realized she was holding. Her hand spread over his chest, pressing against his muscles. His breathing grew ragged as she brought her other hand up, caressing his nipples and down his stomach. When she glanced up from his chest again, he was no longer smiling but staring at her helplessly.

She pulled his body down to hers.

Their lips met full on this time, with his weight bearing down on her. He had her trapped, but he was aware of her, always responding to her.

He slid his tongue along her lips before pushing inside. Avianna froze. Her instinct was to meet him with her own tongue. That's what she would have done with anyone else. Why did she stop?

Thorn drew back. "You don't like that," he whispered.

"I'm sorry."

"No, it doesn't matter. I want to know what you like."

"I don't want to disappoint you."

"You could never, Avi."

Avianna tried to figure out the ideas stewing in her head, ideas she'd never spoken aloud. "Men seem to really like jamming their tongue into my mouth."

Thorn drew back farther, squinting at her. "They do?"

"They all do it. And not even nice like you did."

"But you don't like it."

"I don't think most men pay attention to what a woman likes, Thorn. Or they think they know better."

"Stars." He leaned in to kiss the tip of her nose. "I always want to know."

She peered up into his serious face.

"Promise you'll tell me?" he said.

She nodded.

He flipped the long side of his hair away. "Maybe it's only they lack imagination."

"What do you mean?"

He lowered himself toward her, moving his lips across her cheek. "There are so many other places to jam your tongue." Then he wedged it into her ear.

Avianna squealed, squirming beneath him, but his tongue was teasing her ear and it actually felt kind of nice. He pulled it out and blew into the wetness he'd left.

"Skies, was that in your book?" she asked.

"Mm-hm." He kissed the shell of her ear and whispered, "There was a whole section on tongues."

Then he was licking a path down her neck, with his fingers tightening in her hair, which sprawled across the floor. He held on until he'd kissed his way down to the top of her dress. He let go of her hair and fumbled with the ribbons across her chest.

"Is this okay?" he whispered.

She laughed. "You'd have to try hard to find something that's not okay with me."

"You know you could tell me to stop."

"To stop?"

"Just tell me. If you ever want me to stop."

"Don't stop."

She closed her eyes as the ribbons pulled open, and his fingers trailed down over her loose shift to rest over her breasts. She imagined him as a boy, alone in a dark, underground library poring over a book with drawings of naked women, studying the ways his hands could touch their breasts to elicit pleasure, storing the knowledge away for some future encounter. For tonight.

His fingers rubbed her, drawing out her nipples with the scratch of the fabric against her skin. She kept her eyes closed, stopping her thoughts and feeling only him.

The motion stopped, and his fingers rested on her skin, and then they slowly pulled down her shift. He rubbed her bared breasts in slow circles and squeezed her nipples in twin pinches. Down her whole body ran lightning, waiting for his touch to cover her, but still he went on tormenting her breasts. She wanted his lips on her, and a moment later they were there, sucking as his free hands pulled her shift off her shoulders. Her hands were pulled off his body and became trapped in the folds of the fabric, pulled down to her waist. He bound her up in the dress, still sucking on her nipples, until at last she moaned enough that he moved on, kissing her belly and downward.

And then she guessed where his lips were headed. It had happened only once before, with that young prince who'd been trying so hard but hadn't gotten much right. Thorn was getting it right. He pulled her dress and shift all the way down, taking all her clothing and leaving her naked on the rug as he freed her legs. She waited in anticipation.

He nudged her hip. "Lift up," he whispered. She lifted her hips and a cool cushion slid under her bottom. She settled down onto it with a slight arch in her back. Thorn put his hands under her bent knees and began kissing on the insides of her thighs. His hands slid slowly up, grasping her skin as he kissed on one side, then the other, back and forth toward the center where she ached for him. As he got closer, her knees sank, languid, and came to rest over his shoulders. His lips closed in on their prey.

At first he just kissed her there, but each press of his lips sent tingles into her. Then the kisses changed, pressing deeper between the folds of her skin, until he was sucking on her. Tremors shot through her, threatening to burst, but each time Thorn backed off, never giving her enough to send her over the edge. The book must have taught him this because how else would he have known to make it last this way? Avianna had never had things go on for this long, and she wasn't sure how much her body could take.

She reached down and grabbed a fistful of Thorn's hair, glad he still had one side long enough for her to hang onto. He squeezed against her, and when her shuddering began, he didn't let go. She held onto him like he was an anchor as she pitched on the floor, her body taking over and making her cry out. She bucked against him again and again until the spasms died off. She gave one last twitch before they were gone.

Thorn released her. She lay panting by the fire with his cheek pressed against her thigh. He exhaled loudly against her skin and went silent. She didn't move. She never wanted to move again. She wanted to keep lying, naked and safe, with Thorn between her legs. They lay that way for a while.

The fire finally began to dim. Had Thorn gone to sleep? She tilted her head up and peered down at him. He was staring ahead, and his fingers were tracing the weave of the rug. She moved her leg to nudge him and he looked up.

Thorn was beautiful. How had she not noticed? Maybe his spectacles hid his face, or he hid it with the loose way he walked instead of parading around the village with his chest out. But she saw it now when he stared up at her, not asking for anything but what she might want.

She tugged a little on his shoulder and he peeled himself off her legs and crawled up to lie beside her. She glanced down. The buttons on his trousers were undone. Sneaky Thorn—he'd managed to take his pleasure without interrupting hers. It made her glad.

He leaned in and kissed her cheek. "This is no illusion, Avi," he whispered.

Then he lay back and was silent. She waited, and his breathing changed into the steady pattern of sleep.

Thorn loved her.

She knew it was true. And she believed his words were true, that his love wasn't an illusion. He wasn't the one under a spell, after all. But what had she done to deserve such love? She'd never be suitable for him. She hadn't paid him any attention until he'd used a spell on her. She had to give him credit there—he'd created a masterful love spell. She could easily have believed she was falling for him, if the idea hadn't been preposterous.

But how would his spell hold up as the seasons passed? Thorn deserved someone admirable and pure, someone real, not like her.

And besides, she couldn't see herself as Thorn's wife—living over the print shop or here in the woods, and accepting such a simple existence. She'd spent her life dreaming of gowns and balls and society events. They didn't seem important now, but over time, as the spell faded, would she wish she'd tried harder to achieve her dream?

Avianna contemplated Thorn across the rug where he lay, his head tilted to the side away from her. She could make out his lashes resting on his cheek. He'd changed from a man she happened to run into in the street to someone who was dear to her. She couldn't go down this path with him. Slowly to avoid waking him, she sat up and began to rebraid her hair.

Chapter 17

AVIANNA HESITATED ON THE EDGE of the forest, facing the road to the village. The last lamp of the fairy path glowed overhead. Now that she'd come out of the trees, dawn rose around her in mists from the frost-tipped grasses. The golds and reds of the forest had been hidden in darkness last night. Now the leaves glittered like jewels.

She'd been lucky to find some teen-aged fairies awake in the middle of the night, picking through the scraps of the feast in the clearing. When she'd told them she needed to get to the village, they'd obligingly taken her to the start of the path and lit the first of the lamps for her. The rest had lighted up as she picked her way along the path, as they had when she'd walked the other direction with Thorn.

Thorn. Her heart had been unexpectedly heavy as she'd left the fairy village and more and more so the farther she walked away from the fairies. She felt terrible about leaving him even though she knew it was the right thing to do. Now, with one lamp still glowing, she could turn right around and relight her way back, even as the darkness lifted from the world.

But what good would it do? There was no way it would work between her and Thorn. She simply had to stop thinking about him. Maybe now that they'd been together, he'd get over her and his spell would begin to fade. Remembering their lovemaking, her body heated and her chest ached.

She ignored her physical reactions and focused on the scene

around her. She stepped out of the trees and the last lamp dimmed out. No one was in sight.

Still Avianna stood by the end of the path, not wanting to leave. If she searched overhead, she could see the first lamp even now that it had gone dark. She hunted for the second one and couldn't find it. She'd never be able to follow the path without the lights to guide her. But still she hesitated to leave.

She pulled a ribbon off the end of her braid. Red. That would be easy to spot. She tied the ribbon on to a branch that stuck out near the tree with the lamp.

What would Thorn do when he woke? He wouldn't know why she'd left. A stab of doubt shot through her. What if she'd made a mistake? When she remembered how it had felt between them, she wasn't sure she'd been right to leave him. She remembered the way his hands had touched her, and it made her long to fall into a daydream right there by the edge of the trees. She had to push the memories away.

Avianna sighed, turning to the village. She couldn't change course now. She had come back, and she needed a plan.

All she wanted was to curl up in bed and sleep. The boarding house would be empty—all the better. No one would be there to taunt her or make her work. She'd go home and secure herself inside. If Flo had locked the door, she could break her way in. She'd have food and a bed, and if the pirates happened to come by the house, poking around in their search for treasure or whatever it was they wanted, she could hide herself in a number of places— Flo's linen closet, or under the dirty sheets in the hamper. If Flo noticed the missing food later on, she'd blame the pirates.

And maybe once Avianna was safe, she could indulge in remembering her night with Thorn.

Or she could focus on not thinking about Thorn and on figuring out her next target, now that Jeb Doolihan had turned out to be such a ninny. Who else had she spotted at that dance who might be the right person for her?

Avianna began to walk southward. She kept to the edge of the forest, ready to dive into the trees if she heard anyone approaching. But the road stayed deserted as the sun peeked over the fields. Nothing around her was familiar. She hadn't been this far from the castle since she'd come to Woodglen at fourteen, and she'd arrived from the opposite direction.

She walked on. It seemed she walked miles as the day grew lighter. She had no sense of how far the horse had carried them the night before.

Finally, as the sun shone fully down, the turrets of the castle appeared as she rounded a bend. She scanned more carefully for any sign of the pirates. As she neared, she found only the smoking remains of their bonfire. The castle appeared as it always did, silent with pennants waving high atop the towers. Surely if the pirates had gotten in, there'd be shouting or gunshots or someone about. Far down across the fields, the gate she and Thorn had tried to enter last night still appeared shut. Maybe the pirates had dropped their file off the cliff by accident.

Should she head for the castle instead of the village and try to get the attention of someone inside? There was no cover once the road left the forest—the road ran through open pasture for a thousand paces to the nearest gate. She'd be completely exposed.

She reached the turn to the village and darted across the road and toward the shelter of the first cottage. Then she crept along, staying against the walls of the homes and alert for any sounds, until she reached the square. Hopefully the pirates had been up all night and were now dozing somewhere. She didn't have a cat to guide her safely through the village.

Rather than cross the open square and village garden as Thorn had the previous night, she navigated around the perimeter, past the herbalist's shop and the new flower shop, and past the fancy hat shop and the Boar's Head. The table where she'd sat with Jeb was empty, her scrumptious uneaten fish dinner gone. Maybe the staff had grabbed her plate on their way out the door to the castle. She hoped someone had eaten that delicious-smelling meal.

The grange hall was a likely target for the pirates, but that was quiet as well. Maybe they'd already infiltrated it and discovered it held no treasure. Thorn was right—all the gold the people had taken from the king was hidden in the castle, and the pirates would never breach the walls. They must be angry. Assuming that gold was the reason they'd come.

Avianna headed down the hill toward the wharf, feeling a little braver now that the whole village was quiet. She spotted numerous cats on the rooftops, calmly watching her pass. How many blasted cats did this village have? She'd never noticed them before. Were they all on Finnegan's team?

The salty smell of the shore reached her as she descended, as well as a puff of wood smoke. She breathed again and the air was clear, and the gulls were starting to call from the docks. Yesterday's fog had completely burned off. There wouldn't be any fish today, with the fish-catchers holed up in the castle.

Avianna neared the bottom of the street and turned toward the boarding house. And another whiff of wood smoke reached her.

She froze. Someone had a wood fire. That meant someone else was here.

Go to Flo's, she told herself. Stay safe until the villagers rout the pirates.

But what if the pirates were dashing? Even so, they could still be dangerous . . . . But they hadn't destroyed the village. None of the buildings was a smoking ruin, and they hadn't broken windows or ransacked homes or even trampled the garden. What if they only pillaged because there was no honest work in their homeland? What if they weren't all that bad?

Thorn's voice echoed in her head. They were *pirates*. She had to ignore her childish daydreams and stay away.

Avianna scanned the sky, which was a brilliant blue between the rows of stone and wood buildings. A trace of brown smoke drifted past on the breeze, dirty against the fresh pale blue. It came from farther down the hill, from the direction of Alistair's.

Avianna moved to the wall and crept down to the bottom of the hill. She flattened herself against the stones as the wharf opened up before her. Far across, something flashed near the docks, but when she surveyed the area, no one was in sight. Whatever had moved was hidden below the edge of the wharf.

She closed her eyes and listened, and the low murmur of men's voices reached her from around the corner. She exhaled and made a decision. Thorn was right. She wasn't going to risk being kidnapped because of a silly childish fantasy about a romantic pirate captain. She was going back up the hill a block, straight to the boarding house to—

A woman screamed.

Avianna's heart dropped. The scream choked off, and the men's voices rumbled louder. There was a woman with the pirates. And she was in trouble.

Avianna peered around the corner. No one was in the street. The smoke was puffing out the chimney at the pub. Her heart pattered faster. She couldn't abandon that woman, whoever she was.

Avianna darted across the street and crept toward Alistair's. The door was propped open. She crept closer. When she glanced quickly around, she spotted yet another cat crouched on the rooftop opposite, an orange tabby. If the pirates killed her, at least someone would know.

The voices grew louder. They spoke the common tongue but with an unfamiliar accent. But Avianna could tell by the harsh tone that the men were complaining. She caught snatches of words— "the gold" and "Liege Varjack" and "back to Sarland"—as she neared. The voices became clearer as she reached the doorway. The pirates were in the bar. Avianna edged into the entryway and crouched beside the doorway into the bar room, hiding herself behind Alistair's ridiculous plant.

Figures sat on the stools, large men in Sarlian furs and leather.

One tipped back a glass. Of course—they'd gathered in Alistair's so they could drink his alcohol. The bottle of Esterian whiskey stood almost empty on the bar. She should have smashed it over Rye's head when she had the chance.

A smaller and hunched over figure sat halfway down the bar. Avianna's heart sank as she recognized Mattie.

"The point is," one man said, "we can't return to Varjack without treasure, and there's nothing in this village, liege take it. We need to crack that castle."

"We'll have to crack a door then," the one beside him said, "since Simeon lost the file. Those walls are too thick."

"So we'll go back to the ship and get the hoot. We take some fishing boats to save time. Sound like a plan, Captain?" He addressed someone out of Avianna's sight.

There was a pause, and a deep voice said, "It's a plan. Let me finish my drink."

"What should we do with the captives?" He turned to Mattie and groped her thigh. She hunched further forward.

"Bring them. That one'll be a treat, and we can watch this one sink in the bay."

Avianna's stomach soured as Mattie began to shake.

She had to move or they'd spot her as they came out the door. But how could she hide while the pirates were carting away Mattie for some dreadful purpose and drowning whoever was with her . . . Beck? It must be Beck. Avianna could imagine what Mattie and Beck had been up to in Alistair's to make them miss the alarm when the pirates arrived.

The nearest pirate slid off his stool, his hand clamped around Mattie's upper arm, and he pulled her off after him. She twisted, and he shook her until she stopped. "Don't make it harder, love," he hissed. At the word "love," Avianna's stomach turned again.

She stood and moved into the doorway.

To her left, the pirate captain reclined on the chair where Thorn had sat two nights ago. He sipped whiskey from a glass. He had long hair that was pale as the sun, tied back from his harsh face with a strip of leather. Bands of metal circled his fingers on both hands, one after another fastened in a row. His vest was leather. He might have been handsome but there was nothing romantic about him.

In the center of the room, Beck was tied to a chair, his feet bound to the legs and a rag stuffed in his mouth. He had a black eye. Mattie stared at Avianna in terror. The three men at the bar were all gaping at her.

"I know the best way into the castle," Avianna said.

The captain's face jerked up. His eyes were a watery blue like the suds in the laundry bucket on a clear day, but he blinked and they hardened.

"Witch take it," he said. "What's this?"

Avianna stood as tall as she could, straightening her shawl on her shoulders. "I lived in the castle. I know all the gates and I know where the treasure vault is. I could save you a lot of effort. But you have to let them go."

The captain's whiskey glass knocked down on the table. He slowly unrolled himself from the chair and stood. He was tall, taller than her by a bottle's length, and his arms bulged menacingly, bigger even than Rye's. A pistol hung by his side.

"You lived in the castle? Is that worn-out trap your dance gown?" He leered.

"She did!" Mattie said. Apparently the chance to be freed had given her back her voice. Beck stared at Avianna with an empty face. Behind the rag, a few teeth were missing.

"Everyone in the court was removed from the castle after the revolution," Avianna said.

"Look at her necklace, Captain."

The captain's eyes darted to her neck. "Norlian crystals, eh?"

Avianna lifted her chin.

"You can't fly. We'd nab you before you were out the door. What position are you in to make demands?"

"You can't make me talk," Avianna said. "I've been mistreated all my life. I know what it's like and you won't break me. Let them go or I won't tell you a thing."

The captain scowled, his eyes narrowed to glare at Avianna. Then he turned to his men. "Let them go," he said. "We need that gold, and we don't have time for this. Besides—" He glanced at Avianna. "I think I like this one better."

Avianna swallowed her fear. They weren't going to touch her.

The nearest pirate shoved Mattie away, and she staggered toward Avianna. The other two pulled out blades and began sawing at the ropes tying Beck. Mattie clutched Avianna's arm. Then Beck pulled himself loose and stood, yanking the rag from his mouth. The pirates kept their blades pointed at him. He strode past them without looking up, grabbed Mattie's arm, and dragged her out the door.

Chapter 18

THE PIRATES LOADED PISTOLS AND daggers onto their belts and pulled on fur-lined vests as Avianna waited by the door. They planned to take her with them to their ship when they went for supplies before coming back to break in to the castle.

She had never seen a Sarlian. The rough seas between Sarland and Sylvania made crossing treacherous. She'd seen only pictures in books. She'd have guessed they were Sarlian, though, by the pallor of their skin and their bleached hair.

And she knew their reputation—harsh like their cold climate and tough to survive in a land that had so little sunlight. The former king of Sylvania had married a Sarlian—and exchanged gold, no doubt—to secure a tentative peace. But even then, the Sarlians had not been trusted as trade partners. When long-gone ships hadn't returned, rumors had spread that the crews had been enslaved by the Sarlian lords who ruled the southern land in a loose network. The desire for Sarlian furs and liquor wasn't great enough to make any trader take the risk.

A breeze blew in the open door. The salty air cleared away the acrid smells of the half-drunk men in their sweaty leather clothing. Avianna pulled her shawl tighter. The captain glanced her way with his cold expression and continued buckling his jacket. When he finished, he reached for a pistol on the table and motioned toward Avianna before pushing it through his belt.

Avianna saw the gleam of both his guns.

"Simeon, give her your coat," he said. Avianna turned in surprise. The nearest pirate had frozen, his fur coat halfway on.

Simeon slid off his coat and handed it to her with a silent glare. Avianna didn't want to take it, but the wind would be cold on the bay. She slid the coat on and fastened the front. Then she tied her shawl over her head and around her neck.

The captain led her out of the pub and down toward the wharf, with his three henchmen following. Mattie and Beck had disappeared, but the cat still crouched on the roof outside. Maybe it would tell Finnegan what was happening to her, and Finnegan would tell Thorn . . . but she'd left Thorn in the forest.

Her heart panged with the memory. Had he woken? What would he think of her leaving—would he think that she'd used him for a night of fun? Maybe she had.

Maybe, given his inexperience, he'd simply think it was customary for a person to slip away like she had and not take it personally, but somehow she doubted that. Would he return to the village? He might stay with the fairies to avoid the pirate incursion and, while he was at it, to avoid seeing her, if she had embarrassed him by leaving. She might never see him again! Her heart sank even lower.

As the wharf came into view, the pirates' ship appeared anchored out in the bay under the clear sky. She had missed seeing it before, focused as she'd been on the movement at the docks. The ship was smaller than she'd pictured, with only two masts. The men herded her to the docks, where several figures appeared, rising from their seats and facing the captain as the group approached. Avianna counted ten of them all together.

"You brought us some goods, Captain?" one of the men on the dock said, eyeing her.

"No one's to touch her. We need her help in the castle."

"Is she a maid? She's probably used to it."

Something snapped inside Avianna. She rounded on the man

who'd spoken. "I bloody well know how to talk, you imbecile. Why don't you ask me?"

He stared at her. The captain began to laugh. "Go ahead. Ask her."

"Did, uh, were you a maid?"

"No," Avianna said. "As a matter of fact, I was the princess's lady-in-waiting until the people revolted and overthrew the king. And I was 'used to it' more than any of the maids in the castle, so enough with your ignorant prejudices. Stars help the women of Sarland if the men there are all like you lot.

"Now the people of Woodglen have a stockpile of munitions in the castle, and if you want my help getting past them to the gold, you'd better treat me with respect."

The man stared a moment longer before turning away. The captain was grinning, and someone behind her muttered a curse.

The captain directed the men to steal three of the widest fishing boats to use along with their own two rowboats. Then the pirates split into pairs and boarded the boats. Avianna was put with the captain and Simeon on one of the rowboats. At least there were empty seats and she could keep her distance. She moved to the far end from the captain, which made him smile as he watched her take her seat. Nearby, sails were sliding up the masts of the fishing boats. Simeon sat on the middle bench of her boat and picked up the oars.

As they pulled away from the dock, the wind hit and Avianna huddled down.

"I don't suppose you want me to keep you warm?" the captain said over Simeon's rowing shoulders. Avianna snorted and surveyed the water.

They rowed away from the wharf and out into the choppy surf of the bay. After they cleared the buildings of the village, the garden wall at the castle came into sight. The steep cliff and the rocky shore below made landing impossible—unless one landed on the tiny beach tucked behind the gardens. That would be the easiest way to storm the castle, now that the king didn't have archers guarding it. But Avianna had no intention of telling the pirates that. What *was* she going to tell them? She certainly didn't want to help them steal from the villagers.

Avianna smelled only fresh salt air, not the stinking seaweed smell of low tide. Hopefully the tide was high enough to hide most of the beach sand. Viewed from the water, the stretch of sand would give away the beach's location.

Sitting in the whistling wind, with only the grunting from the oarsman and occasional cry of a gull to break the monotony, Avianna again brooded over Thorn. Thorn, who loved her. Blast it all to the stars, she'd never felt anything like what he'd done to her. Now she was all mixed up. Because she knew Thorn couldn't give her what she needed—a nice house, the life she'd grown used to with enough shells to buy dresses and a carriage to impress the neighbors. But she couldn't stop thinking of him and thinking that maybe she'd be happy with him in spite of it all.

Apparently, their night together hadn't ended Thorn's spell.

The tilting of the rowboat made her queasy. She looked up from the heaving water and out over the sea. The pirate party was about halfway to the ship. From the other end of the boat, the pirate captain watched her, stroking his chin. A villain straight out of a storybook. Gad. What had ever seemed romantic about pirates?

"What's your name?" Avianna asked, mostly to get him to stop staring at her in his creepy, menacing way. "Or do you go by 'Captain'?"

He lowered his arm and leaned forward slightly, as if bowing. "I am Adolfo van der Horne, of the House of Krale. In Sarland, I'm known as The Blackhorne."

Avianna had to stop herself from snorting again. To cover her smile, she asked, "How long was the trip from Sarland?"

"We were at sea a week, with surprisingly fair winds and without rough seas."

"And, this—robbing people—that's what you do?"

The captain considered her, and she feared she had gone too far. But he sat up straight and cricked both sides of his neck and said, "I have other pursuits."

Avianna decided against taunting him more. They were far out in the bay now, nearly to the ship, and the water was rough. She could barely swim in the calm, sheltered water of the beach cove. She didn't want to try it out here, should the captain decide to toss her overboard.

"Well, whatever you do for income, I'm sure it beats doing laundry," she said.

"You're a laundry maid?"

"Yes."

"That's quite a fall from the princess's lady-in-waiting."

Avianna kept her chin up. "I also take care of the elderly who have no families." The captain's eyebrows shot up. "And I'm planning to pursue work as a bookkeeper, now that I'm learning to read." She almost asked if he could read, but Thorn wouldn't approve of her teasing anyone about that, not even Adolfo van der Horne.

In any case, the captain began directing Simeon, and Avianna turned round to find the bow of the pirate ship looming above her. The ship appeared a lot bigger now that it was upon them. Two fur-clad men appeared at the railing and dropped a rope ladder down, and the oarsman held the boat fast as the captain made his way toward her.

"Have you ever climbed a ladder, my dear?" Adolfo asked, holding out his hand.

She glared at it. "Yes," she hissed, and stood on wobbly legs. She grabbed on to the ladder and stepped on. It swayed with the motion of the ship as she climbed, but she held tight and made it to the top. The men on the ship grabbed her arms in spite of her protests and heaved her on board. They held her tightly.

The captain came up behind her, swinging his long leg over the railing and dropping onto the deck. He pointed to the steps leading up to the forecastle deck. "Go sit there," he said, and then he added a threat to his voice. "And don't let me see you move."

"I could tie her up," one of the pirates offered, releasing her and following the captain down the ship, but the captain ignored him.

Avianna stumbled to the steps as the deck swayed beneath her. She fell onto her seat. All the men were clambering onto the main deck from the various boats. She imagined they'd load up their supplies and head back to the village.

But instead, they milled around in apparent disorder. Some fuss erupted with the captain shouting and someone being tossed overboard. The water must feel balmy here, she mused, compared to the icy seas of Sarland.

The captain disappeared below deck, and the sailors' work dwindled until they were mostly sitting on barrels and railings so that nothing appeared to be happening. A few glanced her way, sending shivers down her spine, but no one came near.

What in the skies was she going to do when they reached the castle? Could the pirates break through the castle doors? It was true she knew the location of the former king's treasure hall, but the gold could have been moved. And she had no idea where in the large castle the villagers had hidden themselves away. She didn't want to endanger them.

And the villagers were armed. When they saw the pirates, they were sure to start firing. She'd be shot. Or she'd be used as a hostage. Or both.

She had to get away from the pirates before they entered the castle. But how?

She'd swum in the ocean, but only at the beach with the sand beneath her feet. She could swim a few strokes but not enough to get to land. And if she tried leaping overboard, they'd see her and snatch her back. If she stole a boat, she'd be too slow and they'd catch her in a trice. She'd have to wait until they were back on land and watch for a chance to escape.

She leaned her chin onto her hands, propped on her knees. The ship rolled, back and forth on the waves, and every breath tasted like salt. Two of the pirates hauled a crate across the deck.

"Don't move."

Avianna froze.

"Don't move, okay? Just act normal."

She resisted turning her head toward the voice—Thorn's voice—because she knew she wouldn't see him. Besides, tears had filled her eyes. How had he managed to get here? And why hadn't he given up on her, after she'd left him in the woods?

She sat up slowly and wiped the tears away with her shawl and stared forward. Quietly, she said, "I'll act like I usually do when I'm being held captive by pirates."

Something bumped up against her knee, and his warmth was beside her. The tears returned, and something else began welling up in her heart. He always came back for her.

"Oh Thorn . . ." She closed her eyes.

His fingers slipped into hers, and she realized how cold hers had become. Thorn didn't appear beside her. She wasn't invisible, then.

"How did you get here?" she whispered.

"When I woke up you were gone—" He paused, and Avianna held her breath. "I wanted to make sure you were okay, after—"

He couldn't even say it aloud, what they'd done together. Avianna's face started to crumple, but she held herself together and forced all the feelings back. She couldn't fall apart sobbing now, not when she—they—had to escape the pirates.

"I left as soon as I woke, and then Finnegan reached me," Thorn said. "I made it to the docks in time to slip aboard. Are you sorry?"

She wasn't sure what he was asking about. "Thorn, no."

"I know you have a thing for pirates."

Avianna controlled herself to keep her voice low. "They had

Mattie. I didn't know what to do. But now they think I'm going to help them find the gold in the castle."

"Are you?"

"No!"

A shadow fell across her. "No?"

Avianna jumped to her feet and Thorn's hand slipped away. The captain stood behind her on the forecastle deck. He must have come up from below.

"I was daydreaming," Avianna said.

The captain arched an eyebrow and smiled.

Avianna glared back and tightened her lips. As if she'd tell him her daydreams.

He smirked and came down the steps. Avianna stepped back, but he reached to grip her upper arm. "We'd better put you below," he said. "I've a feeling you're regretting your offer to help us."

The captain marched along the deck, towing Avianna beside him. The few pirates who'd been active stopped to watch them pass until the captain shouted for them to get back to work, and everyone scrambled into motion. At the back of the ship, a door below the quarter deck led to the captain's quarters. The captain opened it and shoved Avianna through, releasing her and following her in. The door snicked closed behind him. Avianna's heart sank. There was no way Thorn had gotten in, too.

A map-covered table stood in the center of the room, and chests lined the walls below multi-paned windows of thick glass. A lantern swung overhead. Behind the table, a doorway led into what must be the captain's sleeping quarters. Avianna shuddered. Maybe it was better that Thorn hadn't been able to follow. If the captain tried anything, Thorn would intercede, and he was sure to be killed if the captain discovered him.

The captain stood beside the table. "I've plenty of parchment," he said. "If you draw a map of the castle, I'll have one of my men row you to shore now. You'd be done with all this."

Avianna squinted up at him. "You really think I'd fall for that?"

The captain shrugged. "I've no wish to hurt you."

"Most men don't, Captain."

"Adolfo, please."

She stood silently.

The captain sighed. "Very well. I'd hoped you'd cooperate."

"I am cooperating."

"Not in the way I'd like."

Avianna's insides lurched. She didn't like where this was heading.

"You were mistreated because you were poor," he said when she didn't move.

Avianna nodded once.

"You had no one to take care of you. No parents?"

"They were poor, too."

"Of course."

He took a step toward her, and she stepped away.

"What about a husband, then? Surely with your looks, someone wanted you?" He stepped forward again and lightly pushed her shawl back off her hair.

Avianna didn't reply.

"They didn't?"

She glared at him.

He snickered. "They wanted something though, didn't they? Just not a wife. Not someone like you, anyway."

The captain's words were the same as the taunts Mattie and Beck used. No one wanted her as a wife because she wasn't good enough. But something had changed since she'd last heard such a jibe. Somehow, with the words coming from Adolfo van der Horne, Avianna could see them for what they were: lies meant to break her.

Thorn had told her she had value, and he was right. Being poor had made her tough and determined. She'd used the little she had to change her situation. Maybe the things she'd done hadn't been ideal, but she'd not had the option of a better path. And maybe it hadn't worked out at the castle, but she had more options now. She had new skills and friends who would help her, and she had the same determination she'd always had.

Adolfo was wrong, just as Mattie and Beck had been.

"Someone like me?" she said.

"Someone who's good to ram, but not a keeper." He took another step toward her.

"Touch me and I won't help you."

The captain's lips parted, and he rubbed his tongue along a row of crooked teeth. "It might be worth it," he said. "How hard can it be to find gold in a castle?"

Avianna tensed.

The captain hesitated a moment, and then he relaxed backward. "I'd think you'd find this situation romantic. Most women seem to like being tossed onto my bed and made love to."

She didn't see the captain being open to the idea that his perception of those women was wrong. Instead, she responded, "I've found it's different when you hear it in a storybook or imagine it, than when it's really happening."

Shouts sounded from the deck.

The captain jerked his head toward the sound. The shouting continued, filled with alarm. Thorn must have done something.

The captain growled, glancing around. Then he grabbed her arm and dragged her into the back room.

"I've no time for you now," he muttered, hauling her to a trapdoor. "And I can't leave you here."

He opened the door. Steps led down into a dark hold. He pushed her in, and she stumbled down the narrow stair to the bottom, bracing herself against the walls to keep from toppling. Light shone down from above. She moved into the hold through a maze of crates and barrels. The captain came behind her and prodded her forward.

A doorway led into a dark passage with light filtering in the far end. Avianna started down the passage, only to be pulled back by the captain. He opened a side door and shoved her in. She stumbled against the crates inside as the ship swayed. The door closed behind her, taking away the light, and a lock snapped shut.

Avianna held onto a crate, scared to move in the void of darkness. Steps pounded overhead.

What had Thorn done?

If he'd waited, the pirates would have taken her back to shore. Then she and Thorn could have simply disappeared and run. Maybe that would still happen. Inept as the pirates seemed, maybe they'd still mobilize and tell the captain they were ready. Unless Thorn had done something drastic.

What if Thorn made the captain angry? The captain's interest toward her had been clear. Would he force himself on her in anger?

Avianna shuddered. She shook her head and whispered to herself, "I will get through this." They wouldn't kill her. As long as they didn't hurt Thorn.

Her eyes slowly adjusted to the dark. Light seeped in at a space on the ship's wall. Now she could make out the crates around her. She checked her balance and tried the door latch, but it clicked emptily. Something held the door closed. She moved toward the light, feeling the wall of the ship until she found a metal bar. She pushed and it slid to the side. A small round window opened onto the sea.

She was in a room stacked with crates, rows of kegs, and larger barrels. With the window open, she could hear waves sloshing against the side of the ship. She was near water level.

She stepped back from the window and tripped over a thick iron loop in the floor. Another trapdoor. She tugged the door up and peered into darkness, barely able to make out more crates in a dark hold.

Voices carried in the window. A new voice rang out, and it was a voice she knew. Her heart faltered. She raced over to peer out.

A man was standing on a fishing boat beside the ship. He wore a vest like one of Jeb Doolihan's with a thick watch chain drooping out the pocket, and he had a neatly trimmed beard. The sails of the boat flapped loosely. They sagged slightly, not quite to the top of the mast, and the bowline trailed in the water.

"Liege take it! Where did he fly from?" said a voice above her.

The man stood tall. "I've come for the girl. I saw you take her at the docks. I'm willing to pay."

No, Thorn, Avianna thought. What was he doing? It was futile. There was no way they'd let him take her, not for what Thorn could pay, when she could get them into the treasure room at the castle. Or at least, they thought she could.

There was more shouting above deck, and someone whined, "I didn't see him, Captain." Then a thump sounded—a ladder being tossed down—and Thorn lifted a chest from the bottom of the boat. He stepped onto the bow and leaned forward out of her sight, and the boat was pulled after him until she lost sight of that as well.

As if rich men in vests knew how to climb ladders one-handed! And if the pirates counted the fishing boats, they'd see that Thorn had appeared on one of the ones they had stolen. This plan would never work. Why hadn't he waited?

Because he didn't want her to be hurt. He'd seen the captain take her inside his quarters. It wasn't enough for Thorn to save her life. He wanted to protect her. To him, waiting wasn't an option. Even if it meant he'd be captured.

Avianna strained to hear anything else, but other than some stomping overhead, she couldn't make out what was happening. Then footsteps thundered on the steps. The door shook and was flung open. The captain himself had come with Thorn, or rather, Avianna's rich, would-be ransom payer. He dragged Thorn in and shoved him down on the trap door, ignoring Avianna. Behind him hovered a pirate with a set of rusty manacles, and Avianna knew she couldn't stand to watch them beat Thorn, but when the pirate stepped forward, he only threaded one side through the hook on

                    Jane Buehler

the floor and locked the heavy iron cuffs on Thorn's wrists, leaving Thorn chained to the floor.

The captain glared at Avianna. "I'm beginning to think you're more trouble than you're worth," he said.

He strode out the door. His man followed, and the door slammed shut.

Chapter 19

THORN'S BEARD DISSOLVED AND HIS vest with the watch chain shimmered away. Avianna ran to him.

She crouched on the floor beside him and raised her hand to his cheek. His spectacles were gone. His lopsided hair hung beside his face, where traces of the bruise around his eye still showed.

"Did they hurt you?"

"Not much." He didn't meet her eyes.

"I saw you offer to ransom me. It was very brave."

He didn't respond.

"What did they say?"

"They said my gold was enough to buy my own freedom."

"Then why did they lock you up?"

"I think they're onto me. They're waiting to make sure it's real."

"Is it?"

"Of course not! Where would I get a chest full of gold, least of all in the middle of the bay?" He stared at the floorboards.

"I'm sorry, it was a stupid question. Did they take your specs?"

He nodded. Avianna had never seen him like this. Even when he'd been fighting off Rye, he'd been smiling, unruffled Thorn. Now he huddled on the floor, staring at the boards without even a frown or a grimace, just a blank stare.

"If we're not out of here by sunset," he said at last, "all my gold is going to turn back into seaweed and they're going to know I tricked them and kill me."

"Oh Thorn, this is all my fault! I only wanted to help Mattie, and now I've dragged you into it."

"No, I'm sorry, Avi. I should've planned something better. We should've jumped overboard in the first place, even if I can't really swim."

"We'd have drowned."

"You can't swim either?"

"Not well."

"Me neither."

He lapsed into silence.

Avianna couldn't let the pirates hurt Thorn. He deserved to live and be happy, if anyone did. Or maybe she just didn't want to live without him. Spell or not.

"Come here," she said, and she smoothed her hand down his back and pulled him up. She helped him sit upright, with his hands still chained in front of him. He slumped forward, but at least he was up. "Maybe there's something in these crates that can help us."

Avianna stood and approached the crates. They were nailed shut at the corners. Without a bar to pry them open, she'd never manage. She hadn't noticed before, but they had letters scrawled on them in charcoal.

"They have letters," she said, "but I don't know the words. Can you read them?"

He squinted up at her. "I can't see that far. They're all blurred."

"I don't know more than the alphabet."

Thorn slumped forward again.

"I'll read the letters," Avianna said, "and you tell me what they say." Avianna studied the letters. "F-L-O-U-R," she read.

"That's flour."

Beside it was a barrel. "W-A-T-E-R."

"Water."

"P-O-W-O, no wait, P-O-W-D-E—"

"Powder."

"Powder?" Avianna asked, thinking of the jars of it the ladies had had at the castle for fixing their faces.

"Gunpowder."

"Gunpowder! That's perfect! We can blow a hole in the side of the ship."

Thorn twisted to stare up at her. He lifted his chained hands.

"Okay, not with you chained to the floor," Avianna said. "Can we blow the manacles off first?"

"Not if you want me to keep my hands."

"Wait, I have a hairpin." Avianna patted her head until she located one. "They can pick locks, right?"

"I've never tried it."

The hairpin was tiny compared to the lock, and when she pushed it into the keyhole, it bent this way and that.

"Neither of us can swim well," Thorn said. "Even if we get out, we'll drown."

Avianna continued poking the lock. "We'll take a boat. Or we'll use one of these barrels to float on. Or you can find a dolphin to help us, like Prince Dustan did when he rescued Rose from Prince Murkel." Avianna's hands were starting to shake. The hairpin was too flimsy to force the lock. "This won't work."

Thorn sighed. He kept staring at the floor—it unnerved her. Had she broken him by leaving him in the woods?

"What about the animals?" Avianna said. "Can one of them bring us a file? Isn't there a fish with a sharp snout?"

"Not that sharp."

"What about a crab with a massive claw?"

"I do know a crab," Thorn said, and he straightened slightly.

"You do?"

"He helped me obtain ink from some squid, when I needed a blue-black shade for a project."

"Do you think he could break a lock?"

"Maybe not, but . . ." He bit his lip. Then he closed his eyes, and a minute ticked past. Avianna sat beside him, forcing herself not to speak.

A grin spread across Thorn's face. "He's coming."

"You reached him?"

Thorn fixed his gaze on her. "Avianna. You'll need to help him in the window."

"Of course. But—"

"Wait, this is important. He's very fragile. You need to hold him carefully."

"Of course I will." She started to rise.

"Avianna. Look at me."

She lowered herself back down until their eyes were level.

Thorn stared into her. "He's fragile, and he's harmless. Promise me you'll be careful, that you won't drop him, no matter what."

"Of course. I promise to be careful. No matter what." Why was Thorn worried?

"He's nearing the surface. Can you reach the water with both your arms at once?"

He must be quite the crab if she'd need both hands to lift him from the water. Avianna stood and approached the window. She had to squeeze to get both her arms out, but her fingertips trailed in the water. A moment later, something bumped into her left hand. She closed her fingers on it. It was hard and thin, like the edge of a pottery plate. Her right hand found another edge. Slowly she lifted the creature up to the window.

She almost screamed. She knew crabs had claws, but this thing had dozens of them, for skies' sake, all waving about atop some kind of skeletal structure. Calm, calm, calm, she told herself. He's not dangerous. As she drew him in the window, a long spike appeared, trailing behind him, and Avianna couldn't help but whimper. The creature certainly looked deadly.

"He won't hurt you."

"Why is he waving his claws like that?"

"That's how he says hello. Turn him right side up so his legs are down," Thorn said. "He has to swim with his legs up."

Avianna gingerly turned the creature over. He didn't have eyes that she could see, just a smooth bowl-shaped brown shell. The top of him wasn't half as scary.

"He says he likes your necklace," Thorn offered.

"Um, thanks? What is he?"

"He's a horseshoe crab. They're skilled with locks. Bring him here."

Thorn moved his wrists together, turning them so the keyholes on the manacles faced upward. Avianna lowered the crab onto his wrists and let go. The crab shifted around, and then it stopped moving, although every now and then a claw would flash out from underneath it.

"Does it have a name?" Avianna asked. She settled onto the floor beside them.

"Not one I can pronounce." Thorn considered her. "Using gunpowder is dangerous. If we succeed in blasting a hole in the ship, the water might spill in too fast and we'll be trapped. Or if we make a crack but it's too small to get out, we'll be in trouble."

"We're going to be dead anyway."

"I am, but not you. They might let you go after you help them."

"I'm not letting them hurt you."

Silence fell except for the clicking of the crab's claws in the keyhole.

Then Thorn said quietly, "Avi, why did you leave?"

Avianna couldn't bring herself to lie to him, not after he'd risked his life to save her. "You love me."

"I do."

"You deserve someone who loves you back. For real."

Sadness crossed his face. "And you don't." She shook her head. "I thought maybe you did, after what we shared. You seemed . . ." His voice trailed off.

She tried to be gentle. "But wouldn't the spell make me seem that way?"

Thorn's head snapped up. "What spell?"

"You don't need to pretend. I know you used a love spell on me."

Thorn's mouth hung open. "A *love spell*?"

"It's okay, I understand why you did it. But I just—"

"Avianna Blackburn." Avianna halted at the growl in his voice. "I would never, *ever* put you under a spell. How could you think I would do that?"

"Well I . . ." Was he telling the truth?

"I love you," Thorn continued, "and I respect you. I would never take advantage of you like that. How could I truly love you if I used a spell on you?"

One of the manacles dropped to the floor with a bang. Thorn slid his hand out from under the crab and flexed his wrist.

All her replies suddenly sounded pathetic. "It was love that drove you to it," she said, faltering. "I thought you wanted me and you didn't know how to manage so you used a spell."

"Real love doesn't work that way, Avi. It's not about controlling someone. It's about making them happy. You really thought that?" He studied her face, and shame washed over her.

"You really didn't use a spell?" she asked in a whisper.

The other manacle dropped to the floor. Thorn stood, unfolding his legs and lifting the crab with him. He went to the window and carefully put the crab through. Then he turned with his empty hands on his hips.

"Avianna Blackburn."

She wanted to flinch when he said her whole name that way.

"I swear on the full moon, on every hawthorn tree in the forest, I did not put a spell on you."

She recognized a fairy oath when she heard one. There was no way he could say such words and lie.

He strode toward her until he stood above her.

"What I'd like to know," he said, and he crouched down until their faces were only a hand's breadth apart, "is what made you think you were under a love spell, cast by me?"

Chapter 20

AVIANNA SWALLOWED. THORN CROUCHED IN front of her, waiting for her answer. She cast about for some excuse, but the truth wouldn't let her escape.

She couldn't avoid looking up into his eyes, and he stared back into hers. All those feelings she'd had for Thorn. They'd been real.

Footsteps pounded on the steps outside the door.

Thorn leapt up and dashed toward the crates, and Avianna scrambled to her feet to help him. Together they slid a crate labeled "FLOUR" in front of the door. Someone was working the lock on the other side.

"Another. Help me lift it," he muttered.

Avianna braced herself and heaved up one side of the crate. They got it on top of the first just in time. The door wobbled behind the crates, then banged forward a finger's width. Curses sounded, and the door banged harder, but the blockade held. Thorn slid another crate into place.

Avianna inspected the powder kegs. How much powder would they need to blow a hole in the ship without blowing themselves to bits? She pushed aside images of sea water filling the hold and drowning her. Thorn appeared by her side. He leaned in close to inspect the stopper in the top of a keg, then twisted it out.

"Wait, Thorn. That one." Avianna pointed at a different keg, with a metal base. "It's metal. It'll do more damage."

Thorn squinted at her. "How do you know about using gunpowder?" he asked, reaching for the metal-bottomed keg.

"I used to hang around the soldiers' training field," she said, "when I got bored with the courtiers." Maybe her uncouth behavior was finally paying off.

They lifted the open keg together and began to pour a trail of gunpowder from the stack of supplies toward the outer wall of the ship, to a place where the wall was thinnest, between the ribs. The pirates continued their futile banging against the door and the blockade of crates. Someone beyond shouted for a hatchet.

When they reached the wall, they gently set the keg down, so that the trail of powder ended below the opening. Gunpowder spilled out, forming a pile that connected the keg to the floor. Avianna held the keg steady, and Thorn dragged a water barrel over to stand beside it. Soon they had it wedged in place. They added more barrels to oppose the explosion, to force the powder keg to shoot toward the ship's wall.

Something—the hatchet the pirates had shouted for?—thunked into the door.

"I think that's the best we can do," Thorn said.

Avianna climbed behind the remaining water barrels. He came beside her and they crouched down. From the loop on his trousers he took a steel band—the one he'd taken from the fairies' supply shed, Avianna remembered—and he reached into his pocket.

Panic crossed his face. "My flint."

"Don't you have it?"

He tried the other pocket. "No. I had it at the treehouse." He cursed. "I left it on the table. I was in such a hurry to follow you and never imagined I'd need it."

The crates by the door shuddered as the hatchet broke through, embedded in the wood, and was yanked out.

There had to be something in the hold, something they could use to create a spark and light the gunpowder. How hard could it be to set gunpowder on fire? But all they had were wooden crates and barrels of flour and water. No rocks, no hard surfaces like a shell or—

"The shackles!" Avianna scurried out and grabbed the chain that had bound Thorn. She worked it out of the hook on the floor and brought it back to him.

He bundled the rusty chain and the cuffs into his hand and struck it against the steel. A lone spark flew out. "They're too rusty," Thorn muttered, trying again. Again, a single spark ignited. "This won't work." The hatchet splintered the door in a long crack.

"Wait," Avianna said. She reached behind her neck and unclasped her necklace. "These should work."

Thorn took the crystals from her. He held the steel over the trail of gunpowder and struck it with a Norlian crystal. The crystal cracked in two and fell off the thread. He held the necklace lower, and struck from a sharper angle. This time the steel sparked. He tried the same angle, harder. Five sparks flew out, and one of them ignited the gunpowder. A flame leapt up, dancing and sizzling, and moved away down the line.

Thorn pulled her down behind the barrels.

"Just hang on, okay? Whatever comes in, we'll fight it until we're out."

She nodded, her heart wedged in her throat. They'd be blown to bits. She'd drown. The pirates would catch them. Thorn's fingers laced into hers, holding tightly.

The flame was three hands away from the barrel. Two. Then only one. It disappeared behind the water barrels, and Thorn pushed her head down beside his.

The powder exploded.

Scraps of wood smashed into the walls of the hold, and a cloud of acrid smoke filled the small chamber. Even before the debris stopped raining on them, Thorn dragged Avianna up. The cursing from the hallway became enraged, with bodies slamming against the door and the captain shouting for them to break it down. Water was pooling on the floor, and they both coughed in the fumes.

Thorn shoved aside the water barrels that had aimed their missile. Water poured in through a giant crack below the smoking keg. It was far too small for a person to pass through.

Thorn reached for the blackened keg and began pounding its metal bottom against the crack. Another board gave way, and the water poured in faster. Icy cold, it swirled over Avianna's ankles. She glanced back—the barricade shook with the pirates' blows, weakened by the lift of the swirling water. Thorn slammed the keg into the crack again, giving a strangled yell as he did. The boards splintered, and the whole keg went through.

He slid down with his feet in the opening, catching himself halfway through. "Lie down, quick." Avianna dropped into the water, keeping her chin above the surface. Thorn faced her, only his top half visible. His hands squeezed her wrists. He nodded. Avianna took the deepest breath she could and held it. Behind her, a crate crashed into the room. Thorn pulled her down into the water. Her skirts caught and ripped as he dragged her out of the ship.

Her heart pounded, and her lungs burned. She didn't dare open her eyes as she focused on not breathing. She held onto Thorn, staying still until he kicked for the surface, and then she kicked as hard as she could, too. His arm came around her, pulling her upward. Her head broke through into the air and she filled her lungs.

They were only a few strokes away from the ship. Waves lapped against her face, and she swallowed salt as she wheezed, catching her breath. The side of the ship leaned with the waves, over them and away, the water slapping its sides. Thorn's free hand grabbed her hand under the water, and she knew he'd made them disappear.

They kicked away from the ship, and a few heartbeats later, one of the pirates surfaced in the water where they'd been. They kept paddling, moving slowly away.

Around them floated broken bits of the ship. Nothing was big enough to support them. Avianna's legs beat through her skirts. How long could she keep it up, keeping her face above the surface? Beside her, Thorn panted.

"I need to move my arm," Thorn whispered between gasps.

Fear surged in when his arm around her let go, but she bobbed and stayed above the surface. He kept hold of her hand. "You'll be seen if you let go," he said. "Don't let go of me, okay?"

"There's no chance of that," Avianna whispered.

The captain appeared on the deck, scanning the water with his spyglass and shouting. The pirates were clambering down their ladders onto the boats. It was too late to take one.

"I can't see anything big enough to support us," Thorn whispered as they passed the last of the flotsam and pushed into clear waves. "And I can't find a big enough creature to ask for help. We have to try to reach the shore."

Avianna nodded. She scanned the horizon to find the closest land—a promontory that jutted out into the bay. "That way."

Slowly they moved through the water, little by little. Avianna's heartrate slowed back to normal, or at least closer than it had been as they'd escaped the ship. With every stroke, they moved another few paces away. Maybe they would actually escape the pirates. The men in the boats hadn't left the ship, but watched the captain as if waiting on him to direct them. He swung his spyglass to and fro, moving along the deck.

The cold sea water splashed her cheeks. The Sarlian coat was heavy, but she probably couldn't get it off even if she let go of Thorn's hand. Her feet were bare—her shoes must have slipped off when she entered the water. Even Thorn's hand on hers was chilled. She glanced back again, watching the pirate ship slowly list to the side. Would it sink? Avianna almost asked Thorn's opinion but stopped herself. They had to save their energy for swimming.

Thorn twisted beside her and his motion stilled. "I think we're far enough," he said. "I need to take a break with the invisibility." They turned back. The captain had moved to the far side of the ship.

As they rested in the waves, drawing in long breaths, Avianna kept ahold of his hand. Did he want her to let go? Was that why he'd spoken? Her fingers loosened and she changed her mind and kept her grip. But the shame washed over her again. How could she have believed Thorn would cast a love spell on her? He was the most conscientious person she knew, yet she'd accused him of doing something abominable.

And why? Because she hadn't wanted to admit to herself that she had feelings for him.

She reflected back over the past week. The way his skin had glowed in the firelight as he made her dinner in his room, when her feelings had been so strong that she first considered a love spell. And the way he'd looked in the firelight last night, lying beside her on the rug in his treehouse. And stars help her, the way it had felt. And it wasn't only her attraction to him. She was happy when she was with him. She could tell him anything and he didn't judge her. She could be herself and he liked her just as much.

She had been foolish. Thorn was perfect.

Maybe he didn't rake in the shells with his printing business, but he never seemed worried about having enough to pay the rent. And potatoes were cheap—she could live off baked potatoes if she was eating them with Thorn. And if they were a team, if she kept doing laundry or found new work, they'd have plenty to get by. She trusted him to stand by her.

All the things that had once attracted her to men, like Rye's buoy-sized biceps and Beck's skin-tight leather pants—maybe her expectations were a distraction. They had led her only to men who weren't worth the dust on the print shop floor.

She didn't know what Thorn thought of her anymore. But she had to make it right. Hopefully when they were back on land, he'd give her a chance.

Now that they'd stopped swimming, Avianna's body had drifted down until she hung vertical in the water, with Thorn's legs churning beside her. She kicked her feet over and over, and each time, the force lifted her up in the water.

Thorn squinted into the distance. "Do you see something coming?" he asked.

Avianna faced the village. The castle towered up in the sky. To the right, something moved at the edge of the buildings—white and tan forms, shimmering in the breeze. Sails were sliding up the masts, and some were moving out onto the water. The fishing fleet was raising its sails and departing the docks!

"The boats are coming."

Thorn pulled his hand from hers, keeping his gaze toward the boats, although he probably couldn't see that far without his spectacles. His hair was plastered to his face, still long on one side the way she had left it last night.

"I'll have to finish that haircut when we're safe on land," she said.

Thorn didn't reply.

"Maybe we can practice swimming next summer," she said. "In case we ever do this again."

He nodded once without looking at her.

The breeze struck her cheeks like icicles. She began to shiver. "I think the water's warmer than the air."

Thorn turned to her. "Are you all right?"

"If I keep moving my legs, it helps."

"They'll be here soon." The first boats were skimming across the water toward them. Thorn lifted his arms and waved them back and forth. He kept intermittently waving as the boats came farther out, and some of them shifted course to head toward them.

Finally, someone shouted and began to wave back. Thorn lowered his arms. The boat sailed closer and closer, the figures inside resolving into the familiar faces of villagers. The dock master was at the tiller. Sitting with him was a man with a gun.

As the boat neared, the dock master turned his sloop into the wind, and the sails flapped, empty of force. Thorn and Avianna kicked over to the boat.

"What in blazes are you two doing out here?" the dock master said.

"We blew a hole in the pirate ship," Avianna said, clinging to the side of the boat. She pulled herself up as far as she could. Over the far edge of the boat, more of the bay was visible. Other boats sailed toward them, while still more headed past toward the pirate ship. The ship had stopped rocking and now sat at a sharp tilt, low down in the waves.

The villager had put down his gun and moved to help pull Avianna up and into the boat as Thorn's hands settled on her waist and lifted her. Avianna sank onto the wood boards, her fingers and her feet shriveled with cold. The wind bit into her.

"Behind that center porthole," Thorn said, hanging off the boat, "the hold is filled with gunpowder." He turned to grasp the side of a second boat that had arrived. He pushed himself up and was helped over the edge into the other boat.

The dock master called out to the boats as they passed, repeating Thorn's words. Now boats were flying past, an armada of them heading to fight the pirates. Pride swelled Avianna's chest. She and Thorn had given them a head start, maybe even saved lives. She looked over her shoulder to find Thorn.

All she found was the open water. His boat had gone.

Chapter 21

AVIANNA GRIPPED THE BOAT BENEATH her as she searched the bay, frantic to spot Thorn. But now the fleet had arrived. So many boats filled the bay, their sails weaving in and out in the breeze, that she couldn't recognize anyone. Had Thorn gone back out to fight? They should go after him. But the dock master held his boat steady, the sails still loose and fluttering.

Another boat pulled up alongside them.

"Alistair!"

"Avianna," her friend replied, shaking his head. "Causing trouble as always. Do I even want to know what you're doing out here?" He grinned as his boat bumped gently into theirs.

The dock master reached out to grab hold of the rigging on Alistair's boat. "Take her in, Alistair, or she'll catch her death out here in the wind."

The woman with Alistair stood, using her gun for balance. She held her arm out to Avianna and put her foot onto the dock master's boat, clearly expecting to trade places.

"Alistair," Avianna said, "I have to go after Thorn." She couldn't leave him out here after he'd come out in the first place to save her. And without his spectacles to see with!

"You're not a soldier or a hunter, Avi," Alistair said. "You'll be in the way. And by the look of you, you've already had quite a day. Mattie told us what you did."

"But Thorn—"

"Thorn's fine. He's a fairy, for skies' sake. He can get out of anything."

They weren't going to listen to her. The villager seated beside the dock master had his lips pressed together as he stared out at the pirate ship, his fingers drumming on his knee. The one leaving Alistair's sloop watched her, waiting. They wanted her to go.

Avianna took the arm offered and stepped into Alistair's boat. It tipped as the other passenger got off. She hunkered down on the seat, hugging her arms around herself.

"Hold tight, gal," Alistair said. "We'll get you in and you can dry off and get warm." The dock master pushed Alistair's boat away, and the sails filled. The boat began to glide across the water, and for a moment they were heading out with the rest of the boats, until Alistair trimmed the sail and pulled the tiller toward himself. He barked a warning. The boat turned and the sail swung round to Avianna's side, flapping a moment before it filled again with wind and carried them toward the shore.

Avianna tried not to look back. She wouldn't see Thorn.

What if he hadn't left, though? Maybe he was here beside her, invisible . . . but she knew that wasn't true either. Thorn would go back to fight. And for sure he had wanted to get away from her. He was gone.

The boat flew across the waves, with Alistair focused on adjusting the sails. Avianna stayed low, waiting for the ride to be over. At least she'd be dry soon.

A gunshot cracked across the water. Avianna's heart jumped. She twisted to peer under the sail. Alistair paused to watch, too. A puff of smoke drifted in the air near the pirate ship, but it wasn't clear who had fired. On the ship, tiny figures moved on the sloping deck.

The village boats had surrounded the ship, which still tilted badly. The pirates scurried along the railing, and now gunfire flashed again, and again, until it was continuous. The pirates appeared to be trying to prop up a cannon, which tilted down, angled at the water.

"Please don't let anyone be hurt," Avianna whispered. She turned to Alistair. "Do you think they'll be able to sink it?"

"Shouldn't be too hard, especially if there's barrels of gunpowder on there. Just need someone to sneak on and blow a few more holes."

Dread filled Avianna. That's why Thorn had gone back. Who better to sneak onto the ship than someone who could turn invisible and who knew just where to go?

What if he blew himself to pieces along with the ship? She'd never get to tell him how sorry she was for thinking he'd put her under a love spell. And she'd never get to tell him how she truly felt about him.

And she'd never get to see him again.

The wind calmed as they entered the harbor. The cracks of guns firing were more distant now, carried away on the wind. Ahead, villagers lined the wharf, and a few headed down onto the docks to meet them. Alistair sailed up alongside a dock and let out the sails. Someone grabbed the boat's rigging and jerked the sloop to a stop.

Avianna forced herself up on wobbling legs, thinking she would have to crawl off the boat. But someone reached down to help her. Flo was coming at her, taking off her own coat and holding it out as she neared as if Avianna had appeared in the parlor naked and needed to be covered immediately. Avianna's mother was beside Flo. She put out her arm for Avianna to lean on.

"Where have you been?" Flo berated her, draping the coat over her shoulders and pulling it around her. "Trust you to take on a ship of pirates."

"I didn't mean to."

"Let's get you dry."

They led Avianna up the docks. The crowd of villagers who'd gathered on the wharf was mostly older folks and a few parents with children, although Avianna spotted someone resembling Jeb

Doolihan ducking behind the dock master's shed. Most of the heads were turned toward the bay, where the distant sound of gunfire crackled. A deeper boom rumbled in, and the crowd gasped. Avianna tried to turn. It was cannon fire. But her mother and Flo held her tightly. As they led her into the lane, her entire being begged her to wait there for Thorn.

Back at the boarding house, her mother helped her change into dry clothes. Avianna didn't ask whose they were, but the dress was new and it fit her perfectly.

"I lost my shoes," Avianna said.

"We'll get you some new ones," her mother replied.

"But I need them now!" A whine crept into Avianna's voice.

"You sound like you're ten winters old," her mother said with a smile.

Flo bustled over with the tea tray, tsking. "Why do you need shoes now? So you can head back to the wharf and catch your death of a cold?"

"You can't help any more today," her mother said, coaxingly. "Stay here and have a cup of tea, and Flo will let us know what happens."

"I promise to return as soon as it's over," Flo said. She deposited the tea tray and padded out into the hallway, where she wrapped her damp coat back on. She hustled out the door.

From the parlor, Avianna could hear the occasional gunshot and once more the boom of a cannon. She paced in the center of the room in the dry stockings they'd put her in. Thankfully the pirates weren't firing the cannon that often. Hopefully they were as inept at operating a cannon as they seemed to be at everything else.

Her mother returned from placing a new log on the fire. She poured the tea and held out a cup. Avianna sighed and took it. She sank onto a chair beside her mother. Even with dry clothes and the fire blazing, she felt cold inside.

Her mother was watching her.

"You must think I'm a ninny, getting captured by pirates."

Her mother smiled. "You gave yourself up to help a friend. That's nothing to be ashamed of."

"Mattie is hardly a friend."

"Even better."

"Where's Da then?" Avianna asked.

"Out fighting."

Avianna's eyes widened. "Da is out fighting?"

Her mother smiled. "He's not a complete lout," she said. "I admit, he used to be. But things have changed. That's why we came to see you. I've been wanting to talk with you, but we haven't had a chance."

With all the excitement, Avianna had forgotten about her parents' reason for visiting. She'd assumed they'd gotten into another of their endless scrapes and wanted her help getting out of it. Maybe they assumed she had shells now. Did they want to take her back to South End? She didn't want to return to their schemes, always hustling for her next meal and a place to sleep.

Although on her own she'd ended up in much the same place.

"You see," her mother continued, "Your father did a job for one of the manor lords after the revolution."

Avianna snorted.

"I know what you're thinking," her mother continued, "but it wasn't bad." She considered. "I mean, no one got hurt at least. And the revolutionaries were making this poor lord give up his extra plots of land, so he gave one of his properties to your father as payment."

"A property?"

"It's a decent house with a garden and all."

"You've got a house?" Avianna could scarcely believe it. Her parents had always been vagrants.

"We've settled down. We're growing vegetables, and you heard your da stopped with the ale. We still do odd jobs, but not like it used to be."

"Where is the house?" Avianna asked. She couldn't believe her parents owning a home—and a fancy-sounding one, at that.

"Down in South End, near where you grew up. You see, if you wanted to return, we'd have a place for you." Her mother twisted her hands together. "I know we weren't the best parents to you, Avi. We never blamed you for running off to the castle. We missed you, but we didn't come after you because we knew you could take care of yourself. We figured you were better off."

"Wait—you knew where I was?" Avianna stared.

Her mother smiled. "Of course we did. Joe Samuels drove the buggy you rode in on. And your father had a cousin who traveled through this way, so he kept an eye out for you."

"He did?"

"What'd you think, we didn't care what happened to you?"

Avianna was silent.

"I don't blame you for thinking that," her mother said.

"Well, I didn't succeed, in the end," Avianna said.

"That's why we came. We never heard you were bonded, and we learned the king's court had broken up. We wanted to offer you a place to live. There are a lot of young people in South End, and some handsome young men. Maybe you'd meet someone."

During Avianna's whole childhood, this would have been a dream come true. But now . . .

"I can't, Ma."

Her mother waited.

"It's not you. I would love to see your home. But there's someone here."

"I see."

"Only I've messed it up so badly, I don't know if he'll give me another chance. He stuck by me time and again, and I . . ." She felt too ashamed to admit what she had assumed about Thorn, and how she'd treated him. "He's the best person I know. And he's out on the water now."

Her mother's arm went around her. "He'll make it back to shore. You'll get a chance to fix it."

"But what if I can't? What if he won't see me?"

"You'll have to try your best. And if he won't see you, at least you tried. It might sting, but you owe it to yourself to try to fix things up. And you owe it to him, it sounds like."

Her mother was right. Facing Thorn again would be worse than anything, worse than the pub full of patrons laughing at her or the entire dance hall thinking she'd caught a merfolk sex disease from tumbling Prince Murkel. But if she didn't do it, she'd never forgive herself.

Her mother squeezed her shoulder. "Drink your tea."

Chapter 22

Two nights later, Avianna stared into the mirror in her room at the boarding house. Her neck was bare without her Norlian crystals, but at least she had a new dress. Two, in fact. It turned out her mother had bought her the one she'd changed into two days before. And the one that now swished around her knees had been sent over that afternoon by the shopkeeper of the fancier dress shop in the village. It wasn't plain linen but something softer, with ribbons gathered into tiny roses that were sewn around the neckline.

It seemed everyone was grateful to Avianna for saving the village from the pirates. Mattie had spread it around that Avianna traded places with her as captive so she could get onto the pirate ship and sabotage it. Now the villagers hailed her as a hero. Thanks to Avianna, the pirates hadn't had a chance to use their weapons against the castle or even to pillage the shops. No one had lost so much as a coin.

No one would listen when Avianna tried to set the record straight. She hadn't meant to sabotage the ship. And Thorn's role had been entirely forgotten—perhaps because there'd been no sign of him.

She'd been past the print shop a dozen times, and the door was locked every time. When she'd peered in the window, there'd been no activity inside, only the counter with its stacks of paper and the sunlight streaming into the back room. Where *was* he?

She'd been down to see the dock master to ask about Thorn,

but he didn't remember whose boat Thorn had gotten into. The dock master assured Avianna that no one had been lost in the fight. But what if Thorn had been invisible? What if he'd been hit with a cannonball without anyone seeing him and had sunk into the bay? Or what if he'd been responsible for the explosion that eventually sank the pirates' ship, and he hadn't gotten out in time?

When the pirate ship had sunk, the pirates had ended up floating in the bay, or halfway sinking in some cases, thanks to their heavy furs and the weapons hung all over their bodies. The army of villagers had pulled them from the water and disarmed them. They'd been taken to the castle. It was the first time since the king's demise that anyone had used the dungeon.

Avianna turned from the mirror. Going to a celebration was the last thing she felt like doing.

Corella burst in the doorway of their room. "Avi! Look who it is!"

Avianna's heart rose.

And then it sank when Elspeth walked in.

Elspeth! Elspeth was here! Of course Avianna was glad to see Elspeth. But she'd hoped for Thorn.

Elspeth took Avianna's hands and kissed her cheeks. Her brocade gown was like one they would have worn in the castle, except that it bulged out oddly in front.

"You're pregnant?" Avianna asked, her eyebrows shooting up even as her stomach flopped over. She'd been drinking bitter tea every morning, but there was still a chance that during her lapse she had gotten pregnant.

Elspeth nodded.

"I can't believe it. Five moons away and you're already in trouble."

"I'm not in trouble, silly. I'm bonded. We wanted to have a baby."

Avianna grimaced.

"You'll want one, too," Elspeth said, "as soon as you find the right person. Just wait."

Avianna doubted that. The thought of a baby to take care of filled her with dread—whether it arrived in nine moons or nine seasons hence.

"Besides," Elspeth said, and her voice changed. "It will be nice to have something to do. Someone to take care of." Did Elspeth's voice quaver on the final words?

"I'd think Drake was enough," Avianna said.

"It's different now."

"Different how?" Avianna tugged Elspeth to sit on the bed beside her. Corella sat silently beside them.

Elspeth plucked at the threads of her skirt. Her voice was quiet. "Drake's busy with the business all the time. He's even talking about sailing with the ships next spring."

Avianna studied Elspeth's downcast face, expecting tears to brim up in her eyes. All along, she had been envying Elspeth's new life, assuming she must be happy in her luxurious surroundings. "When did it change?"

"As soon as he found out about the baby. It's like I'm suddenly not fun anymore, I'm just a mother with a job to do. Like he put me on the shelf with his boxes of Esterian imports."

"You can still tumble him, you know."

"I know! I told him that, but he said he didn't want to hurt the baby. He doesn't know anything. I asked his mother to tell him—"

"You asked Miz Chapman to talk to Drake about sex?"

"More or less. I was desperate! But she said this is how it is once you're bonded. The fairy lights blink out and it's just day after day of normal life. But the baby will be nice."

The mention of fairy lights stirred the unease that had been growing in Avianna's chest since she'd noted Elspeth's despondency. Was it normal for things to change this way? Or was Drake's mother full of cow dung? Avianna tried to imagine Thorn tiring of her or expecting their roles to change once they were bonded. But Thorn wouldn't do that. He'd care about what made her happy.

Miz Chapman was full of dung. And so was Drake, it sounded like, but Avianna couldn't tell her friend that.

Avianna reached to stop Elspeth's nervous hand. "The baby will be wonderful," Avianna said. Not that she wanted one, but Elspeth seemed excited about it. "And I bet Drake will come around. Wait until he sees you holding his baby. You can bet he'll want to make more." Elspeth gave a weak smile.

"Anyway," Avianna continued, "you're here with me and Corella now. *We* know you can still enjoy a party."

"Girls!" Flo called up from the parlor.

Corella jumped up and moved to Avianna's side.

"Almost ready, Miss Flo!" Corella said. She reached for the comb and ran it lightly through Avianna's hair a few times, then began her braiding. "Rest, Elspeth. You must be tired carrying that bundle around. When did you arrive?"

"Just now. I came straight here."

"How did the news of the invasion reach you?"

Elspeth settled onto the bed, and excitement crept back into her voice. "We were having midmorning tea two days ago when Mark Owens came crashing through the gate on his horse."

"He always did," Avianna murmured, "and you always—"

Elspeth shot Avianna a disapproving glare and interrupted. "To hear him shouting, you'd have thought all of Sarland was at our shores. Drake was up in Nor Bay, but his mother and I went to the fort. Mostly it was dull, waiting there with everyone, and Mark didn't stay—"

"Pity," Avianna said.

"Stop it, Avi," Elspeth said. "I'm married to Drake now." She turned to Corella. "We waited and a day later, word came that it was all done, and when he said Avianna Blackburn had saved everyone, I had to come see you. I told Miz Chapman I was taking the carriage and she fussed and I did it anyway."

"Good for you."

"Avi's a hero," Corella said over her head. "The whole town adores her."

"How did you do it?" Elspeth asked.

"It wasn't just me!" Avianna said. "Thorn was there, too, but everyone seems to have forgotten about him."

"Who's Thorn?" Elspeth asked.

"Her beau," Corella said.

"He is not!"

"He wants to be."

"I'm not so sure anymore," Avianna said. "He hasn't been round in two days. I think he finally realized I wasn't worth his time."

"But who *is* he?" Elspeth asked.

"He's the village printer," Corella told her. "He's thin and wears spectacles. And he's a fairy."

"A fairy?" Elspeth burst into peals of laughter. "Avi, you're the last person I'd have expected. After Murkel?"

"I know, but Thorn's different, not like you'd expect. He's teaching the villagers to read."

Elspeth grew serious. "I'm not knocking him. You were just always so focused on, he had to have muscles, he had to have a nice backside. Not to mention being able to shoot things and sweep you into the air—"

"He does have muscles, it turns out," Avianna said, and Corella snorted.

"He always did," Corella said, "but you refused to see them." She turned her face to Elspeth. "Thorn's a hunk, and he's the absolute best person to dance with. The village girls practically fight over him, but he'll still ask the old folks to dance because he's so nice. And he's been trying to catch Avi's eye since before you even left." She pinned the end of the final braid to Avianna's head. Then she reached for the comb the hat-maker had sent over—with silk flowers sticking up from it—and pushed it down into Avianna's hair.

Avianna peered into the polished glass. The flowers poked off the top of her head like a weedy garden. She pulled the comb out.

"Will I meet him tonight?" Elspeth said. "I'm so excited for a dance!"

"I hope he'll be there," Avianna said. Surely he wouldn't miss the celebration.

"Well."

The three women turned to the doorway. Flo stood there in her best dress, her face a smear of pink gloss and rouge.

"Miss Flo! Are you going to the dance?" Avianna asked.

"It's not just a dance," Flo said, and she sniffed. "It's to celebrate our victory, and with you being one of my boarders, I could hardly not go."

"Plus Alistair will be there," Corella said, biting her lip and winking at Avianna.

"In that case," Avianna said, "You're next, Miss Flo. Sit." Avianna rose from her seat and moved to tug Flo into the room. Flo resisted, but Corella joined in. And truthfully, Flo didn't try very hard to resist.

Corella was pulling out Flo's hairpins before she was seated. "Let us doll you up. For Alistair."

"I *was* dolled up," Flo said.

Corella twisted Flo's tresses firmly into place, a sight better than the usual flyaway mess she went around with. Avianna reached for her kerchief and blotted half the paint off Flo's lips. When they finally finished with her, it was time for the dance.

Chapter 23

AVIANNA ENTERED THE GRANGE HALL with her head down, once again missing her Norlian crystals. Her neck felt exposed without them. It seemed she'd never get to dance with them.

As soon as she was inside, she surveyed the room, but she didn't see Thorn.

Alistair approached, his eyes glued to Flo. At least someone might get lucky tonight. Alistair tucked Flo's hand onto his arm and led her away. A few couples swirled around the dance floor, although the music hadn't started yet.

Corella was introducing Elspeth to Tanner, who'd materialized by her side. Apparently Avianna wasn't the only one who'd been busy during the pirate invasion. She scanned the room again for Thorn.

A small hand slid into hers.

"Hi Alfie."

"Hi Avi," Alfie said. He wasn't smiling.

"What's wrong?"

"I'm the only person who didn't get to see the pirates."

"You saw their ship, though, right?"

"No. Da dragged me off to the castle in the fog. We didn't even get to peek. And he left me there with the *children* and went off to fight without me. And they sank the ship before I could see it."

"He loves you, Alfie. He didn't want you to get hurt."

Alfie scuffed his shoe against the wooden floor. "It's *boring*. You were so lucky."

"I was *not* lucky. They could've killed me."

"They wouldn't kill you, Avi. You're too pretty."

"Let's not go there."

"Look, it's food," Alfie said, and dragged her away from the door.

Across the hall, tables stretched along one wall, filled with tureens of stew and plates of biscuits and sandwiches. An image flickered into Avianna's mind of the buffet tables in the forest, left after the fairy celebration, when she'd been there with Thorn.

"Alfie," Avianna said as they filled their plates with sandwiches. "Have you seen Thorn since the battle?"

"He was leaving," Alfie said, reaching for a dish of butter.

Her heart leapt. "You saw him?"

Alfie nodded. Avi's heart warred with itself. Thorn had survived the battle, if Alfie had seen him. But he was gone.

"Did he say where?"

"He didn't have bags or anything. He asked me to watch the shop while he's gone. Not that Finnegan lets me near it. I tried to see in the window, and he was hissing at me from the roof and chased me away."

"Thorn didn't say where?"

Alfie shrugged. "He probably went to his treehouse."

"You know about his treehouse?"

"He took me once after Ma died. He taught me to climb trees." Alfie bit into his sandwich. He tried to keep talking, but Avianna couldn't understand a word. She hushed him so he wouldn't choke. They took seats against the wall.

Avianna again scanned the room as she took a bite, though she knew it was futile. Thorn wasn't going to come to the celebration. Had he left the village because of her? Because she'd rejected him? But he knew the truth now. He knew she had feelings for him, and that she'd been lying to herself. But he didn't know that she was ready to admit it.

Now that no one's life was in danger, she had time to think

about things, and the more she considered the way she'd acted, the worse she felt. Every nice thing Thorn had done for her danced through her memory, night and day. And she'd never once reciprocated. He'd even helped her prepare for her date with Jeb Doolihan, for skies' sake! He'd risked his life with the pirates. He'd probably been ready to help her if it turned out she was pregnant. Everything Thorn had done had been to make her happy, and she had barely even thanked him, much less appreciated him.

She had to try to make it right. But Thorn was gone.

In a far corner, Beck sat scowling at the floor. From the distance, his face seemed lopsided, even without the pirates' gag in his mouth. Mattie stood beside him and stared at Avianna, her hip pressed into Beck's shoulder. Avianna swallowed her bite of sandwich and gave a small wave. Beside Mattie, Jeb Doolihan waved back. Beside Jeb, a smiling Samantha turned to see Avianna, and her smile faded.

What a mess, Avianna thought. She took another bite of her sandwich.

Mattie came over first.

She stopped with her feet apart, as if bracing herself to speak to Avianna.

Avianna tried to finish chewing without being obvious and gave a hard swallow. At her elbow, Alfie swung his feet and made a carrot stick walk around the edge of his plate.

"Thank you for what you did," Mattie said. Avianna guessed it pained Mattie to say it. Mattie couldn't quite make eye contact.

"Anyone would have. I could hardly leave you to the pirates," Avianna said.

"No, anyone would not have. I'm sorry we were mean to you."

"I wasn't very nice either."

"I shouldn't have lied about your tea though. That was low."

"You lied?"

"We didn't really change it on you."

Relief swept through Avianna.

Mattie continued. "Samantha was so worried you were going to steal Jeb."

"I shouldn't have tried. I knew she liked him."

Silence filled the space between them.

"I met your ma and da," Mattie said at last.

"I guess they told you I'm not from a manor then."

"No, they just talked on and on about how accomplished you are."

"They did?"

"They're so proud of you, running away to make a better life."

"They *are*?" Her mother had said they didn't blame her, but Avianna hadn't expected them to brag about her.

"Corella told them what a success you'd been at court, and they kept saying, 'That's our girl.'"

"That's all over now. There's no more court, and no more success." Avianna picked at a crumb on her skirt.

"I never considered what it must've been like for you to lose your whole life all at once."

Avianna didn't know how to reply for a moment. "Why do you live at Flo's?" she asked at last. "Aren't you from Woodglen?" It had never occurred to Avianna before, but being a village girl, Mattie should have a home and family to live with.

"My family's in Knotty Knob. I left them."

"You left them?"

"I wanted something better. I guess we have something in common after all."

"Were they that bad?"

"My da was a drunk and Ma wasn't much better. I hid my coins until I had enough for the carriage to Woodglen. I thought I'd get work at the castle. But they never wanted me."

"Not getting a place at the castle might've been a lucky thing. The king was a bastard."

"Maybe. I was so jealous, and angry, when you and Corella

showed up. Moping about having to work for the rent, when you had it good for so long. But it must've been hard to lose."

"Hard to lose what?" Jeb came up beside Mattie.

"Nothing," Mattie said and stepped away.

"Hi, Avianna," Jeb said. He had a new vest on, plushier than the last one. His forehead was shiny. Alfie stopped his game and stared up at Jeb, eyes squinting with his mouth open. Maybe he was remembering Jeb shouting at him from his carriage.

Avianna could only imagine what the boy must think of Jeb's frippery. She hurried to speak before Alfie blurted out something inappropriate.

"Hi, Jeb." She considered asking if he'd made it home safely after their date but decided not to ridicule him.

"I hoped to have a dance, when you're ready," Jeb said.

"Jeb," Avianna said, pausing to consider her words. It had been a long time since she'd had to do this. And she needed to do it in a way that wouldn't leave him hanging on. "I don't think it's going to work between us. All the adventure of the last few days, it's made me realize. I want a quiet life, not the whirlwind romance we had. My feelings for you are gone."

Jeb stood mute.

"Look," Avianna said. "Samantha is all alone over there."

Jeb glanced over his shoulder. How could she get Jeb back with Samantha?

Jealousy, that's how.

Avianna wet her lips and lowered her voice. "Mattie said Samantha's thinking of visiting Woods Rest to see a carpenter she met at the castle during the invasion. Apparently they hit it off and he invited her to stay at his lodge in the woods."

Jeb turned back to Avianna with his eyes widened.

"I'd hate her to go," Avianna said. "We'd miss her here in Woodglen. You always liked her, didn't you? I bet if you fought for her, she'd change her mind."

Jeb looked again at Samantha. Avianna watched too, willing Samantha not to stare back with her usual lovelorn expression. At the perfect moment, one of the other fellows in the hall stopped to ask Samantha to dance, and, at least on the outside, she burst into a smile. Her partner led her to the dance floor.

"I'll have to get the next one," Jeb said.

"You'd better."

"Thanks, Avianna." Jeb hurried away.

"Blast it," Avianna muttered. "Thank the stars that's over."

"Who was that dolt?" Alfie asked.

"Jeb Doolihan."

"Jeb DOO-lihan?" Alfie asked, snickering.

"Don't you start."

"His name's DOO!" Alfie roared with laughter. "Doo-doo-li-han! POO-lihan!" He continued rattling off crude names between laughs. Avianna smiled at him and leaned back in her chair to watch the dancers.

"Would you care to dance?"

This time, Avianna focused up at a stranger. He was about her age and had neat dark hair and rather piercing eyes. In her lap, her plate was empty. She didn't have an excuse to say no.

"Okay," she said, offering her hand.

She forgot his name immediately after he shared it. Of course, he knew hers. Everyone did now. And no one shied away from her—whether or not they believed she carried a deadly merfolk sex disease.

She tried to enjoy dancing with the first man, and with the next man who asked, and the next. Everyone wanted to dance with her, and this time all the young men asked her. And they wanted to talk with her when the musicians took a break and hear about how she'd defeated the pirates and bring her a cup of punch or a mug of ale. They asked to call on her at Flo's, and one bold young man even gave her a trinket from the village pottery.

All the doting attention—it was exactly what she'd always wanted.

And she was miserable.

Chapter 24

A WEEK PASSED AND THORN DIDN'T return.

Avianna had been down every street in Woodglen. Twice. In addition to her search for Thorn, she and Corella had begun doing Flo's errands all over the village, now that Mattie had moved in with Beck.

On one hand, she enjoyed seeing the village. She had never scrutinized every bit of it as thoroughly as she had the past week. She'd stopped into every shop to ask if anyone had seen Thorn—and been given sweets, and another new pair of shoes to replace the ones she'd lost in the bay, and a shawl for the winter. She'd been over to the castle, past the cottages with their pens full of pecking chickens and the fall gardens. How many times had she passed by the cottages without a glance? She'd always thought them rundown and sad, but now they appeared homey.

And down the hill, nearer where she lived, she now noticed the decorative stonework adorning the buildings—buildings she'd always considered ugly compared to the splendor of the castle. But someone had built them with pride, and the stonework had remained as a symbol of that pride even through the dark days of the king's reign.

On the other hand, Avianna had seen no sign of Thorn. She'd asked after him everywhere. Even at the hemp mill on the far edge of the village, and the paper maker's workshop. He truly had gone, and he hadn't come back. But then, she'd known that. She just kept hoping something would change.

What if he never returned?

Avianna remembered her mother's parting words, again telling her she had to try to reach Thorn. She had to try to fix the relationship she'd damaged, even if attempting it was completely humiliating. And to try to fix it, she had to find Thorn. Even if it meant going into the forest after him.

Now she stood staring at a pair of spectacles in the window of the general store. Thorn had lost his specs to the pirates, just as she'd lost her crystals and her shoes. But everyone in the village had been helping her—new shoes, a new dress, and Flo telling her not to worry about this moon's rent. Had anyone thought to help Thorn?

She could buy the spectacles. Her heart beat faster at the idea. It was perfect. She'd buy them and bring them to Thorn. It was the perfect excuse to hunt him down and talk to him. She knew the secret fairy path—never mind lighting the lights, she'd find her way to him. There had to be a way.

Only she still had no coins. Even without her debts, the specs would take another two moons to save for. Why had she refused when her mother offered her some funds, before her parents headed back to South End?

She turned to face the bay, the chill breeze whipping her hair around her face, and pulled her shawl snug about her ears. Her Sarlian fur coat was warm at least. The fishing boats were heading in. Soon the docks would be swarming with the fish-catchers. The dock master wheeled a barrow down to the end, preparing to receive the day's catch.

Avianna put aside her doubts and marched down onto the docks.

"Miss Blackburn," he greeted her.

"Hello, sir."

"Did you find your young man?"

"No, but Alfie saw him so I know he made it back from the fight. But that's not why I'm here. Or not exactly."

"Oh? How may I help you?"

"I wondered if you might need an assistant."

"An assistant?"

"To help you manage. I've seen you taking tallies. I know my numbers and letters, and I'm working on writing them." Never mind how she'd continue without Thorn's help.

The dock master squinted at her. "As it turns out, the missus has been needing to stay in lately, and the work's been a bit more than I like. Do you know your knots?"

"My knots?"

"You do needlework, right?"

"Yes."

"Same thing but with rope. Get Alistair to show you."

"Yes, sir."

"I'd say it's a tough crowd here on the docks, but I've seen you in action. I think you can hold your own."

"Thank you."

"Tomorrow's our day of rest, but come the day after. A little earlier than this. You can help me get ready for the boats."

"Thank you." Avianna squirmed. "There's one other thing." She twisted her hands together. "I wondered if you might advance me some pay."

He raised his eyebrows.

"Just enough to buy those specs at the general store. It's just, the pirates took Thorn's when they captured him, and when we escaped the ship, they got left behind, and now the ship's sunk. He can barely see without them.

"Everyone's been giving me gifts, only my laundry job barely covers my room and board so I have no savings, and I lost my beads so I don't have anything I can pawn. And I wanted to get the specs for Thorn."

The dock master considered her, his lips pressed tight. Then he glanced out at the bay, where the boats were almost in to the harbor. "Come with me," he said, and he set off up the docks.

Ten minutes later, Avianna and the dock master left the general store. She clutched the package that held the specs—a pair for seeing into the distance, purchased on credit. "See you in two days," the dock master said, and he ambled off to the docks, where the boats were arriving.

Avianna walked back toward the boarding house. When she reached the turn, she stopped. If she went back, she'd have dinner, and she'd lose her courage and put off her task for another day, and who knew what tomorrow would bring. There could be a fall storm, or more pirates, or a merfolk invasion, or a dragon could reduce the whole village to ashes. She shouldn't wait any longer.

She stowed the specs into her satchel, fastened her coat, and headed up the hill to the woods.

Two hours later, the sun was getting low as Avianna picked her way along the edge of the forest. She scanned the brambles for her red hair ribbon, praying to the skies it would still be there over a week after she'd left it, that no squirrel had picked it off to weave into its winter nest.

Not that it would help her much to find the start of the path if she couldn't manage to see the lights. The sun was leaving, but she forged ahead. Her plan was flawed, but an urgency impelled her to keep moving ahead.

A farmer trundled past on the road, coming from the forest with his wheelbarrow filled with acorns, maybe for his hogs for the winter.

Avianna was sure she had missed the spot, but she kept going, unsure how far the horse had carried her and Thorn the night they had come this way. Each time she thought of turning back, another thick trunk appeared ahead. One last tree, she told herself yet again. And finally, there was her ribbon, fluttering on the branch where she had tied it.

Step one accomplished.

Standing at the base of the tree, she searched for the lantern overhead. It would be hard to find when unlit, but if she could find it, and move to the next tree in and find the next lantern, and the next, she could follow the path to Thorn. She tried not to think about how it would be once she was in the forest with all the rustling noises and branches grasping at her, not to mention the nearing darkness.

But she couldn't find the lamp at all. Around her, the sunlight was fading. As the twilight deepened, it would be even harder to see. It was hopeless.

Avianna leaned on the tree trunk. She closed her eyes. There was something comforting about the solid trunk beside her.

Could the tree hear her? She put her arms around its scratchy bark and inhaled slowly. "Please," she whispered as she exhaled. "Please light the lamps for me. I need to get to the fairies." She kept holding the tree, scared to open her eyes and see that she had failed. She took another deep breath and let it out and opened her eyes.

The lamp was shining in the branches.

"Thank you," Avianna whispered, leaning her forehead on the tree one more time.

She stepped into the forest. The next lantern lit as it had the last time. Avianna glanced around, through the thick trees and back at the light and space out by the road. Darkness was already falling under the trees. She listened but the woods were quiet. She had to do this. Just a few hours, and her journey would be over.

Unless Thorn rejected her and she had to walk back out.

She stepped toward the lamp and the next one began to glow. As she walked on, the lamps lit, and after a while the space outside the lamps' circles of light was dark as pitch. She didn't peer into it—if something was watching her, she didn't want to know. Keep walking, she told herself, never letting herself give in to the hints of fear at the edges of her mind. Hopefully the lamps wouldn't suddenly stop working and leave her in the dark.

She focused on the path as the minutes ticked past, counting the lamps as she passed them. If only she had counted them last time, she would know how far she had to go. Cold seeped up through the soles of her shoes, and the musty smell of autumn filled the air. She snuggled into her coat and kept walking.

Her eyes adjusted to the dim lighting. The forest was silent. Maybe the animals had gone to sleep for the winter. She glanced over her shoulder once and started at a light shining far off behind her. Had she followed the wrong path? The light was golden and bright, not like the glow of the fairy lamps. She stopped for a moment.

It was the moon.

Relief filled her. She turned back to the path and continued, knowing the full moon was rising behind her, helping light her way to her destination.

The moon was high in the sky when Avianna suspected she heard voices from the branches. She peered all around and overhead but only dark leaves filled the night. Another lamp lit ahead of her and she continued toward it. And then she came to the place where the lamps spread out and they were all shining, and the track widened. She was almost there.

She'd been focused on getting through the trees without getting lost, and not allowing herself to fear the forest at night. Now her task returned to mind. She had to face Thorn. What if he didn't want to see her? What if he wasn't even here?

He was going to be here. She had the spectacles tucked in her satchel. If he didn't want to see her, she could still deliver them and leave.

Music beat through the trees, and it grew louder as she followed the path toward the clearing. Lights shone as she neared, brighter than they'd been last time, and a crowd of figures moved back and forth in the space. They were dancing! Thorn had said that the fairies danced each full moon. Avianna neared the clearing and ducked beside a tree, peering out. She scanned the dancers in the clearing, hoping for Thorn among them but also relieved each time a dancer wasn't him.

The dance was chaos, not like the neat dances of the villagers. No wonder Thorn had laughed when she'd described the dance at the grange hall as heathen. Here, the music raced twice as fast as at the village dance. And not everyone danced the same pattern. While most couples circled or spun, some others improvised, dipping one another or performing flips like acrobats. All of the dancers were barefoot. And mostly, the dance seemed to have no pattern at all.

And yet the dancers all knew exactly where to go. As Avianna watched, she began to see there was actually a pattern with the dancers moving in lines down the clearing. They were so graceful and moved fluidly. And Thorn danced here—dancing with her must have been awkward by comparison. What had Thorn seen in her? Why would he want her back, when there were all these fairy women? Was that why he'd returned here?

She wanted to keep watching, but she'd searched each dance line and not found Thorn, and she couldn't put off seeing him all night. The sooner she got this done with, the better.

She crept around the edge of the clearing, hoping no one would spot her, until she reached the storage huts and made her way back into the woods. From there, she remembered the way to Thorn's treehouse.

As she neared the base of the tree, she recognized the trunk with the flat rock. Relief flooded her—the ladder hung down. Overhead, lights shone in the branches. She listened but all was quiet overhead.

She looped her satchel across her chest and began to climb, her heart pounding. What would she say to him? Don't think about it, she told herself. Hopefully the right words would come. She'd give him the spectacles and apologize and see what happened.

After half a minute, she paused in the branches at the side of the tree to look up. The platform neared overhead, with the opening in the boards that the ladder passed through. She resumed climbing and was a few hands away when someone spoke above her.

"Stop. I'm fine."

It was Thorn.

"You're not fine. I should have come to get you a long time ago."

A woman. Thorn was with someone else.

Avianna froze, hanging on the ladder and waiting.

"Who was this person?" the woman asked, and Avianna knew the woman meant her.

"Just a girl," Thorn said.

"A human girl." The scorn was evident.

"Don't say it like that. You're so prejudiced."

"She didn't treat you right, though, did she? Not like you deserve."

"It wasn't her fault."

"That's my Hawthorn. Always defending the humans."

"Feel free to leave at any time."

A sigh. "You know I'll never leave you, love."

Avianna felt sick. She clung to the ladder, scared to move and give herself away. Who was Thorn with?

She had to get out of here. She lowered herself down a rung, then another. If they saw the ladder moving and investigated, they'd find her clinging to it and she'd be mortified. The voices resumed but she couldn't make out the words as she moved down. Finally her foot hit the ground.

Avianna fled back up the path, blinking back tears. She'd missed her chance. She'd lost Thorn. He was back with someone else—had he ever even left his fairy girlfriend? Had he truly loved Avianna? He'd said he did, and it had certainly seemed that way when they'd spent the night together. Avianna circled the clearing but with the tears swimming in her eyes, she didn't see the dancers. She hurried to the path homeward.

The lamps were out.

No one was in sight who could help her. She placed her arms around the trunk of the tree with the first lamp and closed her eyes.

"Please help me," she said. "I want to go home. Please light the lamp." She opened her eyes, but the branches overhead were dark. She tried again. Still nothing.

"It doesn't work that way."

Avianna let go of the tree, ashamed at being caught. A fairy stood in the path, her figure glowing slightly in the darkness. She must have had something like the solar lamps hidden about her robe, to give off the glow. She leaned on a staff, but her stance was regal.

Avianna sniffed and wiped her eyes again. "It worked on the way in," she said.

"Maybe you wanted to get in more than you want to get out."

"No, I want to leave." One thought of the voices she'd heard at Thorn's made Avianna's heart sink all over again.

"Did you get what you came for, then?" The fairy tilted her head to one side, and her eyes stared into Avianna's. Avianna couldn't turn away.

She'd come to face Thorn and to tell him she was sorry. And she hadn't done either. Maybe he didn't want her anymore, but she could still apologize—for overlooking him for so long and for refusing to believe her feelings when she felt something more than friendship for him, and for accusing him of placing her under a spell.

Instead of trying her utmost to speak to Thorn, she'd run away.

That was her life, always running away, always avoiding things. She'd had so many chances to find someone at the castle, and she'd kept postponing making a commitment. Then she'd gotten involved with the princes, who'd never be free to court her. And she'd wasted time with Beck, who'd never had any interest in sharing a life with her, and fooled around with Rye and the others, always pursuing her faded, unrealistic ideals.

But those past events paled in comparison with the latest. She'd run from Thorn because he didn't fit into the picture she'd painted for herself, a picture so cracked and chipped at the edges that it depicted a life that was a hollow fantasy. Her world was built on expectations without any solid foundation beneath them.

What if she started over? What if she had a blank page—what would she write on it?

She'd have a decent job, for one thing. She wouldn't place all her hopes on a wealthy partner, and she wouldn't expect to have new dresses constantly or fine food all the time. But she'd make enough to pay for room and board and still be able to treat herself every once in a while. And she wouldn't resent the work, thinking she deserved more than the villagers simply because she'd once lived in the castle.

But mostly she'd write in Thorn. On every page. He wasn't the macho hero she'd thought she needed. He didn't have stockpiles of gold or live in a manor or even a glorified cottage. But his home was filled with love. When she was with him, she knew he cherished her. He respected her and made her smile. He had come after her time and again, when she'd ignored him and pursued her outdated fantasies and been too self-centered to see what was obvious—too self-centered to believe it, even when she did see that she was falling in love with him.

This time she would be the one to go after him.

The fairy hadn't moved a smidge. When Avianna surfaced from her thoughts, the fairy said, "I'll light the lamps for you if you want to go."

Avianna shook her head. "No. I'm not going to run away again."

Chapter 25

THORN WAS STILL TALKING TO the woman on the treehouse patio. This time Avianna knocked on the platform over her head. The voices ceased.

"Hello?" Thorn called.

Avianna steadied herself for a moment in the brisk night air before climbing through the opening.

"Avi!" Thorn was on his feet and by her side in an instant, but he stopped short of giving her a hand off the ladder.

She clambered off the ladder and turned toward him, drinking in the sight of him. Different, without his spectacles on, but still Thorn. Someone had finished cutting his hair.

She couldn't stop her gaze from flitting past him to see his companion, who sat in one of the oddly sloping chairs. Even in the low light, Avianna could tell she was beautiful, with hair the color of Thorn's, cropped above her shoulders. She wore a flowing dress illuminated by the light of the moon, which had ascended high enough to beam down from overhead.

Avianna risked another glance up at Thorn. Without his spectacles, his emerald eyes were luminous and made her breath catch, but she missed him with the specs on—the familiar Thorn from the village. He wore a fairy tunic and britches with suspenders, and he looked marvelous.

"How did you get here?" he asked.

"Through the forest."

"Could you see? Were the lamps on?"

"I asked the trees and they obliged."

Thorn almost smiled.

Avianna fumbled as she reached into her satchel.

"You see, I needed to bring you these," she said, and held out the package.

Thorn opened the paper. He considered the specs in silence for a few heartbeats, and his lips parted but he didn't speak. He lifted them carefully and examined them, then opened the sidebars and positioned them on his nose. He peered around and smiled for real.

"Thank you. I was missing them."

Avianna looked past Thorn to the other woman, still reclining in her chair and watching them with a shrewd glare. It was too strange ignoring her. "Hello, I'm Avianna," she said.

The woman stood without smiling. "I'm Hazel. Since you've arrived, I'll go to the dance." She touched Thorn's arm possessively as she passed him. Avianna stepped closer to Thorn to let Hazel reach the ladder. All her muscles relaxed with relief once the other woman had climbed out of sight.

The music and laughter of the clearing rang through the dark forest, muted with distance. The night felt suddenly crisper and colder. Avianna would have been chilled through without her Sarlian fur coat. She hugged it around her.

"I can't believe you're wearing that thing," Thorn said, shaking his head, but his voice was soft.

"It's my pirate spoils of war," Avianna said. "Besides, it's warmer than anything else I own."

"Will you take it off if I invite you inside?"

She nodded. "Aren't you cold?" she asked as he moved toward the cottage door.

Thorn shook his head. "Fairies sew little chips into their winter garments—like the lamps that store sunlight, but these radiate heat. They'd not been used for a generation, but someone found them and brought them out this autumn—now that we're living outside again." Avianna followed him inside and shut the door. She unclasped the coat and slipped it off as he stoked the embers in the stove into a fire.

"Did Hazel cut the other side of your hair?"

"Yes. She usually cuts it for me but I hadn't seen her in a while."

Avianna tried to stay calm. But after everything she'd believed Thorn felt for her, had she been merely a fling? It was better to know the truth. "You certainly moved on fast," she said.

"Moved on from what?"

"From us."

He paused by the fire to regard her. "There's an 'us'?"

"I thought an 'us' is what you wanted."

He swallowed. "But you don't," he said quietly.

"I was wrong. I was so wrong. I know I messed up, but I thought I could fix it if I came here and talked to you. But then you're already with someone else." Avianna was struggling to keep her voice from sounding like a petulant child's.

"With my mother?"

"Your mother?"

"She's been cutting my hair since I was a kid," he said, turning back to the fire. "In fact, no one else had ever cut it until you did."

"Hazel is your mother?"

"Yes, I promise. Would you like me to swear it?"

Now Avianna felt worse than ever. "She's so young, it doesn't seem like she's old enough to be your mother."

"She's a fairy, remember? That's how we look."

"I haven't met many fairies. And none of them were ever old. Or maybe they were and I didn't know it." Avianna couldn't tell what Thorn was thinking. Was he going to give her another chance? She reached for her beads, but they were gone.

Thorn didn't respond.

"She hates me," Avianna mumbled.

"She isn't too keen on you, not after I told her about how terribly you treated me, but she'll come around. Assuming you stop crushing my heart into the dirt with your fancy new shoes."

"Oh Thorn, I'm sorry, I—"

"I'm teasing you, Avi. I'll stop."

"But I did—I was horrible to you! And I came here hoping to fix it and instead I accuse you of flirting with your mother. I'm a disaster."

"Stop," he said gently.

"Can you forgive me for thinking you'd use a love spell on me?"

Kneeling by the stove, with the firelight flickering on his face, he nodded.

"I don't understand what you see in me. I've been so pig-headed and selfish."

"That's not what I see," he said, but he didn't go on. He stood from tending the fire. "Thanks for the new spectacles."

"You're welcome."

"How did you manage them? I hope you didn't pillage the castle, given your extensive knowledge of the location of the treasure."

He was teasing her, like always. Avianna relaxed a smidgen. "The dock master gave me a job as his assistant. And he asked the general store to give them to me on credit."

"Well thank you."

Silence stretched between them. If only he'd sweep her into his arms and start kissing her, things would be much easier. Where had all their attraction gone? This was so awkward.

But she wasn't going to run away. Thorn wasn't the sweep-her-into-his-arms-and-solve-everything-with-sex type. And where had that ever gotten her, anyway?

"The spectacles were the least I could do," Avianna said. "I made a lot of mistakes, Thorn, and I'm so sorry. I have a lot to apologize for. I know I need to trust you."

"You haven't had a lot of people you could trust in your life, from what you've said. I know it's hard to do after people have let you down time and again."

"You've never let me down."

"I hope I never will. Will you try to trust me?"

She nodded.

"Just talk to me when you have doubts. I'll be honest with you."

"I'll try."

More silence.

"Have you eaten?" Thorn asked.

"I'm not hungry."

"How was the party in the village last week?"

Avianna shrugged. "The best part was talking with Alfie. And I made up with Mattie, more or less. Turns out they didn't change the tea—they were lying."

"That's a relief."

"And Elspeth came. I wish you could've met her. She's been gone only five moons and Drake's knocked her up already."

Thorn smiled. "Maybe I can still meet her."

"You should have been there, Thorn. They're all thanking me for saving them, when it was you! I try to remind them but they keep giving me things, like the shoes."

"You did lose your shoes in the bay after blowing a hole in the pirate ship."

"You lost your specs and no one gifted you a new pair."

"You did."

"That's not what I mean. You deserved the celebration."

"Well, why don't we go to the celebration here in place of it?"

Avianna started to protest. That dance had looked terrifying. But it was what Thorn wanted. Besides, anything was better than their stilted conversation.

"Okay. I'll have to wear the pirate coat, though, or I'll freeze."

"Can I lend you something else? You'll heat up far too much in that coat once you start dancing. Besides, it's trimmed with animal fur. We don't need to give my mother another reason to dislike you."

"Okay."

Thorn disappeared into the back room.

This dance will be okay, Avianna told herself. She could handle attending the dance if that was what Thorn wanted, even if she made a fool of herself.

He emerged with another tunic like the one he wore, loose enough to wear over her dress. Thorn helped Avianna slip it over her head, and the thought flashed in her mind that she hoped he'd be slipping it off her later that evening, but she banished the idea. She was focusing on Thorn and what he needed, instead of being the one always doing the taking.

The tunic had shiny, flat chips sewn around the border as a court gown might have jewels. Avianna fingered one as Thorn moved to the door. These must be the solar chips he had mentioned. Outside, the dark chips radiated a faint heat, just enough to keep the cold at bay.

Thorn moved to the ladder. His feet were bare, like those of the dancers.

"Should I leave my shoes?"

He considered. "You'd better wear them. Your feet wouldn't last long dancing without them." Maybe someday she'd dance barefoot, too. The fact that she looked forward to such a thing made her giggle. She imagined Jeb Doolihan's outrage—barefoot dancers!—and let herself laugh as Thorn disappeared down the ladder. She waited for Thorn to descend and followed him. This time, Thorn extended a hand to help her climb off.

"Is the celebration special for the harvest?" she asked as they set off under the lamps on the forest path.

"No, it's the regular dance. On the night the full moon rises."

"The village dance is every moon, too."

"Yes, but they follow the work schedule. The fairies still plan around the actual moon."

They both looked up to find the moon, smiling down on them with a golden-white light. The sounds of revelry were growing louder.

They came to the clearing filled with the wild fairy dancers. Only this time, Avianna couldn't hide behind a tree. Something panicked inside her. She reached for Thorn's hand. "I can't go out there alone. I don't know the dances. If someone asks me, what'll I do?"

He squeezed her hand. "You're not alone, silly. I'm going with you. But if someone asked you, they'd help you follow along."

He led her toward the end of one row, such as it was with the dancers spinning in and out. "Besides," he added, "here the music never breaks. If you want, you keep going with the same partner."

"If it never ends, how do we join?" she asked.

"Like this." He tugged on her hand, and the last dancers in the row were welcoming them. She gave her hand and was pulled in.

Without ever having learned the steps, she wove in and out, guided by the other dancers until she remembered the pattern herself. Slowly she and Thorn moved down the line together, meeting one couple after another. And over and over, the dance gave her back to Thorn, who took her in his arms and spun her before sending her on to the next step. Each time she found herself facing him, her heart gave a small leap of excitement.

The music shifted, and the dancers responded, following a new pattern. Avianna stepped the wrong way, and someone reached to pull her back and turn her right, and then Thorn was with her again. She didn't care if the steps changed, as long as the moments with Thorn didn't end.

At last, the dance spun them out at the far end of the line. Avianna laughed at having made it. While she'd danced, all her worries about her future and her shame over her past had cleared away. There'd been only the music and the guiding hands of the dancers and Thorn waiting to meet her, every time. This was what she wanted her life to be. Work would be the music, and friends and mentors beside her, and coming home to Thorn every night.

Chapter 26

THE DANCE WENT ON AND on, and Thorn never suggested they find other partners.

At first Avianna had been breathless just following the steps and keeping up. But then she got the hang of the dancing. When she didn't have to focus as hard, she became aware of Thorn. How she moved into the heat around him each time they spun together, and how he gazed into her eyes but never pushed himself into her space. Always waiting on her. The next time she met him, she moved closer, and his hand on her back followed her lead, pulling her in. Her heart sped up.

Once she would have blamed a love spell. Now she knew better.

Between her mounting attraction to Thorn and her sore feet rubbing in her shoes, she needed to stop dancing. The fairies must have gone about barefoot often, leaving their soles callused to dance on the ground, stomping and sliding with ease.

She met Thorn again, their bodies moving in closer together, until their spin was so entwined that they were like one person. How were their legs not tangling? When he spun her away, departing from his arms left an empty place inside her. She didn't want to stop touching him. But she couldn't interrupt the dance to drag Thorn into the bushes to tumble him. If she stopped following the pattern, she'd create a rift in the line and throw all the dancers off.

Did Thorn feel it too?

She came to him again. He didn't take his eyes off hers. Their lips were a hand's width apart. Her breathing came out in pants with the effort of dancing. Or with something else.

Only three more turns to go until the end of the line. His lips came closer to hers, and his leg was between hers as they spun. Before he released her, his leg slid up and rubbed against her, sending sparks through her center. She stumbled through the rest of the pattern, and when she next returned to him, he was grinning at her.

Avianna lost count of the turns. And then she met Thorn and instead of continuing with the dance, he wrapped her around him, and their spin slowed as their lips came together.

Her hands slid around him to pull him closer, and his hands on her back held her tight as his kisses deepened. His kisses were intoxicating. The music became a buzz in her ears, and distantly she heard laughter, and gentle hands pushed her and Thorn away from the line of dancers. They stumbled together and found their footing and kept kissing.

Thorn's touch aroused her, but it was his love that undid her. She could feel it emanating around her, how much he still cared for her in spite of everything she'd done wrong. Her heart welled up and she broke their kiss and buried her face in his shoulder, clinging tightly to him. He crushed her against him until she almost couldn't breathe and pressed his lips to the top of her head.

I love you, she wanted to say. But the nearness of the crowd and the sounds of the dance returned to her. He wouldn't hear her words unless she shouted them, so she pulled him tighter.

He waited until she let go. She wiped at the tears standing in her eyes as Thorn hovered close, watching her.

"Can we go home?" she asked.

He slipped his arm around her and led her straight into the trees. After a short way through the bushes, they emerged on a path.

The sounds of the revelry followed them as they silently walked back to Thorn's treehouse. In the moonlight, she climbed up the ladder ahead of him and let herself into the cottage. The door clicked shut and Thorn was behind her. He rested his hands on her shoulders and leaned in to kiss the back of her neck, the way she'd imagined him doing it the night he'd made her dinner over the shop.

Avianna turned to face Thorn. It was obvious what was about to happen, but he didn't move. He was always going to wait on her. He wasn't going to toss her onto his bed and have his way without being sure she wanted it. She stepped toward him, her hands latching onto the front of his tunic, and she stood up on her toes to reach his lips with hers.

The kiss started gently and moved in concert with his hands, which were caressing her sides so it felt like her whole body was being kissed. She pressed harder, and he pushed back. He gathered her locks to one side and kissed her neck behind her ear, and flames licked up from the fire simmering within her. Her fingers curled and dug into his back and her legs were trying to climb him. He murmured in her ear, "I'll have to remember this spot," before kissing it again, harder, while his lower hand reached under her bottom and pulled her up off the floor. Her legs went around him to hold herself against him. He carried her into his bedroom.

He lowered her onto the bed and went down on his knees before her, his hands lightly on her hips. All above them, the twinkling lights began to glow. Avianna lifted her arms over her head and raised her eyebrows at Thorn. He grinned and shook his head, but reached to take the hem of her tunic and draw it up and off her. She tugged on his tunic, and in one swift motion he had that off as well. She pushed his suspenders off his shoulders and peeled up his undershirt, until he kneeled before her wearing only his britches. She longed to touch him, but she drew back her hand.

Her fingers trembled slightly as she undid the ribbons at the front of her dress. Thorn waited, watching her face. When she met his eyes, she flushed hot at his expression, the way his eyes had flames dancing in them. The fabric came loose across her chest. She lowered her hands.

"You still have your specs on," she said.

"I don't want to miss seeing any of you."

"They're brand new. I don't want to break them when I drag you onto the bed." She reached out and he took them off and handed them to her. "You'll just have to get close enough to see me."

"Can I?"

"Yes." She leaned back and twisted to place the spectacles on the windowsill, and suddenly his arms surrounded her and his body pinned her to the bed, heat searing along her back. Her body responded, but he had her trapped tightly enough that she couldn't turn. His lips found the spot behind her ear, tightening everything inside her as he kissed her skin. As he flattened her into the mattress, his hand caressed her shoulder and moved to her front.

"Is this okay?" he whispered.

"I promise I'll tell you if it's not."

Her loosened dress had slipped down so that only the fabric of her shift covered her breast when his hand found it. He squeezed and began kissing her neck as he stroked her. His other arm held her across the front of her shoulders. He pulled her dress and shift down together to expose her belly. Then he smoothed his way back up her body, gentle now, caressing her skin. Each time his fingertips touched her, she strained against his body, her reason lost to his touch. But she couldn't budge.

Then his hand moved back down.

He hesitated a moment, and then his fingers smoothed down through the small curls below her navel and came to rest between her legs. He gently hooked them against her and pressed. Avianna's fists clutched the bed cover and she moaned.

His cheek was against her neck as his fingers began rubbing her in circles. His body pressed against her, and through the bunched-up fabric of her dress, he was hard against her bottom. His fingers never stopped as the pressure built inside her. They just pushed, little by little getting harder and faster, until the moment neared.

He kept right on as she spasmed in his arms. He held her fast, continuing to rub her as her body jerked out of control, until every last ounce of her tension had been released.

Still he wouldn't let go of her, but held her from behind, his face pressed into her. "I love you, Avianna Blackburn," he murmured to the back of her ear.

"Then let me love you back," she said, pushing against his hold until he let her twist around in his arms. She gazed up at him. Their lips were only a breath apart. "Let me take you inside," she said. "You want that, don't you?"

"Stars, yes."

She reached down to push her bunched-up dress off her bottom, and kicked it from her legs. Thorn gave her space to do it, bracing himself over her. She reached for the fastenings on his britches and unbuttoned them. She lifted her knees, hooked her toes into the top of the trousers, and pushed them down his body.

Her gaze turned back to Thorn's.

"You're really proficient at this," Thorn said. "I hope I don't disappoint you."

"Thorn, you could never." She lifted her knees again and squeezed his body between them and pulled him down on top of her.

Anyone else would've rushed to the finish, but not Thorn. He started all over with kissing her, running his hands over her body. He rubbed himself against her, down between her legs, until her want of him returned. She whimpered and pulled on his waist, and he broke off kissing and smiled down at her, and he might have had tears in his eyes but then he was sliding himself inside her and she stopped noticing anything but how wonderful he felt.

He was being so careful. She reached her fingers to touch his cheek.

"You don't need a love spell," she whispered. "You're perfect."

Then she pressed herself against him and away, and he began to meet her thrusts with his own. His arms framed her head, his forehead dipping to touch hers. She dug her fingers into his back as his breathing grew heavy. She watched his face above her, adoring the pleasure etched there as his control slipped and he moved harder. She waited on him as he lost himself in it, driving into her again and again. When he cried out, spilling heat inside her, she gasped with the beauty of it—of how much joy she could give.

Three moons later

AVIANNA STALKED UP THE DOCKS, ignoring the handful of men who still catcalled her. Most of the fish-catchers politely asked after her health and gave her their tallies, but a few of the men couldn't seem to get over having a young woman in charge to give the dock master a day of rest. She wished they'd get over it already.

"Avi!"

She turned at the call and scanned the wharf as the winter wind skimmed over her face. Alfie stood on the edge, waving frantically. She hurried in his direction and up the ramp. He met her at the top, shouting about a message and all out of breath.

"Thorn wants you to meet him at the castle beach when you're finished," Alfie panted out.

"That's it?" Avianna said. "Skies, Alfie, I thought someone was dying."

"This place is too boring for that," Alfie said, scanning the bay, probably hoping for another pirate ship. Avianna had taken him to the castle to see Adolfo van der Horne and his men on the day they were sent home, but it hadn't been that exciting as the pirates had been stripped of their weapons and subdued. Adolfo's face had been blotchier than Avianna remembered, which made her think he normally used powder. He'd glowered at her but touched his helmet when he'd passed, causing Alfie to cock an eye at his retreating form. Simeon had been grateful at least, when she'd passed him his fur coat over the crowd.

Avianna scanned over her list and over the docks one last time.

Everyone was accounted for. She left the list in the dock master's shed and headed away with Alfie.

"How's the pub?" she asked, rubbing her hands together to warm them.

"Boring. Everything's boring. No one fights anymore, now that you're not around."

"I doubt they were fighting over me."

"Well Rye stopped coming around when Da wouldn't let him go upstairs with girls, and all the new people are dull."

"The new people?"

"Miss Flo convinced him to rent rooms for a long time like she does. She asked if he wanted to run a bottle, and he turned bright red. So now Rye has to take girls home, and he stopped coming, and Beck's bonding with Mattie so she won't let him out, and it's busy all the time but never anyone interesting."

"Run a bottle?"

"With girls, you know. Doing it."

"A brothel," called a voice beside them. They stopped. Prince Murkel crouched on the street before them, huddled under a raggedy coat someone must have given him. For once, he didn't seem drunk.

"Where've you been, then?" Avianna asked. "You've not been around for weeks. And I didn't see you out fighting the pirates, come to think of it."

"I can't go on the water anymore. You know that."

"You could learn to swim like the rest of us. I went out there, and I didn't know how."

"I'll never learn. Not without my tail."

Avianna was sorry she'd begun talking to him. Every time she remembered that she'd had relations with him, and he'd turned out to be a sea monster, she stopped pitying him. It could have been her he'd dragged out into the ocean, instead of the princess.

"Not with that attitude," she replied, and tugged Alfie to keep going. Alfie kept peeking back at Murkel.

"Blimey he's a creep," Alfie said.

"So what else is new?"

"Flo keeps sending us casseroles."

"That's not so bad."

"But Da used to let me eat pie for dinner, and now I have to eat the casserole to get any pie."

"Well Alfie, things could be worse."

He let out a huge sigh before conceding. "That's true."

They reached the square and the turn for the beach. Avianna stopped to catch her breath in the cold air. "Are you coming?"

"No. You and Thorn'll probably start kissing. And he'll get embarrassed if I'm there."

Avianna reached to push Alfie's hair out of his eyes. "Thanks for delivering the message."

He grinned and walked away, then picked up speed until he darted out of sight.

Avianna followed the beach path away from the cottages and out onto the cliff, where the wind off the ocean blew her hair to the side and whipped her skirt around her legs. The sunlight was pale, low in the sky and not quite strong enough to keep off the winter chill.

The stone walls appeared, and then the iron gate, happily standing open. Avianna passed under the once-solid hedge and entered the gardens.

The castle gardens weren't kept up like they'd been when she'd lived here, but that was to be expected now that underpaid gardeners weren't forced to do the work. Thankfully the fairies had supplied some expertise, so now native flowers filled the beds, as well as perennials that would appear each season with minimal human effort. The asters and chrysanthemums weren't as spectacular as the exotic flowers the king had expected, but now Avianna saw the bigger picture.

She would have lingered longer to enjoy the flowers, but Thorn was waiting.

She reached the gate to the beach and followed the stone path into the sand. How many times had she walked this path in a corseted gown and satin shoes? But there had never been anyone waiting for her at the end of it.

She came around the dunes. The salty wind blew harder and waves rolled onto the beach. Thorn sat on the sand just out of reach of the waves. In the stiff breeze, he probably didn't hear her approach. As she neared him, she spotted a horseshoe crab resting on the sand behind him, where the swishing waves washed over it.

Thorn looked up and smiled. "You got my message."

"Yes." Avianna dropped to sit beside him. "Is this the same crab?"

"Yes. He has a present for you."

"For me?"

The crab suddenly lifted up, standing on its row of claws. It was so menacing that Avianna got nervous, even though the thing hadn't hurt Thorn the last time—when it had had all those claws right on his hands. It shuffled forward, dropping its shell and lifting up again to gain another few steps. Its spike of a tail dragged in the sand.

When it neared her, two of its claws came out from under its shell with her Norlian crystals wrapped around them.

A lump rose in Avianna's throat. She held out a hand, and the crab placed the beads across it. Then it turned and made its way back to the water.

"I got a picture of it this morning," Thorn said. "He found it on the ocean floor and remembered it was yours." The crab was wading into the water.

"Tell him thank you."

Thorn reached for the necklace and dusted off the sand with his handkerchief. Then he motioned for her to turn her head so he could fasten it around her neck. This time he leaned in and kissed her skin when he finished.

"I was resigned to them being gone," Avianna said, fingering the familiar beads. "I missed them, but I realized they don't really matter. They were just a symbol."

"For what?" Thorn stood and offered his hand to pull her to stand. They headed back up the beach.

"The life I thought I wanted. Coins, gold. But really I wanted security, and I thought riches would bring it."

"It does help."

"As long as pirates don't show up and steal it all. We have the opposite kind of security. I can see that now."

"How do you mean?"

"Living without much," Avianna said. "It's like you said. No one would pillage from us, and all we have to do is make enough to buy food and the few things we need, and to save a bit for the future." She took Thorn's hand and they walked back along the stone steps to the garden gate.

As the sun neared the horizon, they arrived back at the print shop. Inside, Thorn left the "Closed" sign in the window and locked the door.

"Come upstairs a moment," he said. His voice sounded odd. Avianna followed him.

Upstairs, he moved next to the table and leaned on it, staring at the smooth surface.

"I have to show you something."

"I like the sound of that."

Thorn closed his eyes and smiled. "This is serious."

"Okay. What is it?"

He reached for a pouch in the middle of the table and slid it toward himself, spilling out its contents. Avianna gasped. Gold coins and gemstones clinked onto the table and gleamed in the rays of the sunset shining in the dormer window. Thorn dropped into a chair.

"Where did you get those?" Avianna sat across from him.

"Well, when we had our adventure . . . I had a few extra minutes on the pirate ship before you arrived." Avianna could have sworn Thorn was blushing, but it was hard to tell in the orange sunlight. "I poked into the captain's quarters and pocketed them."

"You robbed the pirate captain? Adolfo van der Horne, of the House of Krale? Known in Sarland as The Blackhorne?" Thorn's face cracked into a smile. Avianna could not believe him. She reached to squeeze Thorn's hand. "That's wonderful."

"I forgot all about it, once we were fighting for our lives. And I hid it away before I left for the woods, and then I got distracted and I forgot about it."

"You forgot about the bag of riches you stole from the pirates."

"More or less."

"What are you going to use it for?"

"I had two ideas. One is I could buy the supplies I need to print my first book." He stopped.

"What's the other?"

"I could buy us a cottage to live in."

Avianna stared across the table at him. Once again, he was making her dreams come true.

But she wanted to make *his* dream come true. "I like living here fine. You should make the book."

Thorn exhaled. "Are you sure? I want you to have the home you always wanted."

"I do have it. It's here with you. And I'll keep saving my earnings, and your book will sell—wait, what book are you going to print?"

"I thought maybe a traditional fairy book would be a good place to start."

Avianna clapped her hand over her open mouth. "No," she said.

Thorn grinned. "The elders let me borrow it from the library," he said, reaching to a shelf on the cupboard to pick up a wrapped bundle. He carefully undid the wrappings. "They figured fairy sex secrets could only help the world."

Avianna stood and moved around to stand behind him, leaning

on his shoulders as he began unfurling the ancient scroll on the table. Beautiful text in a foreign language passed by. Then a drawing of a naked woman emerged, standing as if she were walking along the parchment. She carried a staff with spires of flowers at the top. And her face seemed familiar. Avianna stared for a moment before it came to her. She resembled the fairy who had offered to light the lamps in the forest, who had turned Avianna around and sent her back to Thorn.

"Is that Queen Delphinium?" Avianna asked.

"Yup."

"Wait, did she put *herself* in all the pictures?" A new one was emerging of the naked queen standing beside a man. She no longer had her staff, Avianna noted, but he sure had one.

"You have to wonder who she had draw them all," Thorn said.

"Or who the lucky male was who got to pose with her."

"Males."

"No!"

"Somebody different in every picture. I guess it might be a hard job for one man—"

"I'll say it was a hard job," Avianna said.

"I mean, if all you could do was get close to a beautiful naked fairy queen and you had to hold still for an hour so someone could sketch you."

A third new picture was emerging. It seemed to be an explanation of the female anatomy.

"That looks helpful," Avianna said, nudging Thorn.

"Yes."

"You'll have to figure out the best places to use hawthorn ink when you print that one."

Thorn chuckled.

"Don't you think they really did it?" Avianna asked.

"Who?"

"The queen and her companions."

"With the artist watching?"

"Maybe after the artist finished."

Thorn unbuttoned the top button of his shirt. "I hadn't thought about it."

A few passages of text emerged. "I'll have to translate this," Thorn said, stopping to run a finger over the old fairy script.

"Keep going to the good parts," Avianna said, shaking his arm.

He kept unfurling the scroll and simultaneously rolling up the far side. The walking Queen Delphinium's naked bottom disappeared into the roll on the left as her rapturous face appeared on the right, her eyes closed and her lips parted. Her lover appeared a moment later, hovering between her raised knees with two fingers pressed into her body.

"Ooo, I recognize that one!" Avianna said, squeezing Thorn's biceps.

He shook his head and kept turning. More love scenes scrolled past, with the queen's adoring suitors stroking her, kneading her, and kissing every bit of her. Another diagram had X's marked all over her body, on the places that felt the best when touched, Avianna guessed.

Then finally the man had himself inside her. Avianna could imagine she felt his relief, flowing across the centuries through the artist's pen strokes.

"Look," Avianna said, pointing at his bottom. "You don't think he weaseled his hard self inside her while the artist worked?"

"It does look rather real." Thorn undid another shirt button.

As they kept going, the figures twisted into ever more complicated poses. Just watching the queen tumbling about with her lovers was making Avianna want a tumble. She leaned forward and slid her arms around Thorn's shoulders to point at the book.

"How about that one. What are they doing there?"

Thorn squinted at the text. "It says, 'She lifts her leg to vary the angle of his . . . branch'?"

"Wait, that's *her* leg?" Avianna ran a finger along the picture.

"No, I think *that's* her leg." Thorn pointed.

"I don't know, I can't picture it from that drawing. Here,"—she stepped back, tugging his arm—"maybe if we posed like in the picture, we'd understand."

Thorn's head had turned to keep studying the scroll. "I don't think so." Then he turned to her, and he was grinning. "Not with all these clothes on, anyway. We'll never be able to tell whose legs are whose."

Avianna grinned back and pulled Thorn from the chair. "Thorn," she said, walking backward toward the bed and pulling him after her. "Everyone's going to want your book. You'll make more gold than that pirate treasure you stole in no time."

"Once I do, will you be my wife?"

She stopped when the back of her legs bumped against his mattress.

"Me?" Avianna said. "But I'm not the kind of girl men bond with for life. Mattie's the kind of girl you choose for that." She couldn't stop a smile from breaking across her face.

"No, Mattie's the kind of girl *Beck* chooses. You're the kind of girl I choose." Thorn leaned forward to kiss her.

"I'll be your wife today," Avianna said. "You're more precious to me than all the gold in the castle." And she pulled him onto the bed.

A Note from the Author

DEAR READER,

Thank you so much for reading *The Village Maid*. The story originated with me wondering if I could redeem a "mean girl" by following what happened to Avianna after the revolution that occurs in *The Forest Bride*. Thorn's character developed as I considered how the person who makes a good match can be very different from the person you imagined. (At least this was true for me!)

I love writing stories in this cozy fantasy world, and I'm hoping other book lovers might enjoy reading them. If that's not you, that's okay. If you did like the story, please consider leaving a review online to help other readers with similar interests find the book. I would really appreciate it.

I'm hoping to have the next book in the Sylvania series, *The Ocean Girl*, out in 2023. You can subscribe to my email list at https://janebuehler.com for an email when the new book is available. I send only a few emails each year, so I won't crowd your inbox. When you subscribe, I'll send a link to bonus material. The email list is also how I give away advance review copies.

You can connect with me online on Twitter as @ephemerily or on my Goodreads author page. And you can email me at jane@janebuehler.com.

Sincerely,

Emily Jane ♡

Acknowledgments

As always, I want to give a big thank you to my friends and family. The supportive network you provide keeps me going, as a writer and otherwise.

Thank you to Adrienne M. for always being an amazing beta reader with insightful feedback. And thank you to Angie M. for your intelligent feedback and for repeatedly assuring me as I wade through the process of writing and publishing novels.

And finally, I'm grateful to work with Kelly Urgan as my editor and Cory Marie Podielski as my cover designer.

About the Author

EMILY JANE BUEHLER WAS ADRIFT for many years before realizing she wanted to work with words. She published two nonfiction books—one on the science and craft of baking bread, the other a memoir of her bicycle trip from New Jersey to Oregon—before venturing into fiction. She now writes "cozy fantasy romance": lighthearted stories that focus on a protagonist finding their courage and happiness, as opposed to plots with a lot of fighting and darkness. She also copyedits (mostly science papers) and teaches bread-making classes.

Emily lives in Hillsborough, North Carolina, with a bossy cat named Coco. She is looking forward to becoming the weird old lady who walks around town in a reflective safety vest and fit-over sunglasses. Her favorite things include letters sent through the mail, made-in-the-USA knee socks, and very dark fair-trade chocolate. She is passionate about living waste free and supporting local businesses.

Emily publishes fiction using her middle name, Jane.

www.ingramcontent.com/pod-product-compliance
Lightning Source LLC
Chambersburg PA
CBHW050838190726
48286CB00007B/2137